CHOSEN

What Reviewers Say About Brey Willow's Work

Fury's Bridge

"[*Fury's Bridge*] is a paranormal read that's not like any other. The premise is unique with some intriguing ideas. The main character is witty, strong and interesting."—Melina Bickard, Librarian (Waterloo Library, London)

Fury's Choice

"As with the first in the series, this book is part romance, part paranormal adventure, with a lot of humor and thought-provoking words on religion, belief, and self-determination thrown in.

Tis is a wonderful character, at a significant crossroads in her existence. Kera has no doubts about herself...the connection she forms with Tis is sizzling and very believable. And when they team up for some of the more action-orientated scenes, it is real page-turning stuff."—*Rainbow Reading Room*

Fury's Death

"This series has been getting steadily better as it's progressed." —*The Good, the Bad, and the Unread*

The Afterlife, Inc. Trilogy

"The whole is an intriguing concept, light and playfully done but well researched and constructed, with enough ancient and mythological detail to make it work without ever becoming a theology lesson. ... Brey Willows has created an amusing cast from Fates and Furies to the gods of old. The gods are extremely well done, literally personifying the characteristics we associate with them, drawn with wit and humour, they are exactly who we would expect them to be."—*Lesbian Reading Room*

Visit us at www.boldstrokesbooks.com

By the Author

Afterlife, Inc Trilogy:

Fury's Bridge

Fury's Choice

Fury's Death

Chosen

CHOSEN

by
Brey Willows

2018

CHOSEN

ISBN 13: 978-1-63555-110-5

THIS TRADE PAPERBACK ORIGINAL IS PUBLISHED BY
BOLD STROKES BOOKS, INC.
P.O. BOX 249
VALLEY FALLS, NY 12185

FIRST EDITION: SEPTEMBER 2018

CREDITS
EDITOR: CINDY CRESAP
PRODUCTION DESIGN: SUSAN RAMUNDO
COVER DESIGN BY TAMMY SEIDICK

Acknowledgments

My thank yous must always begin with Rad and Sandy, without whom I wouldn't have a book to put acknowledgments in. Sandy, thanks for trusting in my voice and not scoffing too loudly when I say a book came to me in a dream. Thanks to my editor, Cindy, for making the book better and for telling me to just keep doing what I'm doing, a high compliment indeed.

And to my wife, thanks for cheering me on, being my creative counterpart, and for every suggestion. You keep the stories flowing.

Dedication

To Robyn, my partner in words and my inspiration.

PROLOGUE

April 20, 2050 CE
CDN News, Final Report

Today, the President of the United Federation of Nations confirmed that we are in a global climate crisis. Though anyone inhabiting the planet could have said as much twenty years ago, the UFN has only now put forth a new set of legislative items for each country to follow in an attempt to mitigate our effect on the environment. These are the primary directives that affect daily life:

Travel by car is restricted to military, government, and emergency vehicles. All others must use public transport or make their own way. All solar powered vehicles are to be turned in for emergency services use. Air travel is likewise restricted. Should you need to go to another country, you will have to book onto one of the few commercial flights allowed each year. Due to the increase of communicable diseases, if you do go to another country, you must stay in the quarantine sector for two weeks beforehand. Electricity not provided by solar panels or wind turbines will be available for only a few hours each day. If you haven't already moved to green energy, now is the time. Otherwise, invest in candles.

Top scientists have officially confirmed that global warming has increased by four degrees Celsius instead of the projected two degrees. As you can see behind me, Las Vegas, like all deserts the world over, is a ghost town. Temperatures here now stay above one hundred degrees year-round. In the Arabian deserts, that temperature stays nearer to one hundred and forty degrees. The extreme heat makes places like Las Vegas, once a thriving den of excess, uninhabitable in every way.

Similarly, all coastlines below sea level that have not already succumbed to the ocean's rise will be subjected to storm floods and yet higher waters as the ice caps continue to melt. Those in low-lying coastal areas are encouraged to head to higher ground, taking only what you absolutely need. Should you need assistance, go to your nearest relocation center, and they'll give you guidance.

NASA and NORAD have long been discussing the possibility of colonizing another planet. Sadly, for those of us living here today, this has yet to be seen in practice. We must learn to endure the vagaries of all the weather patterns, from the extreme droughts to the heavy monsoons, to the constant Category 6 hurricanes to the frequent earthquakes and fires.

This will be CDN's final broadcast. For further news, please turn to your radio or go to your nearest information center.

With our final farewell, we send out this message of hope: We will adapt. We will not die. Take care of one another. God help us all.

Chapter One

March 21, 2100 CE

Devin Rossi looked out over the sepia mud bowl that had once been Lake Ontario. Her grandparents had bought this house back when the lake was so big you couldn't see all the way across it. The little dock her parents had played on, dived off, and anchored their motorboat to when they were teenagers, was now a few planks of rotted wood on shaky, weather-worn legs. If she hadn't seen photos of it in the early twenty-first century, she never would have believed how stunning and lush the area was. Now, dense rain fell in sheets too fast for the hard ground to soak in, and the lake water slowly rose once more, though it would vanish with the late spring heat.

She thought about the photos of the area covered in snow. What she wouldn't give to have experienced that. And to have seen the old cities known for their music and party atmospheres, like New Orleans and Miami. But like so many other areas, they were just a good place for divers now. Devin had enjoyed her scuba lessons over old New Orleans, an eerie underwater city with signs still intact on buildings that only housed ghosts and fish. There was no more music.

She turned away from her view and scanned the interior of the house. She'd covered the furniture in sheeting, stripped the walls, and put most everything in the attic. She was only taking a massive duffel bag with her for the journey into the Northern Territories.

Anything non-essential would be left behind. Maybe one day she'd come back for it, but there was no water left in the area, and drought was forcing everyone to the north, where the Gateway Cities had been established. At least up there they still got fairly normal rain. Granted, sometimes it was monsoonal rain, accompanied by floods, but they'd adapted and worked around it. In the Gateways, you could still find some semblance of regular food, and life overall was almost normal except for the heavy security presence, but people living outside the Gateways were reduced to whatever they could manage to grow themselves, which they often traded at little pop-up markets. MREs were widely available in stores, and they weren't too awful.

Devin allowed herself another moment of nostalgia. She'd had so many good times in this house, surrounded by family and friends. Her grandmother's birthday had been around Easter, and the last one they'd celebrated ten years ago had been full of laughter, music, and whiskey.

Not today. She listened to the deserted stillness around her. Easter Sunday 2100 was all about change. It was time to seek a new life somewhere else, and the part of her not sad about leaving her family home was excited to see what the future held. She hefted her duffel bag onto her shoulders and grabbed the white envelope off the table. The outline of the drab gray metal disc inside showed clearly through the thin paper. She folded it and shoved it in her back pocket.

A year ago, a military vehicle had pulled up outside, and terribly clichéd men in ill-fitting, sweat-soaked suits had come to the door with the envelope bearing her name. They'd placed her thumb over the disc and it had lit up, scanned her thumbprint, and pricked her finger for a blood sample. They'd told her to guard it with her life, and they'd be back on the date marked on the expensive stationary imprinted with the government seal.

Today's the day. So where are they? She shook her head at the thought of planning to come get a random person a year later. Still, they'd been the super-serious types, so she took her super-serious mystery disc with her. She'd decided she'd only give them until five, and that time had come and gone. She hated waiting around, and there was no guarantee they'd come back at all.

She closed her eyes and thought of her long gone family. *I'll miss you guys. Watch over me, huh?* She smiled and turned to the door. *Time to go.*

She'd barely made it to the street before the two-truck military convoy turned the corner and stopped in front of her. When a man in uniform jumped down and saluted her, she saluted back and grinned. "How's that for timing? I was just headed to the store."

He smiled back at her. "Yeah, our timing is impeccable that way. Lieutenant Rossi?"

She raised her eyebrow. "Haven't been called that in a while. This an official visit?"

He looked back at the trucks and then at her. "Afraid so. Do you have your PID on you? I need to check it before we go."

"My PID? What the hell is that?" She reached into her back pocket and pulled out the creased envelope with its distinctive circle. "This thing?"

"Yes, ma'am, your Personal Identification Disc. Do you mind?"

She handed it to him and he slid the innocuous little disc from its home. When he motioned for her hand, she held it out and he pressed it to her thumb. When it intoned confirmation of her name, date of birth, and blood type once the damn thing had pricked her thumb again, he nodded and handed it back to her.

"Thank you. If you'll jump in back, we'll head out."

"Name, Sergeant?"

"Sorry, ma'am. Walker, Air Force, First Northern, Division Seven."

Devin nodded. She'd recognized the First Northern insignia on his arm patch. She'd worn the same one for a long time. "Well, Walker, before I jump in with you, want to tell me what that little disc is and where we're going?"

He swallowed and shrugged slightly. "I'm sorry, ma'am. We're solely on pickup duty, and we've been instructed not to tell anyone where we're headed, as it's classified information. I only know the discs are necessary identifiers, and anyone who has one comes with us."

The information made the hairs on Devin's neck stand up. "And what if someone has their disc but doesn't want to come?"

"Orders are that those with discs come with us. Force will be used if absolutely necessary but as a last resort." He winced. "I assume you won't be one of the ones who fight, Lieutenant? You're a legend in the Force, and it's an honor to escort you. I'd hate to ruin that."

She laughed and clapped him on the back. She'd been in the military for a long time, and although this was somewhere beyond weird city, life was often like that if you were open to opportunity. "Hell no, Sergeant. I've always been one for taking my chances when they come up, and this sounds more interesting than the Montreal Gateway anyway. Let's do it." His relief was clear, and she wondered just how many people had put up a fight. She hadn't missed the stunbar in his belt.

"Damn glad to hear it. I could use some higher ranking support. Jump into my rig. Still plenty of room."

Devin nodded to the sergeant holding up the rear door of the truck and got a sharp nod in return. Two other pairs of travelers were already seated inside. One couple looked calm, if curious, but the other couple looked frightened. Two charred holes in the man's shirt told her the stunbar had been used to get them into the truck, and she felt for them. *Nothing like being kidnapped by the military to scare the shit out of you.* She slid onto the bench opposite the frightened couple, and the sergeant lowered the back door with a thud and click, so the only light came from the few small windows at the top of each paneled wall.

The man with the charred holes in his shirt leaned forward. "Do you know where they're taking us? Or why?" His eyes were wide and his hand stayed protectively on the leg of the woman next to him.

"Did they check your little disc thingies, too?" Devin asked, leaning back against the cool metal wall. Thankfully, the truck had aircon, a luxury afforded hardly any vehicle or home in the last fifty years.

"They did." He leaned back to put his arm around the woman beside him, who began to cry. "But our thirteen-year-old daughter didn't have one, and we refused to leave without her." He motioned to his shirt with his free hand. "But they put me down and dragged me into the truck, and my wife came with me."

Devin frowned. Maybe she should have put up a fight after all, if they were taking parents from their kids. "And your daughter?"

He shrugged and shook his head. "We're hoping she'll make her way to my mother's place, about ten miles away. Probably go to her friend's house first, but most everyone around us had already joined the migration north. We were headed that way ourselves, next month."

"They made us leave our baby." His wife sobbed against him. "Where are they taking us?"

Devin looked at the other couple, who were sitting close together but not actually touching. "You came quietly?"

The woman, wearing clean slacks, a polo shirt, and her hair in a tight bun, tilted her head when she answered, looking almost puzzled. "It didn't seem wise to fight, and we were in the flood zone beyond the Hudson. We were getting ready to leave anyway. We'd rather have done it on our own terms, but we're hoping they're taking us somewhere better."

Devin noticed that although the woman spoke matter-of-factly, the man's eyes were tight and his lips pressed into a white line. *He's not so blasé about it.* She looked at the canvas drape at the back and moved to look behind it, holding on to the ceiling straps to keep her balance on the bumpy road. The tower of supplies told her it wasn't going to be a quick ride. She stepped up onto the bench to look out the window and watched until she couldn't see the dry lake beds any longer.

Home was behind her. The question was, what was in front of her?

CHAPTER TWO

Goddamn water. Gets in goddamn everything." Karissa Decker piled a few more sandbags around the three-foot-high stack at the back door. They'd hold for a little while. But if the storm kept up, and she knew it would, sandbags would be nothing more than a few pebbles in an angry river.

"Baby, you've done all you can. C'mon in here and have a drink."

Karissa smiled and went to join her mom at the worn kitchen table she'd spent so many years at. "There's already four inches out there."

"Yeah, well, thanks to you pretty much all the furniture is upstairs. We'll get some new watermarks down here, that's all. Don't worry so much."

Karissa's mom patted her hand, and she couldn't help but notice how paper thin her skin had become. Her hair, once thick and glossy brown, was now lank and dull. But it was her eyes that scared Karissa most. The small red dots in the whites of her eyes were an indication of *prion nocoma*, more commonly called the melting fever, or just fever, thanks to the way the brain, once infected, began to melt inside the skull. And that was after it infected all the other organs in the body. All that destruction, caused by a malignant mosquito brought over on a ship carrying rotten tomatoes. *Ludicrous*.

She took her mom's hand in her own. "We should get you to a hospital," she said quietly, unable to look directly at her.

"Darlin', you and I both know there's no point. Once someone's got the fever, that's all there is to it. Your dad has promised he'll dose me up on morphine before the pain gets too bad. What we need to talk about is what you're going to do next."

Karissa sighed and pulled her hand away. She hated having this conversation, which had certainly become more frequent of late. "I'll figure it out when the time comes."

Her mom pushed the white envelope across the table. "Your bags packed?"

Karissa pushed the envelope back at her. "I've got my emergency bag, like always. But I'm not going with some clandestine government group just because they said they'd be back to get me. It's not like they can force me to go." She got up and moved around the kitchen, drying dishes and putting them away, more for something to take her mind off things than because it needed doing. They could all be under water tomorrow anyway.

Life was so fucking complicated. She'd given up her job at the CDC a year ago in order to move in with her parents. Columbus had been hard hit by the storms over the last few years, and when the crops failed and the water supply became contaminated, most people had left for non-contaminated pastures. But her parents had moved into the house forty years ago, and they weren't about to leave. It wasn't a mansion, but it was theirs. *And that's why Mom is going to die of the fever. Because they refused to go even when we heard the mosquitoes had made it this far inland.* Karissa knew it was useless to be angry with her mom, but she couldn't help it. If they'd only let her move them up north to one of the Gateway cities, maybe they would have been okay.

The sound of a truck engine could be heard over the lashing storm outside and Karissa's heart raced. *No way. No damn way.* Her mom gripped the table and stood unsteadily, just as Karissa's dad came pounding down the stairs with Karissa's emergency bag in hand.

"You can put that back. I'm not going."

Her parents followed her to the front door, which she yanked open to the obvious surprise of the young military man standing there with his hand raised.

"Dr. Decker?"

Karissa crossed her arms, trying to look less frightened than she was. "Yes. But I'm not coming with you."

"I'm sorry, ma'am. But orders are to pick up everyone with a PID. I assume you still have yours?"

Karissa thought quickly. "Nope. Threw it out the day I got it. Guess I can't go after all."

He looked disappointed as well as unsure what to do next. He looked out at the two trucks parked in a growing river of water on the street and shook his head at someone she couldn't see.

Just as she felt a victory lap coming on, her mom ducked around her and handed the soldier the white envelope with the disc in it before Karissa could stop her.

"Here you go, young man. She really did throw it out, but I thought she might need it one day." She smiled at him sweetly and shoved away Karissa's hand on her arm.

"Mom, why would you do that?" Karissa glanced at her mom, stunned, before she turned to the soldier. "And it doesn't matter if you have it. You can't force me to go with you."

He sighed and looked genuinely apologetic, even as he reached for the stunbar at his waist. "I'm sorry, Dr. Decker, I really am, but I'm afraid we *will* force you to come with us, if that's necessary. It would be much better if you came willingly."

Karissa's dad tapped her on the shoulder and gently turned her to face him. "Honey, I heard you say just a minute ago you'd figure out what to do next when the time came. That time is now, and this is what's next."

She stared at him, confused, before turning to her mom. "I don't understand. Mom—"

"No, baby. Listen." Her mom took Karissa's face in her hands, which were covered in thin white gloves to keep her sores from infecting anyone else. "I'm on my way out. And when I'm gone, your dad is going to go up to your auntie's place, and they're going to head north with the rest of the family." She smiled even as tears ran down her face. "Sometimes you don't have a choice when your fate comes knocking. You just have to follow that yellow brick road to the end. Something inside tells me that your destiny is part of this mystery."

"Ma'am, I'm sorry, but I really have to insist we head out. The storm is getting worse, and we have several more stops to make before we get to where we're going."

Karissa threw him a dirty look over her shoulder. "You know what? You can wait. I don't care about your damn schedule or the other people you're kidnapping. In fact, if you're in a hurry, feel free to go without me. I won't keep you." She turned back to her parents. "I'm not going—"

She felt a big hand on her shoulder, pulling her backward. She wrenched away from the soldier, but he grabbed her arm again, this time pulling her off the porch step and into the rain. It soaked her through instantly, making it hard to see, but easier to slide from his grip. Her pulse raced and blood rushed to her head, making everything seem like it was happening in slow motion. She kicked the soldier in the shin and elbowed the other who'd come to his rescue in the chin. When the stunbar came up, the blue lights zapping between the small, pointed prongs, she felt her knees weaken, but she still pushed them away. When the bar was close enough it made the raindrops glow like evil neon darts as they hit her shirt, she heard a woman's voice.

"Wait. Stand down for a sec, guys. Let me try."

The woman, also soaked to the skin, her short dark hair plastered down and dripping, stepped in front of the soldiers, close enough that Karissa could hear her over the rain, but the others likely couldn't.

"Look, I know this is scary. Downright terrifying, really. But these guys are going to take you, no matter what. Instead of making this even harder on your family, give them a proper good-bye, and go with them. Don't leave them with the final memory of you being dragged away unconscious."

Karissa swallowed hard and looked back at her parents. Her mom stood next to her dad, pale, trembling, her hands clutched in front of her chest. She looked so fragile, so scared. Her emergency bag hung from her dad's hand, his other arm around her mom. She turned back to the woman in front of her. "How can I leave them? I don't even know where we're going, or when I'll be back."

"Leave with your head high. With dignity. We'll get answers, eventually. But damn, don't leave them wondering if you woke up."

The woman's expression was empathetic, and Karissa knew she was right. Her pulse slowed, but the feeling of dread grew. She nodded and turned to her parents, noticing when the woman held up her hand to stop the soldiers from grabbing her once more. *Is she one of them?* She gathered her parents in a tight hug. "I love you both so much. I'll call and let you know where I am as soon as they let me."

Her parents hugged her back, their love fierce and strong as it had always been. "We love you too, baby. They've come for you because you're special, just like we always said you are. So go do special things." Her mom pulled back and smiled sadly. "And never forget how proud we are of you."

Karissa sobbed as she hugged them closer, the storm waters rising rapidly around their legs. When she felt the woman's hand gently tap her shoulder, she took her bag from her dad and backed away.

"I love you," she whispered, and though it was whipped away in the wind, she knew they heard her.

She turned and followed the woman to the back of one of the military trucks and climbed in after her. She stopped and waved at her parents one last time, memorizing everything about the moment—the driving rain, the water nearly to their knees, the way the gray light of the storm coated the whole scene in a sense of imminent nostalgia…and then the soldier pulled down the truck door and the sounds of the storm were muted, her parents gone. She barely noticed when he pressed her thumb to the disc to verify her identity; the needle prick was nothing compared to the way her heart was breaking.

She slid onto the seat beside the woman who had come out into the rain with her and absently accepted the towel she pressed into her hand. The truck engine rumbled to life, jerked forward, and Karissa began to softly cry as she left her world behind.

CHAPTER THREE

"F uck. Shut the storm doors and open all the venting systems. Keep an eye on the CO and O2 levels." Van Stein jogged from one long corridor to the next, shouting orders. Before long, she couldn't smell smoke anymore.

"It's the second big fire this year. We'll need to make sure we give the vents a good clear out when this one passes." Liz Como, Van's second in command, joined her in her jog through the halls.

Van stopped and threw one of the steel doors shut. It was an internal fire door, but it would help keep the heat out too. "Fortunately, there's not a lot left to burn thanks to the last fire. It should burn itself out on what's left of the spring flora pretty quickly. If you've got a few people to spare, have them check for spot fires around the property."

"Will do." Liz tugged on Van's shirtsleeve. "Can I talk to you in the office for a minute?"

Liz rarely asked to speak to Van privately, which meant it was serious. There weren't a lot of secrets, something Van felt was important. When things became opaque, people got nervous. And nervous people led to stupid actions. But there were a couple areas Van had decided to keep quiet. "Yeah." She didn't ask anything more. If it was something important, it was best done in the part of the building that acted as their combined office. When they went in and Liz closed the door behind them, Van opened the solar powered cold box. "Drink?"

"Yeah, thanks." Liz sat on the edge of Van's desk and pressed the bottle to her forehead.

"Another headache?" Van had watched Liz suffer for years with severe tension headaches, made far worse by stress.

Liz nodded. "We've had news from our source at the Ohio Gateway. There's a convoy headed our way with a new batch. And the Subtrop could really use supplies before tornado season starts."

That explained the need for a private conversation. The people who dealt with the supply raids were a select few. It was an ethical issue Van wasn't open to having a democratic conversation about. These days, moral high ground wasn't a place many folks could inhabit, and she sure as hell wasn't going to let people starve over a few idealistic convictions. While the Gateway cities in the north were able to produce crops and even still had real dairy products, they were heavily guarded and surrounded by walls. Van opened her own drink and sat behind her desk. "The spring storms are bad."

"I know." She shrugged and sipped her beer. "But that might make it easier to surprise them. And we don't know how many others are coming through. We might not have a lot more chances."

The last time they'd made a supply raid they'd managed to free a truckload of people who'd been forcibly taken from their homes, and most had been grateful. A few had been pissed off, since they had nowhere to go and no way to get to where they were being taken. So they'd come back to the Mesa Verde settlement with Van's group, and the few who wanted to continue on had been given supplies and sent on their way. But supply raids were dangerous, something she never took for granted. "How long?"

"Two days, probably. A new weather system just moved in, and they're probably going to have to wait it out somewhere. A group followed them and said they were headed down Cincinnati way. The subgroup there is on the lookout and will let us know."

Van considered her own team. "Okay. Get a few of the old-timers and see if they're willing. With the storm floods I don't want to take any new blood out there and have to keep our own people from drowning." She pointed at Liz. "Ask, don't tell. I want people going of their own accord, got it?" She loved Liz like a bratty little sister, but she knew she could be too demanding.

"Psh. Whatever. You'd make a shit dictator." Liz finished off her drink and tossed it in the recycler. "Set off time?"

"Four a.m. tomorrow. We'll take shifts driving and we'll keep in comms with the regional teams to get updates on locations."

"Will do. I'll let them know and then I'm going to lie down." Liz opened the door but turned back. "Oh, and speaking of lying down, Kelly is looking for you." She laughed and ducked the file Van threw at her as she stepped out and closed the door behind her.

Van stared at the massive road map of the USA on the wall. Egghead convoys, as they were often called, were hard to catch. They zigzagged along old roads, picking up people in various cities and towns all over the place. There was no telling where they were headed, so her teams had to be ready and in constant communication when one was spotted. Too often they missed them altogether thanks to not knowing what side roads they'd taken. Hopefully, they'd be able to grab this one, get the supplies they needed, and get out without any major problems.

Like it's ever that easy. She traced possible routes with her fingertip, trying to anticipate the various options. "Come in," she said when someone knocked on the door, but she stayed focused on the map, memorizing the different roads and possible terrain.

"It's like you're hiding from me." Kelly's wiry thin arms encircled her waist from behind.

Van groaned inwardly. *This is what I get for not keeping my hands to myself.* She'd slept with her once after a night of hard drinking on the upper decks. Hell, she barely remembered much more than the theatrical thrashing and screaming that had eventually made her head hurt more than the impending hangover. Ever since, she'd been dodging Kelly's advances. *Liz probably told her I was here.* It made her think about playing a bongo outside Liz's door for an hour or two. She gently disengaged Kelly's arms and tried to step back, but bumped into her chair and tripped. She managed to get her chair between them and leaned on it casually. "Hey, you. What's up?"

Kelly's bottom lip came out in a way Van had thought was cute while in a drunken haze, and now just found incredibly infantile.

"I've stopped by your room and tried to catch you at meals, but you're always gone. Didn't you have a good time?" She unbuttoned the top button of her blouse, and then moved to do the next one.

Van wondered if she could make it to the door before Kelly leapt on her like an underfed coyote. She held up her hand to stop her from undressing. "I did, I really did. Thank you. It was nice." *Nice. She'll love that.* The frown darkening Kelly's pouty face said she was right. "The thing is, I'm insanely busy. I really don't have time for more than some fun here and there. I'm sorry, I just can't give you anything more." *And now for the screaming...*

Kelly glared at her but re-buttoned her shirt. "What, the rest of us aren't busy? You weren't too busy to fuck. You can't just use people like that, no matter how important you are around here. And it's not like the place is crawling with lesbians. You're going to want me back."

Nope. Not true. She wasn't about to say that women's sexual identity didn't seem to hold much stock around there. Plenty of supposedly straight women had enjoyed her bed over the years. And she probably shouldn't explain that a lack of something didn't mean you took what was on offer...

Fortunately, Kelly slammed out of her office before she could say something stupid and dig a bottomless hole. Van had told her the truth, after all. She really didn't have time for anything serious. The world above them was literally going up in flames, and when it wasn't burning right outside their door, they had plenty of other catastrophes to deal with in the meantime.

She turned back to the map. *Where are we going to find you, little eggheads?*

CHAPTER FOUR

Daylight filtered through the windows at the top of the truck walls. Devin watched the shadows flit over the other occupants in the truck, highlighting the tight lines around their eyes, the pinched lips, the pale skin. They'd made two more stops after hers, but only the fighter had gotten into her truck. The others had joined the second van. The sergeant had told her they still had several more stops to make, and she wondered just how crowded it would get by the time they reached their destination. *Wherever that is.* No matter how she'd cajoled, hinted at, and even outright asked, the guys weren't giving up their destination. Beyond that, she believed they didn't know why they were picking up their human cargo. Orders were orders, and that's all they knew.

She looked down at the fighter, who had curled into the fetal position and fallen asleep a few hours into the drive. She hadn't said a word the whole time, and Devin wondered how pissed off she'd be once she was up and about. Now, with her head pillowed on her arm and wisps of chestnut brown hair over her cheek, she looked fairly peaceful, except for the light frown line between her eyebrows.

"It's rude to stare," she murmured, her eyes still closed.

"Sorry." Devin grinned. "I've been watching that bit of drool to see if it would actually slide off and hit the floor."

"Gross. I don't drool." She wiped her hand across her mouth and grimaced.

She stretched and Devin couldn't help but notice the way her T-shirt pulled tight over her full breasts. She was on the short side, but built exactly the way Devin liked her women—curvy and solid. Heroin chic was never a style Devin could get into. It always seemed like those women would break with even minimal passion thrown their way. But women built like this one were made for long weekends in bed.

She grinned again when the woman cleared her throat and gave her a disbelieving look.

"Are you seriously ogling me when I've just been kidnapped?"

Devin shrugged. "I see it as an adventure, and when destiny throws a beautiful woman on your path during said adventure, I'm all for it. It's like a fantastically fucked up fairytale." Devin held out her hand. "Devin Rossi."

She shook it and pulled on it so that Devin helped her off the floor and onto the bench seat. "Karissa Decker."

The man who had been on the truck before Devin, the one with the stunbar holes in his shirt, leaned forward. "Dr. Karissa Decker?"

She nodded, looking surprised. "Have we met?"

"Not exactly. I was at a lecture you gave at KSU last year, on dynamic environmental epidemiology. It was fantastic." He motioned at himself. "Edward Canto. This is my wife, Sheila."

Devin watched the exchange with interest. They hadn't done any talking on the way to Ohio. She knew that because of her discussions with the soldiers the others didn't trust her, and she didn't blame them. Outgoing by nature, she was a little bummed at the lack of company, but figured it would settle out eventually. Listening to them now, she started to put the pieces together.

"You're the atmospheric physicists who figured out how to contain some of the carbon dioxide leakage from the ice caps." The woman who had initially looked like something out of a J. Crew catalogue now looked like a rumpled, tired housewife who'd found an interesting documentary to watch. "It's because of you two that people had time to evacuate from the coastal regions."

Edward smiled at his wife and nodded at the woman. "We got lucky. Hit on the right formula. You know how it works. Are you scientists too?"

"I'm a plasma physicist. Natasha Kalkova. This is John Berman. He's an engineer."

"Not just an engineer." Devin smiled at him. He still looked on edge and had hardly eaten or had anything to drink since they'd been on the road. "John is one of the most sought after satellite engineers in the world. He figured out how to use gravitational pull and the topography of the planet to create better signals in space. Groundbreaking stuff."

He finally cracked a smile and the tension around his eyes eased a little. "Thanks. Like Edward said, I got lucky." He shifted so he could sit upright and looked at Devin. "That leaves you."

"Chemical geologist. I play with rocks and see what they can turn into. I'm just a big kid with a cool job."

Karissa looked around the group and then back to Devin. "They're kidnapping scientists? That seems pretty ominous." Her eyes narrowed slightly. "Back at my place, they deferred to you. Are you military?"

Devin inclined her head slightly. *Bummer. It was just starting to warm up.* "Kind of. Retired air force lieutenant. But I've been in science for a long time."

Everyone was quiet and Devin sighed internally. The military hadn't been popular for decades. While it was acknowledged they kept people safe, particularly when mobs attacked villages and towns, it was also universally acknowledged the military had played a massive part in the destruction of the planet during WWIII. It had only lasted a year and a half, but the damage had been devastating. Had it gone on any longer, there wouldn't have been a world left to defend.

"Thank you."

Karissa had said it so softly Devin almost missed it. "For?"

"For calming me down. For getting involved when you didn't have to. For making it so I didn't get stunned and dragged onto the truck like a sack of potatoes." She took in a shuddering breath and gave Edward a small smile. "For helping me to give my parents a proper good-bye."

Devin wasn't sure how to respond. She'd known she needed to help, so she had. "You're welcome."

The simple exchange was all that was needed to ease the atmosphere once more. The truck slowed, gears grinding and thudding, and soon stopped. They all waited expectantly, and when the door opened, hazy sunshine lifted the chill and shadows from the truck.

Devin breathed in the fresh air and stood. A day into the journey, the aircon had failed, which meant it was stuffy and warm in the back. She jumped down and gave Karissa and the others a hand as they all filed out. Edward was last, and she stopped him before he moved to join the others. "Hey. I know you're probably thinking about nothing but your daughter. But don't do anything stupid, okay?"

He looked at her searchingly. "How did you know?"

"Because if it were me, I'd be looking for a way out of this and back to her. But these guys are serious, and it's going to be a bitch of a ride if they have to restrain you the rest of the way to wherever we're going."

His shoulders slumped and his eyes filled. "I just wish I knew she was okay."

Devin squeezed his arm and turned him toward the group. "And at some point, we'll find out. I'll help in any way I can. But be cool, okay?"

He gave her a small nod before taking his wife and walking a little way away with her. The group from the other truck got out as well, and everyone stretched and chatted while the soldiers put food and drinks out on the picnic tables.

Devin watched as Karissa helped unpack the food and handed out plates to everyone else. It had been heartbreaking to watch her fight the soldiers to stay with her parents in a house that looked like it could tumble down under the next gust of wind, but even from a distance Devin could see the ravages of the fever taking her mother. Combined with the storm waters rising around the house, it was clear why Karissa's parents were practically pushing her into the truck themselves. It made Devin glad she hadn't had anyone to leave behind. Emotions weren't practical or fun. They were hard work and unreliable.

She accepted her plate from Karissa with a wink, and when everyone was settled and eating, Karissa came over with her own plate of food and sat beside Devin under the oak tree. "This seat taken?"

"Well, old Joe over there said he'd give me a foot rub after lunch, so you can only stay until he's ready to get to work." Devin moved her heavy boots from side to side and nodded sagely.

"Far be it from me to keep old Joe from those big feet of yours." Karissa ate slowly, looking around the group. "Any thoughts on where we're headed?"

"Now that I know there's a whole lot of smart people around? No idea. But I'm guessing it will be some kind of B movie facility filled with guys in uniforms and suits."

Karissa sighed and set her bowl of rice down, only half-eaten. "That sounds about right." She rolled a bottle of water over her forehead with her eyes closed. "I recognized your name, too, you know. You were too cool for school in there, but I know the truth."

Devin swallowed the last of her soda and set it aside. "Oh yeah?" She doubted anyone knew the real truth about her, but then, no one needed to.

"You created new terrestrial environments that could withstand hurricane-force winds and avoid flooding. Thanks to you, a lot of serious research could continue in places that would otherwise be uninhabitable now."

She held up her finger to stop Karissa. "Nope. I didn't create them. I posited them as theories and let other people do the grunt work. Totally different."

"The humble hero. A cliché, but I like it nonetheless." She stood and took Devin's plate from her. "I'm glad you're around."

She walked away, and Devin appreciated how her jeans hugged her ass just right, the T-shirt lifting just enough to show a bit of her back when she went to throw their stuff in the recycle unit. *Hot and smart. Always a dangerous combination.* The soldiers rang a bell and everyone gathered their stuff and headed back into the trucks. Although no one made a run for it, Devin had been around enough people in dire situations to know that eventually, someone would. She hoped like hell it wouldn't end in body bags.

For now, she'd climb back into the truck and get to know her travel companions a bit more. Hell, maybe she'd even offer her lap as a pillow for Karissa tonight. She climbed in and grinned when Karissa looked at her and rolled her eyes. *Busted. I must be wearing my lust on my sleeve.* But then, why not? They'd been taken from their homes and were being bussed to who the hell knew where, for some mysterious reason. It wasn't like it was the kind of place for a relationship to bloom, so she didn't need to worry about that. But that didn't mean other, more pleasurable options, wouldn't be available. *No reason not to have some fun while I can.*

Chapter Five

K arissa yawned and pulled the sweaty shirt away from her back. Everyone was asleep, including Devin. She lay on the bench, her arm over her eyes, her other hand resting on her duffel bag. She was sexy in that rogue, devil-may-care kind of way. Back when Karissa had worked at the CDC in Georgia, Devin would have been just her type. For a night, anyway. She'd been focused on getting through college and then leapfrogging up the ladder of her career, and relationships hadn't been an option. And then when one of the diseases encapsulated in the ice caps for thousands of years managed to not only thaw, but find a host, the world of infectious diseases had started to spin off its axis. She'd worked twelve-hour days, seven days a week. When she'd gotten the call from her parents saying they didn't know what to do about the flooding, the drought, and the fever, she'd been almost grateful for the reason to walk away from the job she'd worked so hard for.

And now I'm on a train to nowhere. John, the quietest of the group, settled onto the floor beside her.

"Doing okay?" he said quietly.

"I think so. As okay as possible in this insane situation." She looked at him, but his face was shadowed and he picked at a thread on his jeans. "How about you?"

He shrugged and was silent. Karissa had a feeling he needed time to sort an answer, but the fact that he had moved to sit with her suggested he had something to say, so she waited.

"I had a partner. Have, I mean." He sighed heavily. "Tasha and I were working in the home office, playing with a new project idea. We've been friends for years, since we went to school together in Sweden. My partner, James, was baking in the kitchen."

Karissa could feel what was coming and took his hand. "And when they came for you?"

"He's a baker. You wouldn't believe how amazing his lemon cake is, even though we hardly ever get real lemons anymore…"

He was silent for some time, and Karissa wondered if he'd just needed some company. And then he started talking again.

"He'd packed my bag, and Tasha kept hers in her car. That letter and disc we got, you know? We all took it seriously, but I didn't think…I guess I didn't believe it, not really. James had a bag packed too. We figured if they were going to take you, they'd have to take your family." He looked at Karissa and tears streamed down his face, falling from his chin onto his crumpled shirt. "He tried to push past them. Tried to shove them aside and climb into the truck with me. They held me back in the truck when they used the stunbar on him."

He broke into silent sobs and Karissa put her arms around him and held him close, her heart breaking for him.

"The last time I saw him, they'd thrown him into our yard. He was unconscious, lying in the grass like a discarded mannequin."

Karissa let him cry, holding him tightly until he fell asleep against her. *Thank God Devin stepped in, or my parents would have a memory like that. Who the hell do these people think they are?*

She looked around and settled on Devin, who was looking right at her. She glanced at John and shook her head slightly, her frown clearly one of empathy, before she put her arm back over her eyes.

John's silence and pain were echoed in most of the people around them, including herself. She could see, in that brief moment, that Devin saw it too, and wondered if she was leaving anyone or anything behind. Karissa closed her eyes and rested her head on John's. For whatever reason, they were all in this together. Maybe, if they worked as a team, they would make it through. Maybe, one day, they could even get back to their families. As she fell asleep, that thread of hope seemed anorexically thin.

"The road is wiped out. We're going to try some of the old back roads."

Devin nodded and accepted the bottle of water from the young sergeant. Only major roads were maintained, and were almost exclusively for government or military vehicles, which meant they made good time when they were able to use them. But the smaller roads they'd taken in order to make stops for other pickups were often in a bad state of disrepair; fallen trees, sinkholes, and storm debris sometimes blocked the way so they had to go around. Devin had gotten good at balancing on a crate so she could watch their journey from the windows at the tops of the truck walls. Eerie emptiness was all she saw in several of the smaller towns they went through. Vehicles with trees growing out of them, buildings missing rooftops, walls covered over with foliage, and houses with hollow, empty-eyed windows were all that was left of storm and drought ravaged areas.

"Where's the next stop?" Devin asked, letting the cold water soothe her parched throat. The back of the truck was stifling in the late afternoon heat, and everyone was sweaty and on edge. Small talk had dwindled with the need to conserve energy, and most everyone had dozed off. Sadly, Karissa hadn't needed the lap pillow Devin offered. She still held out hope for later.

"Cincinnati. Then on to St. Louis, and from there to our final destination. Not too long now."

Devin considered the mileage and the roads. What once would have taken about twenty hours if they drove straight through would probably take closer to thirty or thirty-five, if they were headed where she thought they might be. Still, he was right. They wouldn't have to endure too much more time in the back of the truck. "How's the other truck doing?"

He grimaced and drank down his own bottle of water. "They're not as nice a group as you guys. Lots of arguing in the back, lots of angry questions. The guys are doing their best, but…"

Devin knew. "Let me know if you need any help." She clapped him on the shoulder and went to join her group. It was always interesting the way people bonded in extreme situations. She'd seen a lot of it in the military, and it was one of the things that made it possible to depend on each other. Her group had come together, and although they were cordial to the other group, there wasn't any desire to mingle. She sat next to Karissa and listened to the conversation.

"I heard he was thrown out of the academy for sleeping with a student," Sheila said with a small smile.

"I heard he was a nightmare to work with and took credit for his student's ideas." Natasha pushed her sandwich at John, who shook his head.

"Who are we talking about?" Devin whispered theatrically.

"Ivan Igorovich." Karissa nodded toward the other group. "He's an infectious disease specialist with a god complex. I've had run-ins with him a few times over the years. He asked me to work on a project with him once and I turned him down. I don't think he's ever gotten over it."

Ivan's voice could be heard over the rest of his group. "If we refuse to leave without an answer, they have to tell us. I *demand* they tell us. They can't stun us all."

Devin watched him try to stir up his group, but most of them were clearly trying to ignore him.

"I bet he'd change his tune if it were him they stunned." Edward held his wife's hand and kept running his thumb over her knuckles. "I'd like to watch that."

Sheila shushed him with a smile.

"I just talked to the sergeant. We're headed for Cincinnati, then to St. Louis. That's it before our final destination. He said it won't be much longer." Devin smiled at John as she took the abandoned sandwich in front of him and ate with gusto. Balancing on that crate to watch their journey took a lot of energy.

There was silence as everyone took that in. Only a few more days, and they'd know why they'd been the ones picked up.

"I wonder how many other convoys are making their way to wherever we're headed," John said. "How many people are they taking from their lives?"

Devin had heard of other people being picked up. Rumors on the wind mostly, but now she thought of the many scientists she'd worked with over the years. Maybe some of them would be at their final destination. It would be like a really fucked up reunion.

"One is too many." Karissa stared thoughtfully at the other group. "At least we don't have to wait much longer to find out. Maybe then we'll get the choice about whether to stay or go."

Devin didn't think there'd be any choice. They wouldn't go through all this trouble, planned years in advance, to just let people walk away once they had them in hand. But saying so out loud wouldn't do anyone any good. They needed hope, and she wasn't about to take it from them. She looked around the area where they'd stopped and then jumped up. "Be right back."

She went to the sergeant, who was listening patiently to a petite woman from the other truck berate him about civil liberties. Devin tapped his shoulder and smiled sweetly at the woman. "Sorry to interrupt. Could I talk to you for a second?"

Devin nearly laughed out loud at his relieved expression.

"Yes. Absolutely." He walked a little way away with her and sighed. "Thanks for that. Were you just saving me, or did you really need something?"

Devin motioned toward the building across the street. "You know what makes people happy? Junk food. What say you and I do some quick shopping?"

He laughed and turned to another soldier. "Hey. We'll be right back. Watch table two for me?"

The other guy nodded, looking utterly uninterested, and he moved toward the table, but not close enough that he wasn't in the shade.

Devin and Sergeant Walker jogged across the street to the convenience store. This town, like most others, had been abandoned, and by the looks of it, pretty recently. They went around back and found an open window. Walker boosted Devin through, and she went around and opened the door for him. The shelves still had plenty on them, and Devin whistled happily as she and Walker filled several baskets and bags with whatever snack foods they could find. Mass production food had been gone for a long time, but local places like this one still had crackers and sweets made by local farms. The drink fridges were turned off and warm, but they grabbed bottles of root beer and lemonade anyway. Before they turned to go, Devin sent a silent thanks to whoever had owned this place. The fact that it hadn't been looted yet meant the town hadn't been empty that long. Homelessness and desperation had created bands of roaming groups who cleared out entire areas like locusts on a crop before they moved on. Stories of violence and theft were common when it came to travelers trying to make their way to cities that were still thriving. *The way I was about to.*

Weighed down, she and Walker made their way back to the group and were met with a chorus of appreciation as everyone dug in and grabbed their favorites. Leftovers were divided into the two trucks, although there was grumbling from the people in the other truck that theirs got the "better stuff."

Devin watched as Karissa ripped open a bag of apple chips. She crunched down and sighed happily.

When she saw Devin watching her she shrugged. "Yes, I know they taste a lot like papery dirt. But I don't care. I've always liked them."

Devin laughed and opened her own package. "Hey, no judgment here. Any food product that has ties to something written in the Bible three thousand years ago has to have some merit." She stuck her face in her own bag and pulled out a chip with her teeth, wiggling her eyebrows at Karissa as she did so.

Karissa laughed and choked on her chip before turning away.

Once more, they piled into the trucks. Knowing there wasn't much farther to go put everyone in Devin's truck in a better mood, and there was plenty of chatter.

"What's your favorite element?" Edward asked.

"Cesium." Sheila smiled down at her husband, who was resting his head on her leg. "Soft and explosive."

He laughed. "Yeah, that's you." He turned to the others. "What about the rest of you? What element best describes you?"

"This is probably the geekiest game ever played." Devin came down off the crate she'd been standing on and sat on the floor, her legs stretched out in front of her. "If we're comparing ourselves... calcium. Useful in just about every way, and good for the body and soul." She grinned when the others started laughing.

"Is there anything you're not good at?" Natasha asked with a smile.

Devin pretended to think. "Humility." When the others stopped laughing she said to Natasha, "So, what element are you?"

Natasha looked at John. "What would you say?"

He looked surprised, but his smile was more present than it had been. "Hydrogen. Most needed to make up the sun and stars."

She touched his hand. "How lovely."

He ducked his head and looked at the floor.

"I'd say you're platinum. Rare, precious, and lasting."

He looked up at her and they shared a private smile that left Devin feeling like she'd seen something far too intimate for public consumption. She turned to Karissa, who looked equally uncomfortable.

"And you?"

Karissa twisted a piece of her hair around her finger, a habit Devin was beginning to recognize as something she did when she was thinking. "Silicon, I think. Brittle on its own, but strong with others."

Devin shook her head. "See, I would have said tungsten. Can be stretched to the extreme without breaking."

Karissa blushed and looked away.

Interesting how we see ourselves differently from how others see us. Devin moved so she could lean against the door, and when Karissa moved from the bench to the floor, Devin scooted sideways. Karissa curled up on the floor next to her and rested her head on Devin's thigh.

Devin ignored the rush of lust that heated her skin. This wasn't exactly make-out territory. She rested her hand in Karissa's soft hair and closed her eyes. Damned if it didn't feel awfully nice, though.

CHAPTER SIX

The wind howled and hailstones pummeled the metal roof and walls of the truck, making it sound like the storm was a garrulous passenger riding in the truck with them. Karissa pressed her ear closer to Devin's thigh and put her hand over her other ear. Her hearing had always been incredibly sensitive, and the pounding noise was reverberating in her skull.

She felt Devin shift slightly, and then Devin's coat pressed against her ear. She squeezed Devin's thigh gratefully and smiled a little when Devin flexed her muscle beneath Karissa's hand. The coat muted the noise further, and she felt some of the tension leave her head and neck. She relaxed her jaw and sighed with relief.

Devin's thigh was solid under her cheek, and she'd enjoyed the closeness, even though she hadn't had any intention of giving in to Devin's flirtation. Physical contact had been a big part of Karissa's life. Her parents had always been full of hugs, and her mom in particular had been good at stroking Karissa's hair whenever she was upset, or cuddling up with her on the sofa to watch movies. She missed that terribly, and the little bit of contact with Devin had eased the ache.

The truck swerved and jolted everyone to the side. Devin's hand was firm on Karissa's back, holding her in place. When the truck slammed to a stop, Karissa sat up and waited expectantly with the others for the door to open. When it did, the sound of the storm was deafening.

Sergeant Walker yelled over the lashing storm. "There's too much debris flying around. We need to stop and wait it out." He turned, squinting, and pointed to the left. "There's a building about two hundred yards that way. Get ready, and when we shout, make a run for it. Watch yourselves, though. There's all kinds of stuff in the air!"

Karissa looked at Devin, who shrugged back into her jacket and grabbed her duffel bag. Karissa did the same and huddled with the others. When Walker came back over, he handed Devin a flashlight. "We'll be right behind you!"

She nodded, jumped down, and held out her hand to Karissa, who took it gladly. She waited just beyond Devin as she helped the others jump down, and then they all followed her as she jogged forward. Karissa didn't know how Devin could see where she was going. The flashlight lit the sheets of rain around them, creating a strange halo effect, but Karissa couldn't see any building. She did see flashlights headed their way from the other truck, though, so Devin must know where she was going.

Suddenly, she stepped into a hole and lost her footing. She reached out and grabbed for purchase, and just managed to grab Devin's jacket. But that yanked Devin backward, and she slipped and landed on her butt beside Karissa.

"Are you okay?" Devin shouted.

"Fine. Sorry." Karissa struggled back to her feet. She was soaked through and her knee hurt, but she wasn't injured.

Devin nodded and got them underway again. Within a few minutes, they were all stumbling through the entrance of a small abandoned hotel. The storm waters were already a foot high inside, and everyone made for the stairs. Squelching shoes combined with dripping water to announce their presence. But once they made it to the second floor, the noise abated drastically. All the windows were still intact, and there was furniture in every room. Although it smelled a bit musty, it wasn't too bad. Karissa would just be happy to sleep on something that wasn't moving for a night.

As everyone started to shake off their wet clothing, Walker spoke, the flashlight making his face look eerie in the dark space.

"We'll bunk down here for the night." He shined his flashlight down the hall in both directions. "I think there are enough rooms for everyone to be two to a room. We'll be here in the hallway if you need anything."

People started pairing off into rooms, though there was plenty of grumbling from the other group. Karissa was so glad that if she had to be kidnapped, she'd ended up with the non-bitching group. Devin tapped her on the shoulder.

"Slumber party in room three?" She grinned and pointed over her shoulder at the room behind her.

Karissa laughed, incredibly relieved she'd have someone nearby overnight. "It won't be much of a slumber party without pizza and alcohol our parents don't know about, but I'm in."

Devin held up her bag. "I have corn tortilla chips and a bottle of hooch the owner left behind. Will that do?"

Karissa followed Devin into the large room and dropped her bag on the desk. "That most definitely works." She looked into the bathroom and saw the antique claw-foot tub. "Do you think they've got running water?"

Devin peered over her shoulder and Karissa tried not to notice the way her hard body felt against her back.

"I think it's worth a try. It hasn't been vacant that long, and I'm sure I saw some solar panels on the run in."

Walker knocked on the open door. "Hey. I found some candles. Not many, but enough for each room tonight." He tossed one to Devin. "You have a lighter?"

She caught the candle and nodded. "Yeah, thanks. Need any help out there?"

He shook his head. "Nah, I think we're good. Water is getting higher, but we'll be fine. The guys have moved the trucks to a high ridge so they won't get waterlogged. Now we wait." He waved and moved off down the hall.

Devin dug through her bag, still holding the flashlight Walker had given her, and pulled out a lighter. She lit the candle and closed the door before turning off the flashlight and bringing it over to Karissa.

Karissa liked the way Devin moved. It was economical, like every movement had a purpose. Her wet clothes clung to her, outlining a chiseled body that looked more soldier than scientist. Her wet hair stuck to her face, outlining her high cheekbones and the darkness of her eyes. Karissa ignored the flutter in her stomach. She hadn't been around such an attractive woman in a very long time. "Hooch, I think you said?"

If Devin's smirk was anything to go by, she knew exactly why Karissa wanted some.

"Absolutely. Should we try and get dry first? I hadn't planned on taking that little swim with you in the watering hole." She looked beyond Karissa into the bathroom. "No towels. We'll have to air dry. Just run around naked."

Her grin made Karissa's stomach do that flippy thing again. "Yeah, sorry about that. I tried to save myself and reached for you." She realized how that sounded and hurried on. "I've got an emergency towel. I'll share."

"Damn. Foiled again." Devin laughed and went to the door. "Actually, I'm going to see if I can find a supply closet. I'll be right back."

She closed the door behind her and Karissa leaned against the doorjamb. *I'm being an idiot. Stop being an idiot.* She turned to the tub and let the water run. *Come on...come on...yes!* Hot water flowed freely, and she quickly plugged the tub to let it fill. She added some body wash she grabbed from her bag and soon had a fabulous bubble bath. She threw off her clothes, climbed in and sank beneath the water, letting the heat flow through her chilled body. When she heard the door open she called out, "I'm in the bath."

"Is that an invitation to join you?" Devin said from just outside the door.

Karissa laughed and pulled the bubbles higher to make sure she was covered. "I'm not sharing this bath with anyone. It's all mine. In fact, I might just stay here forever and keep running hot water until I dissolve. But you can come in."

Devin peeked around the corner and then groaned. "Damn. A girl can hope." She waved a couple of towels. "I found a stash so we don't need to get your emergency one yet. There's no electricity, but there's a fireplace in a living room they must have put in up here because of the flooding. The guys are trying to find a way to get it going, so we can dry our clothes."

Karissa's eyes closed as she listened to Devin's husky voice. She liked the way it caressed her senses like an autumn breeze. She opened her eyes when she sensed the shadows from the candlelight shift. Devin handed her a plastic cup with a shot of homemade alcohol before she sat down beside the tub and opened a paper bag of organic tortilla chips.

"I think this could be the most creative, romantic date ever." Devin downed her alcohol and poured another.

Karissa drank her own shot and felt it burn all the way down, warming her from the inside the way the bath was warming her from the outside. She wasn't a drinker, but tonight felt like the right time to become one. "I'm pretty sure you can't be on a date when you've been kidnapped. But as dates go, yeah, it would be a good one."

They drank and Devin passed Karissa handfuls of chips when she asked for them. Eventually, Karissa was so relaxed she could barely keep her eyes open. "I think I'd better get out before I drown."

Devin stood and grabbed a towel. "I wouldn't let that happen."

She held the towel out, and there was no mistaking the sultry look in her eyes as she opened the towel for Karissa to step into.

It might have been the alcohol. It might have been the desire for connection. It might have been the fact that Devin was the sexiest thing she'd seen in, well…maybe ever. Whatever the reason, Karissa slowly got up from the bath and loved the way the bubbles slid over her warm, naked skin. To her credit, Devin didn't take her eyes from Karissa's face, which was vaguely disappointing. But when she stepped from the tub, Devin wrapped the towel around her, standing close enough that Karissa could smell the alcohol on her breath.

"Feel better?" Devin murmured.

Karissa closed the small distance between them. "Much." She raised her face for a kiss and felt Devin's soft lips touch hers for a too brief moment.

"Why don't you go lie down? I need to wash up too."

Karissa backed out of the room, but caught a glimpse of Devin's naked back, adorned with a black animal tattoo of some kind, before she made it all the way into the bedroom. She slid beneath the covers on the bed that was far more comfortable than the truck bench or floor and curled into a ball to wait for Devin.

She's so insanely hot. Karissa closed her eyes and pictured the various moments she'd really watched Devin. The way her eyes crinkled at the corners when she smiled or laughed, which was often. The way her biceps bunched under her T-shirt. As she struggled not to fall asleep, she tried to picture the tattoo she'd just seen, but it faded as the world drifted away.

CHAPTER SEVEN

Van wiped the rain from her eyes only to leave a thick smear of mud on her cheek. Sheets of hot rain made it hard to see five feet in front of her, which was part of the reason they were digging the front tire out of a pothole they hadn't been able to avoid.

"Give it a try," Liz yelled to the driver.

Van stepped back and watched as the tire spun, caught, and the truck lurched forward. *Thank fuck for that.* She climbed in and rested her head against the seat. "Thanks." She took the towel Liz pressed into her hands and tried to get the mud from her face.

Liz and the others did the same. When it came to roads like this, no one was exempt from helping out unless they were genuinely unable, and Van didn't ask people to go who wouldn't hold up in the field. And she damn well never expected anyone to do anything she wouldn't. Being unprepared out here could cost you your life, and she wasn't about to put anyone in that position.

"Find shelter six, Mac. The road's not passable. And if we're hunkered down, they probably will be too. Hopefully, we'll still catch them."

Mac nodded but didn't respond, his full attention on the mess of flooded, debris-strewn road ahead. Within a half hour, he turned into what had been the parking lot of an ancient stadium. He stopped the truck just outside one of the crumbling entrances and they all dashed inside. They followed Van as she moved through the corridor to the right, down a long hallway, to a locked room. She entered the padlock code, pressed her fingerprint to it for recognition, and then used the key. When the lights came on, she sighed with relief. While their safety spot would be dry and comfortable without electricity, it was always better with the lights and heat on.

"I get first shower." Liz waved off the guy's protests and darted past them into the bathroom, her duffel bag slung over her shoulder.

Van and the guys quickly changed out of their sodden clothes. Modesty wasn't an option on raids, and they'd been through too much together to be worried about a bit of nudity.

"You'd think that woman would melt if water touched her skin." Mac Tracey wasn't really bothered by the cold, but he hated being in second place.

Ray Villa, their scout and resident forager, laughed. "Like it matters to you who showers first. You haven't had one since the last ice age." He ducked the wet sweatshirt Mac threw at him and it hit James Quintero, the team's weatherman, in the chest.

"Damn, this shirt was clean and dry. Thanks a lot." James threw the wet shirt back at Mac, who inclined his head apologetically.

"Coffee's on." Van set out mugs and the powdered cream and instant coffee beside the kettle. "And I get next shower." She ignored their grumbling and threw her bag at the end of her cot.

"What was that?" Mac held up his hand for silence.

It came again. A shuffling, metallic sound echoed beyond the door of the room Van had stocked for emergencies. For all the security on it, people rarely came this far out of the way anymore. "Animal?" she asked Ray.

He shook his head. "Not unless it's injured and tied to a tin can."

James pulled a gun from his bag and moved to the door. Van moved across from him, counted to three, and followed him into the hall, ready to face just about anything.

Anything, that is, except the dirty, bloodied woman lying crumpled in the hallway, her suitcase broken and battered behind her.

James tucked his gun away, and he and Van knelt next to her. James checked the hallway in both directions, but there was no one with her. Van felt for a pulse and was relieved to feel the faint thumping under her fingertips. "Let's get her inside."

She and James carried the woman into the room, and Mac dragged the suitcase in behind them. Liz emerged looking decidedly smug from her shower, but immediately went into work mode when she saw what they were doing. "Five minutes. I leave you for five minutes and you kill someone."

"She dropped outside the door."

Mac moved them aside and started checking her over. "Let's get her dry. May be in shock. Superficial cuts to her face and arms, bruising on her left cheek. Pulse is faint but steady."

Van and Liz quickly got the woman out of her clothes and tucked under the blankets while Mac got out the med kit they kept for emergencies. He hooked up a saline drip and easily inserted the needle into the woman's thin, dry skin.

No one spoke, letting Mac do his job in silence. He lifted her eyelids and checked the whites of her eyes. "No sign of fever."

Van watched and took stock. That the woman didn't have fever was a blessing. She'd been in that situation a few times already, and most certainly didn't want to go through it again. The woman's suitcase looked like it had been dragged halfway across the country, and items were spilling out. She was slight and bedraggled, but the quality of her clothes suggested she hadn't always been that way. Van knelt beside the suitcase and started searching for ID, a common practice when they came across injured or unconscious people. Lately, that seemed to happen more than it had over the last decade.

When she saw the white envelope she sighed. "Shit." She pulled it out and waved it to the others, the outline of the little gray disc clear under the fluorescent lights. "Dr. Susan Sandish, pharmacologist."

"Heard of her?" James asked, looking around. Everyone shook their heads.

"We won't know if she's an escapee or someone whose pickup date got missed because of the storms until she wakes up. We'll keep to our plan until we know." Van slid the envelope into her back pocket. If the woman didn't wake up, she'd send it on to the facility with a death notice. She hoped the officials who got it would then find a way to notify her next of kin. *More likely they just throw it in the trash and move on.*

Ray grabbed his bag. "I call next shower."

Mac and James grumbled but were soon placated by Van pressing steaming cups of coffee into their hands.

"James, can you check the radar on this storm? See what we're dealing with?" Van knew there was a good chance radar wouldn't work if the storm was thick enough, but it was always worth a try. James had developed his own tech that was better than what some of the government agencies used.

He nodded and set up the system they stored in a backroom cabinet. Van and the others relaxed in the meantime. Silence was always comfortable in this group, none of whom ever felt the need to chatter just to fill the void. Liz had chosen a good team, and Van was grateful for the chance to clear her mind and consider their options. She glanced over at the unconscious woman and wondered what her story was. These days, everyone had a story that involved hardship of some kind. *Unless you're one of them.* Them: the rich, the entitled, the ones with enough food and electricity that they were only inconvenienced by the lack of imported cheese or good wine. *Not one of us, living in caves and hoping to hell our gardens grow so we can feed everyone.*

"Plan?" Liz asked, looking at Van over her mug of coffee.

Van glanced at Liz but didn't answer. These situations were always played by ear, but Van never wanted to leave people stranded if she could help it. Some were determined to go their own ways, though, and she wouldn't force anyone to take her help. "We'll decide once we know what path she's on."

"And if she doesn't wake up before we need to head out?" Mac asked.

James came in and poured himself another cup of coffee. "I doubt she'll be out that long. It's a cyclone Category Six, a good thousand miles wide, and it's right on top of us. We'll be down for twenty-four hours, if not more."

Liz groaned. "Good thing we made it to our breakpoint. Ten more miles and we'd have had to use that shithole cabin."

"Hey, I like that shithole cabin. I had my first sexual experience there." Mac laughed and ran his hand through his steel gray hair. "It's amazing it's still standing."

"It might not be after this storm. Although nothing will wash that image from my mind." James grimaced and held his stomach like he was going to be ill.

A soft moan caught their attention, and Van moved to the woman's side. Her eyes fluttered and opened wide when she saw Van standing over her. She pulled the blanket to her chin, her expression full of fear.

Van tried to smile reassuringly, though she'd been told more than once that her bedside manner was more dictator than nurse. "You're safe, no need to worry. My name's Van, and this is my team." She motioned behind her. "We were on our way to St. Louis and had to stop because of the storm. You collapsed outside our door."

The woman looked around and appeared to calm. "I really thought I was going to die. I thought I'd rather die in a building than out in the storm. I don't know why. It sounds stupid now. Then I saw people ahead of me and thought maybe I could reach them. But then…" She sighed and closed her eyes. "I guess I passed out."

"Well, good thing you found us." Mac moved next to Van. "You wouldn't have lasted much longer. How long has it been since you ate or drank anything?"

The woman opened her eyes. "I don't remember. I kept looking for food and water, but everywhere I went the water was brown and the food was long gone or rotten."

Van pulled the white envelope from her pocket. "So. Escape? Or something else?"

The woman looked at everyone in the room and then back at Van. "You're not in uniform. So you're not with a convoy?"

Van shook her head but didn't offer anything more. She knew better than to trust a stranger with details about their organization.

The woman seemed to relax again. "I didn't escape, *per se*. I left before my pickup date after I heard what was happening with other people who had discs. I saw a convoy take away a colleague from work. They didn't even give him time to go home and get his things. And when he fought…" She swallowed and tears filled her eyes. "I don't know what's going on, but I know I'm not about to be part of some government plan or conspiracy or whatever. History has taught us a lot about quietly going along with people who herd you onto transport for their own reasons."

The statement was both true and unnerving. It had happened in the nineteenth, twentieth, and twenty-first centuries. A lesson humanity refused to learn, apparently. *And she doesn't even know where they were taking her.* "Well, Susan, we're not government. We're something else altogether, but we do have food and shelter, if you're looking for a place to land. Unless you were headed somewhere specific?"

Susan looked suspicious. "A cult?"

Liz snorted and Mac outright laughed. James shook his head and went back to his weather equipment.

Van smiled, thinking of herself as a cult leader. "Definitely not. Just survivors doing our best to keep going." Van would let Susan find out the truth of what they were when she arrived there. If she didn't like it, no harm no foul. But if she did, her skills could be useful. The disc proved she knew what she was doing. And if Van were honest with herself, Susan was easy on the eyes. Even with her hair tangled, dirt on her face, and bags under her eyes, she had a certain classic softness Van always found appealing. She also liked her determination to do things her way.

Susan's shoulders slumped. "I don't have anywhere to go. The Melengue Virus wiped out my whole family. I was just…going. I hoped I'd find somewhere safe in the north. Like everyone else on the continent. But then I realized I'd have to check in at a Gateway city, and they'd find me. So I was just kind of…wandering."

Van considered their situation. Susan wasn't in any shape to travel again yet, and they couldn't take her with them on the raid. But she was a lone survivor, and clearly not good at it. "If you'd like to go to our camp, I can have someone take you. Then if you figure out you want to head somewhere else, you're free to do so."

Hope flared in Susan's expression. "That would be amazing. I can travel with you?"

Van turned to her group, and all of them looked grim.

Liz crossed her arms and shook head vehemently. "Not me."

"Nor me, lassie." Mac pointed at the saline bag. "You have no idea what you're walking into, and you might need my help."

Ray shrugged. "I know where we're going and how to find them. But I'll do what you tell me to."

James sighed from his place in the doorway. "Why is the weather guy always the expendable one when it comes to these situations? I mean, the weather is the bad guy, right? Aren't I the superhero in this scenario?"

Van went over and clapped him on the shoulder. "Thanks, James. I appreciate it, you know that."

He waved her off. "Yeah, yeah. I've heard it before." The smile he gave her was understanding despite the truth of his words. "But I like when you owe me favors."

Van turned back to Susan. "We have to keep going to St. Louis. But James will stay here with you until you're able to travel. If we can pick you up on our way back, we will. If you're already able to go before we get back, James can radio for a pickup that will take you both back to camp."

Susan looked at James, who gave her a half smile and nod. "You won't be coming with us?"

Van sighed inwardly, reminding herself to be patient. *A little appreciation wouldn't go amiss.* "No, sorry. We're on an important supply run. But James is great. You'll be in good hands."

Susan lay back again, clearly thinking, but Van was tired and not in the mood to convince or argue. She'd take their help their way, or she wouldn't get it at all, no matter how attractive or determined she was. That was the way the world worked now. Survival was far more black-and-white than she'd like it to be, but she wasn't about to let down a hell of a lot of people for the sake of one who didn't appreciate what it meant to Van to lose a team member on a job like this. But then, it wasn't about appreciation. It was about doing what was right. *Lucky me.* Van turned away and lay down in her own cot. She'd shower later. For now, she just wanted the blank bliss of sleep.

She started when she felt a hand on her shoulder. The room was dark and she could hear the noises she'd come to know as those made by her team when they slept. She rolled over and looked up into Susan's eyes. She'd obviously showered, and she looked far fresher than when she'd collapsed outside their door. She leaned close enough that Van could smell whatever lightly scented, spicy lotion she was wearing.

"I just wanted to say thank you," she whispered. "I needed to say it now, in case you're gone in the morning."

Van rolled onto her side and propped herself on her elbow. "You didn't need to do that."

Susan flinched slightly, looking embarrassed. "I did. I probably came across as ungrateful. I needed you to know I'm not. I can't believe how lucky I am to have come across you."

Van didn't miss Susan's quick, not so subtle glance at her body. She liked the flare of appreciation she saw in her eyes and grinned when she met her eyes again.

Susan swallowed but didn't look away. "I'm looking forward to seeing you again, at wherever this mysterious camp of yours is." She tentatively touched Van's arm again. "Thank you."

With that, she turned and left, deftly moving past the sleeping team and back to the bunk she'd been given. Van watched as she snuggled down beneath the comforter, her back to the rest of the group. With a sigh, Van turned back over too. *That was unexpected.* She had to admit that although she didn't do entanglements, she was looking forward to getting back to Mesa for more than just the usual reasons now.

CHAPTER EIGHT

Devin woke to the too familiar sound of someone vomiting, a sound she was used to from living in the military barracks when the fever arrived the first time. She rolled over and squinted against the hazy gray light slipping through the blinds. Her head felt like it was full of angry kids from band camp. The space beside her was empty, leading to a logical conclusion about the identity of the vomiter.

When it went quiet in the bathroom, she got up and grabbed a bottle of water. She tapped on the door. "Hey. Can I come in?"

"By all that lives and breathes, please don't." Karissa's voice was hoarse and she sounded like she might be crying.

"Okay. Let me pass you a bottle of water?" Devin waited, but there was no answer, so she cracked open the door.

Karissa sat on the floor with her arms around her legs and her cheek resting on her knees. Tears tracked slow, winding trails down her cheeks. The bathroom smelled like sour tequila, but Devin had experienced worse. She squatted in front of Karissa and opened the bottle of water before handing it to her. "That bad?"

Karissa took the bottle and drank half of it down before stopping to breathe. "How are you still upright? Why aren't you right beside me?"

Devin laughed and smoothed a piece of Karissa's hair from her face. "I can hold my own when it comes to alcohol. And throwing up together isn't a good enough bonding experience to attempt it with you, sorry." She stood and wet a towel under the sink, then folded it and put it on the back of Karissa's neck.

"Mmm. That's nice."

Devin didn't know what else to do with her hands that was appropriate in this situation, so she decided to do something else. "I'm going to talk to the guys and see if we're heading out soon. I'll see about breakfast, too. Back in a minute."

Karissa gave a halfhearted nod but kept her eyes closed.

Devin pulled on her jeans and sweatshirt and left the room. She could hear voices in the other rooms as she passed, but no one else was up and out yet. She met Walker at the top of the stairs. He looked exhausted, and the two soldiers beside him were sleeping like babies; uncomfortable, contorted ones in stiff chairs, but still.

"Morning."

"Hey, Lieutenant. Everything okay?"

"Fine, thanks. You been on duty all night?" The bags under his eyes were dark, and he looked like he could barely keep his eyes open. She knew the signs of extreme fatigue.

He motioned at the guys next to him. "Thought they should get some rest."

With a nod, she kicked the boots of the soldier next to him, who startled awake. "Time to rise and shine, beautiful. Your superior needs some sleep too."

"Yes, ma'am." He struggled awake, yawned and stretched, then looked at Walker. "Why don't you find a real bed? We've got this."

Walker stood a little unsteadily. "The storm is only in a lull. It'll start up again any minute, so we're staying put until we know it's safe to get moving and the floodwaters have receded some." He spoke to the soldier Devin had woken up. "I'll be in room one. Get me if you need anything at all."

Devin gave him a light push toward the room. "They've got this, and I'll be here if they need anything. Get some sleep or you won't be worth a damn once we get back on the road."

Without another word, Walker headed into the empty room and closed the door behind him. Devin turned to the other soldier. "Want to wake up your friend so we can get breakfast rations going? We can set things out in the living room up here."

He jumped to, waking up the other guy and calling out to the guys at the other end of the hall to tell them what they were doing. Even though Devin wasn't in active service, her reputation meant they took orders as though she was, and she didn't mind a bit. They'd had the foresight to bring in the boxes of food the night before, so Devin helped them carry the food containers to the living room. She knocked on doors as they passed, yelling, "Grub time! Food's on in the living room!" After she'd deposited her batch on the table she went back to her room.

This time Karissa was on the bed instead of on the bathroom floor, and her color looked slightly better. Even suffering from a hellish hangover, she was gorgeous. "Feel like anything to eat? Maybe just bread and coffee?" She pretended to sniff the air. "We could do to air out the room a little…"

Karissa half-flung a pillow at her. "Coffee sounds divine. I'm not eating anything until we get to wherever we're going." She finally opened her eyes and looked at Devin sheepishly. "I'm sorry about last night."

Devin hoped her disappointment didn't show. The last thing she wanted was an apology. "Hey, no problem. That homemade hooch is a wicked mistress. It was just a kiss, right? And not even a good one, really. Far too quick. I've kissed relatives longer than that—"

Karissa held up her hand to stop her. "I wasn't apologizing for the kiss. I was apologizing for passing out before you got out of the bath."

"Oh." Devin gave her a lopsided grin. "In that case, the kiss was really nice. And maybe tonight we won't have so much to drink before we go to sleep."

Karissa laughed and slowly got to her feet. Devin grabbed her as she swayed and reached out.

"I don't think I'll have anything other than water tonight, thanks. And I'll never eat those tortilla chips again. Way too disgusting tasting them a second time."

Devin grimaced. "Too much information, too early in the morning." She put her arm around Karissa's waist. "Come on, let's get coffee."

When they got to the living room most everyone else was there, already eating and chatting. They took seats next to the Cantos, who were in conversation with a young man from the other truck.

"I wish I could ride with you guys. Whenever everyone is awake in our truck, it's nothing but talk about how wrong it all is and how they're going to protest." He shrugged and picked at his eggs. "Seems like a waste of air to me."

Edward patted his shoulder. "We can ask if you'd like us to?" He looked at the others in the group, who nodded assent. "This is Zeke Shan. He's a computer guy."

Devin shook his hand and liked that it was firm. She always thought you could tell a lot about a person by their handshake. She didn't miss his lingering glance at Karissa when she introduced herself, though, and she found it mildly amusing when she felt a tickle of possessiveness. A raised voice got her attention.

"You've already got us. We can't go anywhere without you now, thanks to the storm and the fact that you took most of us without even letting us bring a bag." Ivan stood with his hands on his hips, glaring at the soldier standing in front of him, his entitled, angry voice filling the room. "You may as well tell us where we're going."

"Sir, I just asked if you wanted orange juice." The soldier sighed and held up the glass.

Ivan grabbed the glass and tossed the contents into the soldier's face. There were several gasps and Devin swore she heard someone chuckle. She was surprised when Karissa jumped up and strode over to the pair. She sat back to watch. Having seen the way Karissa had reacted when she'd been taken from her home, she was pretty sure she could handle this.

Karissa handed the soldier a towel and then turned to face Ivan. "That was really not cool. He was being nice."

Ivan looked her up and down as though trying to determine if she was worth the breath it took to answer. "They've kidnapped us.

Ripped us from our homes, our lives. And they won't even tell us where we're going." He looked at her disdainfully. "Forgive me, princess, if I don't have sympathy for our captors."

Devin nearly laughed out loud when Karissa got right in Ivan's face.

"Listen to me, you entitled bag of douche backwash. None of us likes what is happening. We all want to know what's going on. But behaving like a rabid rat-face who should be put down isn't going to make this trip any easier on anyone. They're just doing what they've been told to do, and I, for one, am grateful they've been damn accommodating when they can. So save your narcissistic bullying for the people who ordered this to happen."

Devin broke into applause and a few others joined in, especially Zeke, who had probably had his share of Ivan's vitriol. Ivan stomped from the room with his head held high, but he was clearly shaken by Karissa standing up to him.

The soldier thanked her quietly and then offered orange juice to the others, who were far more gracious, and a few shot Karissa a nervous look as they went out of their way to be grateful.

Karissa nodded and sat back down next to Devin. When she saw Devin's raised eyebrow, she looked a little embarrassed. "I hate seeing people treated like crap. Someone needed to say something."

"Sticking up for the little guy, huh?" Devin laughed. "Even if the little guy is in charge and carries a stunbar."

"I think in various circumstances we all face the possibility of being the little guy. If no one is willing to take a stand, we all fall together."

Devin thought about that as she finished her coffee and pre-packaged bread roll. She liked Karissa's idealism. There hadn't been a lot of that around in the last century, and with every natural disaster it decreased yet again. Most people were out for themselves now that survival was the primary target. That Karissa would put herself between a bully and a soldier to protect the soldier made her someone Devin could respect. It also made her even sexier.

After breakfast, most everyone wandered back to their rooms, and Devin and Karissa grabbed another cup of coffee before heading back to theirs. They propped the pillows up on the bed and Karissa sighed over her coffee mug.

"I miss the real stuff. Brewed in a glass pot, that filled the whole room with the scent of coffee. I liked to add a bit of chicory to mine."

Devin could imagine it. "I miss broccoli. I used to love it when I was a kid. All those tiny green trees. I felt like a giant eating a forest."

"And apples. Apples were amazing. I loved the way they crunched." Karissa sighed. "Did you leave anyone behind?" she asked tentatively.

Devin shook her head. "Honestly, I was getting ready to head to a Gateway city when the truck came for me. No family, no friends. I was already on my own, so this is just part of the adventure for me. I'm interested in seeing where this leads. Maybe they'll have real coffee and broccoli, wherever we're headed."

They sat in silence for a while, and Devin wondered what she was thinking, but she looked so immersed in thought she didn't want to intrude. When tears began to fall, though, she set down her coffee and moved closer. She raised her arm and Karissa slid under it to curl against her.

"Want to talk about it?"

Karissa wiped her face with her sleeve. "I miss my parents. I miss my messy office with my messy desk and my egotistical co-workers." She shifted so she could look up into Devin's eyes. "Do you really not know where we're going?"

Devin gently caressed Karissa's hair. "I have some guesses, but no, they haven't told me, and as much as I'd like to know, I've always liked surprises. I'm sorry though, that you've left so much. I can't imagine how hard that is." She smiled gently. "But I can definitely say a benefit to the craziness of it is that I've gotten to meet you, and that makes all the riding around in that god-awful truck and getting pulled into puddles worth it."

Karissa shifted again so she was comfortably pillowed against Devin. "I think you're a smooth talker, but I like the way that sounds."

Devin felt her breathing slow and her body relax. She really liked the way Karissa fit under her arm, like a puzzle piece sliding into place. She closed her eyes and just let herself enjoy the warm comfort of it. Her last relationship had gone up in dramatic flames, and she hadn't troubled herself with another one for several years. *Not that this is a relationship. Or could even be one.* Like Karissa said, this wasn't a lesbian pleasure cruise. They were lucky to have guards who were kind, but they were still, essentially, prisoners of some sort. As she drifted to sleep as well, Karissa snuggled closer and Devin held her a little tighter. Whatever was ahead of them, she damn well wanted to keep Karissa safe. She thought again of the way she'd gotten in Ivan's face, and smiled when she thought of Karissa's special use of adjectives. She'd noticed him watching Karissa several times, and it was a look she recognized. Did Karissa have any idea Ivan had a crush on her? Probably not. And given the way she'd stood up to him, she wouldn't have cared. *She may end up keeping me safe.*

CHAPTER NINE

Karissa tried to snuggle into the warmth that kept receding from her back. The chill of the room touched her only briefly before the cover was tucked back over her again. When she tried to fall back asleep, though, sounds of running and loud voices filtered in and drew her away from the sensual dreams that involved moonlight and shadowed kisses.

She blinked and realized the warmth behind her had been Devin tucked against her, but Devin wasn't in the room now. She sat up and listened.

Footsteps pounded down the hallway, and someone was yelling at someone else. She threw off the covers and pulled on her sweats before going to the hallway. A guard ran past and she quickly moved out of his way. Devin was talking to two of the guards at the end of the hallway, and she was standing in what Karissa had come to think of as her military stance. Shoulders back, head high, looking like the person in charge. Sometimes Karissa realized she'd forgotten that Devin, too, had been taken the way the rest of them had. She just didn't mind. *Or she doesn't seem to, anyway.*

She went to Devin and listened in from behind her.

"The storm broke around four this morning. If they left around that time, they could have a four-hour head start, and you have no idea which direction they went. You could chase them exactly the wrong way."

Sergeant Walker sighed and rubbed his eyes. "I hear you. But I can't very well go back and say someone escaped and I didn't even bother looking for them."

"Who's gone?" Karissa asked.

Devin turned around. "That couple from the other truck; they were Latin, I think?"

Karissa thought about it. "They hardly ever talked to anyone. Not that I saw when we stopped, anyway."

Walker shrugged. "That's part of the problem. We picked them up in Pittsburgh. They weren't a couple, either. They were colleagues. We don't know if they'll try to get back there, or if they'll head somewhere else. To family, maybe."

Devin moved to the window and Karissa followed her while Walker went to talk to his soldiers.

"What are you thinking?" Karissa asked softly. She could almost see the thoughts moving in Devin's eyes.

Devin kept looking out the window. "Do I try to help them find these people? Or do we wish them well and hope like hell they get away?"

Karissa wasn't sure what the answer was. "If there wasn't a storm, and there weren't insane floodwaters, I'd say wish them Godspeed. But conditions are terrible, and they could get into trouble if they run into a flash flood or undertow situation." She felt awful. If she'd decided to run, she'd hope that the people who'd been taken with her would let her go. "No...I take it back. If they wanted to chance it, if it was that important to them, then they should be allowed to get as far as they possibly can. We all know the risks of travel."

Devin nodded slowly. "You're right." She turned and went back to Walker, who was laying into the guards who had fallen asleep at the top of the stairs, and not woken when the pair had snuck past. "Sergeant, I'm fully aware I'm not in charge here. But if you want my opinion, I'd say do a small perimeter search so you can cover your asses. Check a local grid, and then get us back on the road as soon as the floodwaters make it possible. You've got other pickups, right?" He nodded. "And you've got dates for those pickups. Staying here to search is going to delay you, and the people you're after could be gone. You could miss the two that have left, and you could miss the others we have yet to get. You'd be shit out of luck on every side."

Walker was silent as he considered Devin's idea. He turned to the other guards. "Do a circular sweep within a mile. Be careful. The floodwaters are draining and there's a wicked pull. Check in every ten minutes. When you're done with the sweep, get the vehicles as close as you can so we can load up and head out the moment we're able." The guards, looking subdued, nodded and headed out without a word.

"Thanks." Walker motioned down the hallway to the living room where several people stood at the doorway watching them. "I'm worried that if people think those others can escape, they can too. I don't want to have to restrain or hurt anybody."

Karissa felt for him. He looked too young to be in a position of authority like this, where he had to forcibly take people to an undisclosed location. He also seemed too kind. He was lucky Devin was there to help him through it. She was a steady presence in a crazy situation.

"Try not to stress about that now. Take one situation at a time, right?" She patted him on the back and took Karissa's hand. "Let's grab some breakfast."

Karissa liked the way Devin's hand felt in her own. Strong, firm, but soft, too. Still, she didn't want to start developing feelings for someone just because they were in a crisis together. She gently pulled her hand away but gave Devin a smile when she looked over at her. Devin gave her a small smile in return and didn't seem fazed.

They grabbed bowls of oatmeal and joined their group.

"Something, huh?" Edward said, looking thoughtful. "Who would have thought you could just sneak away in the night?"

Devin shook her head. "I don't think it was a good idea. Floodwaters were nearly five feet. They'll have had to swim most of the way to higher ground, and there was a lot of debris out there."

Sheila frowned and leaned forward. "I'm wondering whose side you're on. Don't you think it's worth trying? Or do you think we just go like lambs to the slaughter?"

Karissa wanted to jump to Devin's defense, but the truth was, she wasn't entirely sure where Devin stood either. She really liked her, but that didn't mean they had the same outlook on things.

Devin tilted her head in acknowledgement. "I don't think there's any slaughter at the end of this. I agree it's all messed up, and the way it's being done is shit. But I also know that out there, on your own," she pointed at the window, where humidity was already steaming it up, "you've got a whole host of bad things waiting to happen." She sipped her coffee and looked around the group. "I say, if you're going to get out of this, you do it in a way that doesn't mean taking your life in your hands."

"And what if by the time we get to where we're going it's too late to do anything about it?" Karissa asked. She knew full well Devin didn't have the answers, and she knew Devin had a point. Still, it was worth asking whatever questions came up. There could be a time when any questions they should have asked were no longer relevant.

Devin sighed heavily. "I don't know. I have to believe that there will be some kind of choice at the other end of this tunnel. I mean, look at what we are—scientists and engineers at the top of our game. We're wanted for something specific, and you don't kill people you need."

The group finished their meal silently, and Karissa contemplated everyone's journey. Apart from Devin, they'd all lost someone or something. She wondered what her parents were doing, how her mom was feeling. She wondered if the couple had managed to get to higher ground—

"Sarge, come in."

The echo of the radio call was stark in the silent room and everyone looked toward Walker. He turned his back but didn't leave the room, and Karissa knew he was willing to give people answers, even if it didn't do him much good with regard to their behavior.

"Go for Sarge."

"Found them on the south side of the building. Both deceased. Looks like the floodwaters got them before they made it very far."

There were a few gasps and swears from people listening, and Karissa felt sick. *That will certainly keep people from trying to get away.* She didn't even know their names, but her heart broke a little at their desperate grasp for freedom that had ended so terribly.

"Bury them on the ridge. Get their PIDs and bring them back." Walker's shoulders were hunched and he rested his head against the wall. Karissa got up and went to him.

"It's not your fault."

He glanced at her. "It is. If I hadn't picked them up, they wouldn't have tried to leave."

She nodded. "That's true. But the fact is, they didn't have to try to leave in the aftermath of a storm. That was their choice. They chose wrong." She touched his hand. "You're doing your job. We were warned a year ago, and we didn't take it seriously enough. That's not your fault either."

Devin came up beside her. "She's right. You could be an asshole, shoving people around, shouting, tying people up. Instead you're being human, and we're grateful for that. I bet other convoys don't have it nearly as good as we do."

He stood a little taller. "Thanks." He turned to the others in the room. "Look. I know you don't want to be here. Truth be told, I don't want to be here either. But this is the situation we're in. You've seen what can happen if you try to make it on your own. Stick with us to the end. We'll get you where you need to go in one piece. Okay?"

There were a few nods and some murmurs of assent.

Karissa turned to Devin. "Can we get to the roof, do you think? I'd love to get some fresh air."

"Great idea." Devin looked at Walker, who nodded.

"I'll shout when it's time to start packing up. It'll be a while." He walked away, and conversation resumed in the room when he'd gone.

Karissa went to the others in their group. "Anyone else want to go to the roof for some fresh air?"

They gathered their cups of coffee and juice and Devin led the way to a back stairway that led to the roof door. She and Edward had to put their shoulders to it to get it open, but when it did the fresh air that hit Karissa was more than welcome.

They headed out into the sunshine and she closed her eyes. It was never really cold anymore, but it could get damp and chilly when the sun disappeared for a few days at a time. There was nothing like the fresh air after a storm blew through. It cleared the smog and humidity for a little while, and made her feel as though there was hope; the promise of better days ahead slid down the rays of the sun and into her skin.

Devin took her hand, and this time she didn't pull away. She wanted this moment, this feeling of peace and promise, for just a little while longer. Until they got into the truck and headed once more for the unknown.

CHAPTER TEN

St. Louis was in the process of becoming a Gateway city. Shops were open, though people had to climb over floodgates to get in. People walked and cycled down wet, steamy streets just beginning to dry out. Rainwater barrels were covered and brought inside to be used during the drought season. And everywhere there were armed guards watching as laborers built the wall that would eventually surround the city, encapsulating the crops and the people. It seemed like a concrete cage, and Devin knew she'd rather live out in the open and scratch by than get better food but be under surveillance and cut off from the outside world.

They made their way into the suburbs and it seemed surreal that kids were kicking a ball around on the street. They stopped playing to watch the convoy pass, and one boy plucked up the courage to throw a stone at the back of the truck before it had passed too far. The driver tapped the brakes and the kids ran off, shouting.

Sunlight flooded the truck when the soldiers slid the doors open. They'd begun doing that as often as possible to allow some of the humidity out. Everyone in the back was sweating and miserable as the clouds cleared and the heat set in, and the fresh air was a huge relief. Devin had stripped down to her tank top and wasn't about to object when Karissa did the same. The thin material pulled tight over her generous breasts and hugged her waist, and the sweat droplets on her chest gave Devin something entirely different to concentrate on than the stifling truck.

But the door had only been open a few minutes before Walker came back, shaking his head.

"Gone. House is boarded up, but I don't think it's been empty long. We probably just missed her."

"So do you track her down like an animal? Capture her and take her into her cage?" Ivan asked from where he leaned insolently against the side of the second truck.

Walker rolled his eyes at Devin before he turned around to face Ivan. "No. We keep moving forward. We let base know she's gone and they put out an alert to the other convoys to keep an eye out. We keep going."

Ivan shrugged like it didn't matter, but clearly he didn't have a retort at the ready. He glanced at Karissa and looked away.

Devin looked at Walker. "Any chance we can ride with the door open for a while? No one on this truck is going to jump off." She knew it was a slim chance, but she had to ask. The smell of seven humans in an airless truck was like being stuck in the world's worst locker room.

"Sorry, boss. No can do. It's not so much that I'm worried about anyone running, as much as we have to be aware of roadside ambushes. Better you've got a door between you and anyone who comes after whatever they think we've got."

Devin sighed and nodded. That made sense, even if it sucked.

"Just out of curiosity, who were we picking up?" Karissa asked. She hadn't moved from her position on the floor, and she looked exhausted.

Walker looked at the paperwork in his hands, then looked at Karissa. "Can I ask why?"

She barely moved her shoulders in a shrug. "We seem to have heard of one another in some way. I'm just wondering if any of us knew this one."

"Dr. Susan Sandish." He waved to the other driver who started up the second truck, and their own quickly came to life as well. "We're heading to our final pickup, and then we'll be on our way to our final destination. Hang in there."

Devin resumed her position on the floor of the truck, the soles of her boots against the soles of Karissa's. It was way too hot to be physically close to anyone, but she wanted that little bit of contact. She was worried about how tired Karissa looked. She'd hardly eaten anything and the dark circles under her eyes suggested she hadn't slept the night before either. Not that it was easy to do on the road, but still. If they stopped tonight, she'd try to talk her into eating more, and maybe even curling up with her to sleep.

She drifted off, used to the resigned silence surrounding them now, and lulled by the shadows passing over the small windows.

She had no idea how long she'd been asleep when the truck jolted to a hard stop, slamming them all forward.

Gunfire made her freeze. There was shouting, screams, and return fire. She could tell from the windows that it was dark outside, but flashes lit the truck walls with angry lightning. Thunder combined with gunfire rattled around them.

"Move to the middle and stay low." As the others crouched around her, Devin raged that there wasn't a handle on this side so she could get out and help.

Edward put his arm around his wife, who cried softly. When someone banged on the door, she cried out and Edward pulled her tighter. Karissa pressed against Devin's back and she reached back to hold her hand.

"We're opening the door. We are armed, and we're not looking for a fight. Stand down, let us get what we need, and you can be on your way!" The voice shouting from outside sounded female and pissed off.

"We're all unarmed and won't be a problem," Devin shouted back.

The truck door opened to reveal a scene of chaos. The second truck lay on its side, tires in tatters. Smoke curled into the wet air amid sheets of heavy rain, backlit by regular flashes of lightning.

Three people were silhouetted against the flickering headlights from the second vehicle. The one at the front motioned with her gun. "Sorry, you'll have to get a little wet. We'll make this quick."

They filed out of the truck, and Devin tried to keep herself between the gunmen and people she'd come to think of as her responsibility. Once everyone was out, two of the gunmen jumped into the truck, ripped down the canvas sheet at the back, and started hauling out boxes of provisions that they piled into a converted military vehicle.

Devin stepped forward and didn't flinch when the woman in charge leveled her gun at her. "Leave us enough to get wherever we're going, would you? There's no need to starve people who haven't been given a choice in this whole thing."

She couldn't see the woman's expression in the darkness, but she appeared to consider Devin's words. She turned and yelled, "Leave two boxes. That will get them there."

Devin inclined her head in thanks and stepped back. She put her arm around Karissa and didn't move away when Zeke pressed closer to her too. Rain soaked them through and they watched as their rations disappeared. Devin craned to see the front of their truck, and saw Walker and another soldier on their knees with their hands on the backs of their heads, a gunman behind them with a rifle. Both front tires were blown and smoke rose from the hood. She turned and looked at the second truck, which was in far worse state than their own. No one moved over there, and a sick feeling rose in her throat as she wondered if they were all dead.

"Shit! Van, look north!" One of the gunmen loading boxes stopped and pointed.

The gunman by Devin turned, and a flash of lightning showed death headed their way. The massive tornado in the distance meant time was up.

"Evac, now!" the one called Van yelled, and all her gunmen turned and headed to their vehicles.

Devin grabbed her arm and once again didn't back down when the gun was leveled at her. She'd faced worse. "You can't leave us here with no cover and no wheels!"

The woman jerked her arm free. "Sorry, egghead. No room at the inn. But there's a silo about a mile away. You should make it in time if you hoof it." She pointed. "Head that way and turn left when you get to a tree painted blue. Follow the blue trees from there." She walked backward. "Good luck."

Devin watched as they got in their truck and drove off, quickly lost from sight in the driving rain. Every minute of survival training she ever had took over. Walker and the other soldier ran over. Blood ran in thin rivers from a cut on Walker's head, and the other soldier's eye was puffy and darkening.

"The others?" Devin yelled over the howling wind. They had precious little time.

"Soldiers are down. I don't know about the rest," Walker yelled back. "Take your group in the direction the raider told you about. I'll get the survivors from the other truck and follow." He stuck out his hand and Devin grabbed it. "No matter what happens, I'm damn glad to have met you, Lieutenant." With a final squeeze, he and the other soldier moved off to the other truck.

Devin turned to the others. "Grab your belongings. We'll need to move as fast as we can to get to shelter before that comes our way."

Karissa let go of her hand and climbed into the truck, as did the others with bags. Edward and Sheila stood shaking and waiting beside Devin. Within moments, the rest were back with their bags, and Devin set off at a jog with everyone behind her. She could only hope the raider hadn't been feeding her bullshit in order to get her to back down, but somehow she knew instinctively the woman's words had been true.

They dodged wildly swinging branches and debris flying through the air. Devin leapt across a hole and reached out to help the others do the same. The air was heavier, the rain sharp, the wind screaming oaths of revenge for the ravaging of the planet. She very nearly missed the blue paint on the old oak, but when she saw it, the knot of dread that the gun-toting woman had lied unraveled, giving fresh energy to her exhausted legs. She turned as directed and saw a line of blue trees leading the way beneath the snapping and crashing of the tornado's winds as it ripped through the land.

When they made it to the last blue tree in the line there was a red arrow painted on it. Devin turned and could barely make out the pitch-black hole at the bottom of a long ramp. Just as they started toward it there was a horrifying crash followed by a scream. Devin looked back and saw Sheila on the ground, her leg pierced through with a tree branch.

"Go!" Devin pushed Karissa toward the ramp and safety. "Get the others inside! I'll be right behind you."

Karissa's eyes were wide and Devin could tell she was close to panicking, but she grabbed Zeke's hand and the small group ran forward. Devin scrambled back to Edward and Sheila. He was cradling her head in his lap, telling her to hold on. He looked at Devin, fear etched into every line in his face.

"We have to get inside!" she shouted, her words whipped away by the gale. "Take one arm. I'll take the other."

They lifted Sheila to her feet. She was mercifully unconscious, but it meant they had to drag her, and Devin winced as the branch impaling her leg caught more than once on the ground, forcing them to unstick it before they could move forward.

Down the ramp and into the mouth of darkness, the tearing sounds abated as they were surrounded by thick concrete. Ahead of them, Karissa and the others waited with a single flashlight between them. The water was only ankle high here, but it could rise fast.

"Let's move as far into this thing as we can. There's no telling how long the storm will last." Devin managed to catch her breath but could hear Edward struggling. Between his fear and the weight of his wife, he wouldn't last much longer, and she couldn't carry two people. "Zeke, take over for Edward." When Edward started to protest, she shook her head. "Ed, you need to watch that branch. Make sure it doesn't catch on anything we can't see and try to keep it steady."

Zeke replaced Edward without saying a word, carefully taking Sheila's weight. Edward stayed close and his hands fluttered around the branch as he walked backward in front of them.

"Ed, I think you need to do this from behind. If you trip and fall, we could fall over you," Devin said, hoping to get him behind her so she could see clearly ahead.

"Sure, Dev, no problem." He ran around behind them.

Devin could see the group ahead of them clearly now, and the flashlight highlighted the old cement walls covered in moss and streaks of rust from ancient fittings. The group stopped, and Karissa turned around to look at Devin.

"I hear voices. Toward or away?"

Devin weighed the options. There could be safety in numbers, and there was a chance someone with medical training could be there. There was also a good chance the voices belonged to the gunmen who would shoot them as soon as they saw them.

Sheila groaned and Devin's decision was made.

"Toward."

Karissa nodded and turned left, and Devin could see a sliver of light at the far end of the corridor. The sound of the storm was faint, and Devin could feel the slight slope that told her they were heading underground. As they moved toward the unknown, Devin hoped to hell she hadn't just led people she'd come to care about into a trap. Karissa glanced over her shoulder at Devin, and Devin gave her a quick smile. *Please don't let me have made a deadly mistake.*

CHAPTER ELEVEN

In the eerie glow of the flashlight, Karissa looked at the bedraggled group behind her. Devin's brief, encouraging smile gave her the courage she needed to turn and face the hall in front of her. She'd never been as terrified as she had been running through the woods to a shelter they weren't even sure existed.

If it hadn't been for the tornado bearing down on them, she would never have considered entering the hole in the hillside, but the people behind her had needed to follow someone. Devin was playing hero in the dark behind her, so she'd done what she had to. But knowing Devin had gone back to help Sheila, away from safety, away from the group, had left Karissa's heart in her throat. Aside from the fact that Karissa really liked her, Devin was trained to survive. The rest of them were lab rats. *They could be Navy Seals for all I know. No, not likely.* If so, Karissa wouldn't be the one leading them into an underground shelter of some kind.

She paused at the doorway and listened. It would be impossible to recognize any of the voices of the gunmen thanks to the howling of the storm, if, in fact, they'd come here too. She heard what sounded like several men and at least one woman.

"You may as well come in now that you've made it this far."

Karissa froze at the voice but moved forward with the others behind her. There weren't a lot of options. She just hoped this was a lesser evil than the storm outside.

Two men and two women sat around a cylinder fire. They were dry and dressed casually and didn't look at all like the menacing people with guns who'd attacked them. Karissa breathed a sigh of relief. "Our convoy was attacked. Can we join you?"

The group exchanged glances and Karissa wondered if she'd missed something. She'd never been great with people, preferring a microscope to social interaction, and sometimes cues took her a while to figure out. But the taller woman stood and smiled slightly.

"Sure. Come on in." She pointed to the back of the room. "Grab a towel and dry off."

"One of our group is injured. Is anyone medically trained?" Karissa motioned behind her at Devin and Zeke, still holding Sheila between them.

The oldest man came forward, his bushy gray eyebrows furrowed. "That's me, lassie. Let's have a look."

Devin and Zeke moved forward with Sheila, whose skin had a sickly beige color to it now.

"Nasty one. Bring her in the back." The man led the way, and they followed him into an adjoining room, Edward hovering close behind.

Karissa got a towel and gratefully dried the water from her sopping hair. Natasha and John joined her, and they sat with the others around the makeshift campfire.

"Thank you for this. Are you taking cover from the tornado too?" Karissa held her hands in front of the fire, glad for its warmth.

The slight woman glanced at the tall woman, and there was an odd quirk to her smile.

"No one should be out in this weather. Spring is a bad time to travel," the taller one said. "I'm Van. This is Liz and Ray."

Something wasn't right, but Karissa wasn't sure what to do about it. The conversation felt weighted, like a trapdoor hidden just a few steps ahead. What if they'd made it away from the gunmen only to fall into the hands of someone worse?

"We've got food, too. It'll be out in a second. Liz, why don't you throw in some more for our guests?"

Liz saluted mockingly and went into another adjoining room.

Natasha and John were strangely silent, but she put it down to the terror of the night. Karissa directed her questions to the tall woman, who was clearly in charge.

"What is this place, anyway?"

Van looked at her like she was studying a specimen. "It's an ancient missile silo, built back in the nineteen sixties. It's been abandoned for more than a hundred years, but it's a perfect storm shelter. Deep underground with lots of exits, and the drainage system is still in great condition, meaning it doesn't flood often."

Karissa took that in. It seemed somehow fitting they'd escaped a kind of war zone and taken refuge in an old war building. "How did you know about it?"

"Because it's a safe house for them." Devin came in, toweling her hair, and sat beside Karissa.

Karissa looked between Van and Devin, who were clearly sizing each other up. "Who is *them*?" Her stomach sank as she guessed the answer.

"They're our friends who turned our rides into unusable crates and stole all our food." Devin's hands were white around the towel.

"And told you where to find shelter, thereby saving your lives." Van glanced at the towel in Devin's hands and raised her eyebrow.

"And what about the lives of those who didn't come with us? The ones in the other truck?" Natasha asked softly, her eyes staying on the fire.

That's why they were so quiet. Natasha and John had known they were the same people. It was only Karissa who hadn't. She'd been so focused on the gun she hadn't paid attention to the person holding it, and had hardly listened to the conversation. *I knew. I just didn't want to.* Self-deception was a silly habit, but one she'd used over the years in order to cope with things beyond her control. Doing so now could cost them their lives. She focused.

"We hadn't accounted for the storm debris under the tire spikes. The driver over corrected and hit a tree trunk." The one named Ray shrugged like it was no big deal.

"Oh, so it was the driver's fault?" Karissa nearly stood, but Devin's hand on her arm kept her in place. Guns or not, how dared they attack innocent people?

"Where do you think they were taking you?" Van leaned forward, breaking into the conversation. "Do you know?"

Karissa hated being backed into a corner but didn't have an answer. She looked at Devin, but Devin was looking at Van.

"Do you know?" Devin leaned back and crossed her legs, as though the answer didn't matter. "Is that something to do with why you raided the truck?"

Karissa was so pissed off she'd gladly forgo answers just to punch someone. She didn't always communicate with people well, but that didn't mean she was a doormat either. Anger could be an excellent communication tool. But she reined it in and listened. Knowledge was power, and right now, they needed every scrap of information they could get.

"Sure you want to know? Because once you do, you'll have some serious decisions to make." Van looked at each of them in turn.

Karissa and the others nodded. They were scientists, and truth was more valuable than fear.

Van settled back and accepted the mug of coffee Liz offered. "Twenty-five years ago, the government, aware we'd passed the critical point to prevent massive climate change, began serious development of a new space station. One had already been in place since the late nineteen hundreds, but this one was special."

Mac and Edward came in, got drinks, and sat with the group. "Got the branch out. Lot of blood loss. Pretty critical, but we'll have to wait and see." Mac closed his eyes. "Go on."

Van nodded. "The new space station was farther out and temporary. It was only a stopping point to the next step."

"To where?" Karissa's curiosity was piqued, despite her wanting to cause the woman bodily harm.

"To 128D."

Karissa stared at her, stunned. "What are you saying?" Technically called Ross 128D, the exoplanet had been an astounding discovery in 2028. Only eleven light years away, it had an atmosphere similar to Earth's and was in exactly the right position to its star. Water ran freely, and the temperature, although far colder due to the distance from the sun, wasn't unlivable. Theories had abounded about visiting it, but research had shut down once climate change dictated spending money and resources on the planet they already had, rather than on one they didn't. Or, that's what had been reported.

"They not only kept exploring possibilities, they began full development of the space station. And then five years ago, the space station was completed." Van's eyes were dark, her expression grim. "Not only that, but they'd sent drone explorers to the planet, and word came back that it was inhabitable."

Everyone was silent as Liz left the room and then came back with food. Karissa couldn't touch it. For days, she'd been thinking of her parents, of the life she'd left behind. Now…

"What does that have to do with us? Specifically?" Karissa shook her head when Devin tried to press a bowl of food into her hands.

"You specifically? I have no idea. But there have been egghead convoys moving to Colorado and other classified sites around the world for nearly two years now. Military trucks full of lots of smart people go into the facility at Cheyenne Mountain and don't come out again."

Devin ate slowly, laser-focused on Van. "Why scientists?"

Liz handed Van her portion of food, and then looked down at Devin. "They chose the best and brightest of every field so they could take them away to build their new world. There have been others, too. Builders, plumbers, architects, etcetera. People to actually build the shit the scientists come up with when they send you away." She pointed toward the sky.

Karissa felt like she might throw up. "They're sending us into space?"

Van nodded and slurped her noodles. "That's right. Our government contact told us that you'll live on the space station first, and then you'll go to 128D when it's your turn. A whole planet of smart and talented people. While the rest of us are left to fend for ourselves." Her voice was hard, her eyes slate.

"Doesn't seem like you should be pissed off at the people chosen. It's not like we had a say in it." John shoved his bowl away, his eyes full of tears.

"Oh, we have nothing against you guys. Far from it. This wasn't about you. We only do supply raids when we have to, and we try to do it clean and quick." Van emptied her bowl and set it on the concrete floor beside her. "You'll get all the food and care you need at the facility. But those of us left here need help, so we take what we can from the convoys, because we know there's plenty where you're headed. And we're not willing to risk lives by attacking any of the Gateway cities. Once the populations in the Gateways hit capacity, those of us living outside them will have to learn how to survive whatever comes at us next. Right now, we're grabbing what we can, when we can."

Karissa was processing the situation as fast as she could. The others looked just as shell-shocked as she felt, which made her feel a little better. At least she hadn't been the last one to figure this out too.

"And who are you? You're way too organized and calm to be regular bandits."

Liz grinned. "I like being thought of as a bandit. Robin Hood and her merry band of misfits."

Van grinned back at her before answering Devin's question. "We're part of EART."

Natasha scoffed. "That group is an urban myth. Today's version of the Illuminati from the twentieth century."

"Then you've got mythological beings sitting in front of you, lass." Mac raised his drink in a toast.

"I like the idea of being mythological. Like an avenging goddess." Liz posed like she was shooting a bow.

Zeke, the youngest of the group, looked baffled. "What's EART? I've never heard of it."

Van smiled at him. "Myth indeed. It stands for Earth Action Response Team. It was created as a militant environmental group in the early two thousands. The people behind it were a strange combination of scientists and humanists, brought together by a belief in the eventual tipping point of climate change. They were hardcore radicals who did whatever they thought necessary to try to make a difference."

"Including killing people." Devin's jaw clenched. "They blew up buildings without giving a damn whether anyone got caught in the crossfire."

Van tilted her head in acknowledgement. "And so they went underground. Methods became more sophisticated. Computer hackers would get in and shut down operational mainframes. Team members would go undercover and pose as workers, who would find ways to create organizational chaos behind the scenes. Every day major manufacturers weren't operating meant a little less pollution."

Karissa listened attentively, trying to take it all in and create patterns from the information. "But after the twenty fifty summit, all that changed anyway. Why stay in existence?"

"Just because governments say something doesn't make it true." Ray, who'd been quietly eating, finally spoke up. "All the summit did was dictate measures to slow down the train that was about to hit us. And the people with money continued to do what the hell they wanted to. Nothing new there. EART kept going to shut down the assholes driving the train."

His eyes were sad though his words were angry, and Karissa felt an illogical desire to reach out to him. Instead, she turned back to Van. "But major manufacturing has been shut down for years now. Corporations exist on solar power and desalination, for the most part, and only in the Gateways." She glared at Van. "Does that mean you're remnants of a regime that once tried to do something important, however misguided, and now all you do is attack innocent people and take their provisions?"

Liz stood, her face flushed and her eyes blazing. "Look, lady, we could have left you all out there to die—"

Van put her hand on Liz's arm. "Relax. It's a valid question."

Liz sat back down, still grumbling. "I'm not a damn remnant of anything…"

Van smiled at her as she rubbed her eyes. "Even when everything pretty much shut down, EART believed in the need to keep being proactive. So they began developing their own type of technology while still keeping an eye on the world overall. They recruited people skilled in every aspect of what it takes to survive and created a global network meant to develop protocols."

"Weren't those kinds of people made fun of a century ago? Survivalists or something?" John asked.

"In a way, you're right. But this wasn't about a possible Armageddon. This was about extinction."

Van paused, and no one said anything. The possibility of human extinction had become a topic in shadowed conversations. No one wanted to say it too loudly, not even the scientists who could see it on the horizon. It wasn't so much a question of if, but when. And everyone knew it.

"So EART is all about keeping the big brains here, and the government is all about taking them away to colonize a new planet." Karissa's shoulders hurt from the tension in them. She felt like she could split apart from the monumental concepts in front of her.

"Correction. EART is about helping humans survive. We believe we can, if we learn to work with the planet instead of against it. Perhaps our great-great-grandchildren can play outside again one day. But we're not about to tell the eggheads what to do. If you want to jet off to space, off you go. Your choice." Van shook her head and the hard look returned to her eyes. "But the Space Surveillance Center, along with the Global Science Network, have other plans. They don't think anything more can be done here. So they want to take the best and brightest, and leave the rest to die. You won't have a choice. You were chosen, and once you step foot in that building, your fate is decided. It's that simple."

The silence was oppressive, broken only by the sound of the fire and the occasional slurp of coffee. The faint whistle of the wind from the tunnels was like a soundtrack in a horror movie. All of it was a strangely rhythmic backdrop to the confused chaos raging in Karissa's mind. Finally, Van stood up.

"It's late. We're going to get some sleep. I suggest you all do the same. Two doors down the hallway is a room with a bunch of bunk beds. Feel free to use them. We're going to try to get out of here tomorrow even if it's stormy so we can get the supplies to the local branch." She stretched and looked at Devin. "If you decide you want to come with us, we'd be glad to have you. But we need to know before we leave, so we know to pick you up on our way back."

"And if we don't go with you?" Karissa asked, knowing the answer wasn't one she'd want to hear.

"Then you're on your own. Go whichever direction you want, and good luck to you."

That was the answer she didn't want. If she didn't go with them, she'd have to figure out how to get back to her parents on her own, and she didn't have a whole lot of faith in her ability to live in the open. Before Van left, Karissa said, "Hey, do you have a phone we could use?"

Van looked at Ray, who nodded. "Sure. We've got a portable comms unit in the back room. Storm might make the connection rough, though."

Karissa nodded. "Thank you. I'll still give it a try."

They filed out of the room, and Mac put his hand on Edward's shoulder. "I've put a cot in there for you, so you can sleep next to her. Come wake me if anything changes."

Edward nodded, his eyes filled with tears.

And then they were alone. Just the small group of them from the first truck, with one severely injured. Devin took Karissa's hand in her own and stood.

"What say we head to our bunks and have a chat?"

The others stood and a few got more coffee before they walked down the dimly lit concrete hall to the bunk room. Karissa was pleasantly surprised. She'd pictured bare mattresses on rusted frames, but there was clean bedding on each wooden bunk, and there were even pillows. A fire canister was alight in the middle of the room, chasing away the dark chill that threatened to consume her. She huddled near it and was glad when the others crowded around too.

"Well, it sounds like we've got two options, folks. Stay with them, or go our own way, on foot." Devin looked around. "I have a feeling this is something we should sleep on, and maybe meet up in the morning to talk about it."

Zeke held up his hand. "Why wait?"

Frown lines were etched at the corners of Devin's eyes, and Karissa knew she felt responsible for the group. She also knew what Devin was about to say next. It was logical.

"Because it's not a group decision, Zeke. It's an individual decision. Everyone has to make up their own mind about what direction to take." She rubbed the back of her neck. "And I have a feeling we're going separate ways in the morning."

Karissa felt the tears well in her eyes. She'd come to know these people, to like them. But after tomorrow, she might never see them again. She tugged on Devin's sleeve. "I'm going to try to call my parents."

Devin nodded, and Karissa saw the question in her eyes. She didn't ask it.

"Sure. I'm going to turn in." She gave Karissa that teasing smile she used so often. "Feel free to share a bunk with me. It'll be tight, but combined body heat would be worth it."

In a burst of emotion, Karissa stood on her tiptoes and kissed Devin's cheek. "Thank you. For everything." She turned away and quickly headed to the room with the phone, not wanting Devin to see her cry. Again.

Her hand was shaking as she picked up the huge mobile phone unit. Satellites were unstable now, but comms units like this one were still pretty reliable, unlike regular cell phones. She dialed and closed her eyes. It had only been a few days, but it felt like years since she'd kissed them good-bye. When she heard her dad's voice, she finally let the tears fall.

"Dad. It's me."

He exhaled sharply, the relief in his voice clear. "Hey, baby. It's damn good to hear your voice. You in some chichi hotel, drinking champagne?"

The levity in his voice was forced, and Karissa slid to the floor and curled up against the big comms unit. "No. Things have gone pretty sideways. I'm safe, but my convoy is wrecked. I can come home."

She waited for his exclamation, for his questions about how long it would take, but nothing came. "Dad?"

"Where were they taking you, Kar?" he asked softly. "Tell me the truth, baby."

She never liked to lie to her parents, and she wouldn't do it now. "To a government facility. They're ready to colonize another planet, and they want scientists to lead the way."

"Well, damn. My baby, shooting out among the stars. Isn't that something?"

Beneath the pride, she heard the pain. "I'm not going. I'm coming home to help with Mom. Then we can go north together."

His sigh was filled with a sadness that made Karissa ache to her bones.

"Baby, there's nothing to come home to. Your mom…baby, the fever took her not long after you left. And I've got the first symptoms myself. I cut myself when I was helping her…"

Karissa sobbed silently, curled into a ball, and rocked as the waves of anguish bled through her soul. "Then I'll come home and take care of you."

"Listen to me, baby." His voice was firm. "I'm not going to hang around while this eats at me. I'll do what I need to do. And you do what you need to do, my girl. Learn. Help humanity, just the way you've always wanted to."

She was nearly choking on the scream she was holding back and couldn't say anything.

"Baby girl, we knew you were destined for something special. You need to take whatever path is in front of you and see where it leads." His voice cracked. "There's nothing left behind you, baby. Everything now is in front of you."

She finally managed to get the words beyond her trembling lips. "I love you so much, Dad."

"And I love you, baby girl. Be brave. Be strong. Just the way we raised you to be. Never forget who you are."

A shrieking buzz made Karissa hold the phone away from her ear, and when she brought it back, the line was dead. She frantically tried to redial, but the signal had been totally lost.

She collapsed back to the floor, sobs so strong she felt like her body could shatter into a million crushed pieces. When Devin's arms came around her, she sank into her and cried until she was empty. Her legs shook when Devin helped her up and led her back to the bunk room. She felt like she was watching from a distance as Devin took off her shoes and coat, then drew back the blankets and ushered her under them. When Devin climbed in behind her and pulled her close, she pressed against her and prayed for sleep. This was a nightmare she wouldn't wake from, and the future held all questions and no answers.

CHAPTER TWELVE

Van and Liz dressed silently. They were used to waking up early, and even though they'd stayed up late discussing options for the rest of the run, both were wide-awake. Van knew Liz well enough to know she was strategizing the same way Van was.

If one or more of the egghead group wanted to go with them, that was fine. They'd leave them here and pick them up on the way back from the supply drop. There was always a chance they wouldn't make it back. That's the way the world was now. But even if the worst-case scenario came to be, whoever stayed here would have a roof over their heads and food to last a good while. It was more than a lot of people had these days.

But for those who didn't want to go with them, the path was different. They'd give them what supplies they could, but the moment they left they were on their own. It couldn't be any other way. There were people depending on them for survival, and they had to take care of their own first. She respected anyone who made the decision to take their destiny into their own hands, but she didn't have the resources to help everyone she came across who had their own path to take.

The group from last night had been a new experience. A raid had never gone as badly as this one had, and she'd had nightmares about that overturned truck. Had they killed people? One of the guards had gone down for sure. That, sadly, had happened before. But they'd never killed the people being moved. Bile rose in the back of her throat, and she drank down half a bottle of water to wash the bitterness from her mouth, though it wouldn't do a damn thing for her mind.

"Here." Liz handed her a cup of coffee.

"Any thoughts on the final spread?" Van asked, taking that first sip of coffee that always made her glad she had taste buds.

"No clue. Hard to read group." She motioned toward the back room. "But there's no question about that pair going anywhere."

That was another thing Van wasn't sure what to do about. The injured woman wouldn't be able to move, assuming she lived. The man clearly wouldn't leave her side. The devastation in his eyes was exactly the reason Van didn't get close to anyone. Life was cheap now, and she wasn't about to care about someone to the point of not wanting to live without them. So what was she supposed to do with them? Maybe Mac would have a suggestion.

"Devin, the military one. She'd be a good addition to the team."

"How do you know she's military?" Liz turned on the flame on the canister and sat close to it.

"Come on. Seriously? She's got jarhead all over her. She can probably cut up a tree and make an entire apartment building out of it." Van pictured the way she'd looked in her tight shirt, her biceps defined under the material even when she wasn't flexing. *She'd be a good addition to the complex, too.*

"Air force, actually." Devin came in and poured herself a cup of coffee, looking far more tired than she had the day before. "And I'd need more than one tree."

They sat around the canister in silence, drinking coffee. Van didn't want to push and figured Devin would probably wait for the others before stating her own decision. She had that cocky hero thing going on. Van was interested to see how it played out when it came to the feisty little long-haired scientist who'd been ready to kick her ass the night before. She'd bet a night on a real bed that they had some kind of connection.

Mac came in, got coffee, and went into the medical room. He was gone a while before he came back. He shook his head slightly at Van but didn't say anything more. She heard soft sobs coming from the other room and knew the verdict. Now it was just the man who had to decide where to go next. She couldn't, wouldn't, imagine his pain.

Slowly, the others filtered into the room. One by one, they got drinks and spread out. Karissa sat beside Devin, who put her arm around her protectively. *If they stick together, looks like I won't have a chance. Too bad. But if they don't...* When everyone was there, Liz raised an eyebrow at Van, as though asking when she was going to start. She'd just wanted to give them time to wake up and settle before the talks began. *May as well get it over with.*

"So. Any decisions?"

"I'm going." John Berman looked determined. "I'll find my way back to my partner. We'd already discussed an evacuation point, just in case we got separated. That's where I'll go."

Van nodded and looked at the woman beside him. Natasha or something.

"I'm going with him. Once he's safe, or with a group traveling that direction, I might try to find my way to the Colorado facility. I don't have any family to go back to, and I'd like to see what this is all about. But John and his partner have been my family for a long time, and I'm not letting him go alone." She smiled and took his hand, and he squeezed hers with tears in his eyes.

"That's two." Van looked at the other three.

Karissa's eyes were puffy and her skin pale. Van had heard her crying from the comms room and figured it hadn't been good news. It rarely was anymore.

"I think I'll go to the facility." Karissa nodded toward Natasha. "I want to know more, too. And there isn't anything behind me..." She stifled a sob and rested her head on Devin's shoulder.

Devin nodded while stroking Karissa's hair. "Me too. I don't have ties, and I want to know what the next step is, what they're developing. I'm all about adventure, and this could be the ultimate one." She looked at Zeke. "How about you, kid?"

Zeke looked like a frightened teenager, and Van couldn't fathom him making it on his own. Fortunately, he seemed to know that too.

"I'm sticking with you. I was chosen for something, and I want to know what it is." He swallowed hard. "If it's okay if I travel with you. I don't want to try it by myself."

Devin smiled at him and clapped him on the shoulder. "Of course you can come with us. Long as you can hold your own, I'd… we'd, be glad to have you with us."

Karissa nodded but didn't lift her head from Devin's shoulder.

"What about Edward and Sheila?" Devin asked.

Van looked at Mac. Better that kind of news come from the medical guy.

"Sorry, folks. She didn't make it through the night. Too much blood loss."

Karissa began to cry again and Devin held her close. The others were silent. Van had grown used to senseless death, and she'd forgotten to some degree how hard people still took it. She felt for them, but she also knew the injured woman might be better off. Medications weren't easily available anymore, and antibiotics had long since stopped working. Gangrene or sepsis were horrible, drawn out deaths. Fast was definitely better.

"Do we know what Edward is going to do?" John finally asked.

"I imagine he'll try to find his daughter. We're all from back East. Maybe he could travel with you guys?" Devin said.

John and Natasha both nodded.

"Well, that's everyone." Van stood and tugged her sweatshirt down, feeling the need to do something with her hands. She hated emotional, awkward situations and couldn't wait to get out of this one. "Guess no one is going with us."

Ray stepped forward from where he'd been leaning against the wall. "We'll give everyone food and packs to take with you. We've also got old-fashioned compasses so you can keep heading the direction you want to go." He looked at Devin, Karissa, and Zeke. "If you can get to a main road, you may be found by a convoy that can take you the rest of the way. We don't know how many convoys are left, though. Seems like they're slowing down."

Devin nodded and looked at Van. She tilted her head slightly toward the other room and Van indicated she got the message.

"We're going to try to get our weather guy on the comms to find out the storm's status. We'll let you know what we find out so you all know when to hit the road. We need to lock up behind you, so I'm afraid you have to go when we do. Sorry."

They all looked like the world was sitting on their shoulders. Van didn't envy the position they found themselves in. She hadn't been one of the chosen, so she hadn't had a choice to make. Though, if she had, she knew she would have chosen to stay. But she wouldn't wade into a philosophical argument now. They'd made their choices, and she had a schedule to keep.

She headed into the other room, and Devin soon joined her.

"You sure? We could really use someone like you on the team." Van gave it one last try.

"I'm sure. And the other two are, so even if I wasn't, I'd go with them."

There's that hero complex. "Okay. So what do you need?"

"Weapons." Devin said it softly, her hands shoved in her pockets. "We both know you're not the only raiders out there, and the others would have shot us before letting us into a shelter with them. By my calculations, we're still about five hundred miles from Cheyenne. That's a lot of ground to travel without protection."

Van led the way down the hall, knowing full well Devin would follow. She made her way into the complex, down one hall to the next, before finally stopping at a massive metal door. She pressed her thumb to the scanner and entered a code.

She pulled the door open and pressed the click-light that dimly illuminated the weapons room. "Take your pick."

She watched as Devin carefully considered the armory covering the shelves and walls. She grabbed a carbine rifle and slung it over her shoulder, then pulled a PEP gun as well as a Mauser 98 from the wall.

"Nice choices. Carbine for ease, which means you've probably got some kind of sniper background. A PEP for non-lethal control, and a Mauser if you run into the sort of trouble that fires back. I approve."

Devin rolled her eyes and loaded up on ammunition too. "Gosh, I'm glad to hear that the raiders approve of my need for self-defense."

Van grinned, not offended in the least. But when Devin turned to her, looking deadly serious, she straightened. This was a bad place for a confrontation, if she'd read things wrong.

"I want to ask you something, and I want a straight answer."

Van relaxed and nodded. Words were fine. "Shoot. Figuratively, of course."

Devin moved closer. "Why are you so opposed to what they're doing in Cheyenne?"

She wasn't expecting such a simple question, and it took her a second to formulate the answer. "Because they're leaving the rest of us to die. It's elitism at its absolute worst. They're taking the best brains away from us, and they don't care about the millions who are left behind." She gritted her teeth, the old rage building. "Don't you see? It's genetic selection. It's a forced evolutionary jump, weeding out those of us who aren't good enough." She pressed her hand to the cold metal of a shelf to ground herself. There wasn't any point in getting angry at an egghead. "Who are they to determine who is good enough to live and who deserves to die?"

Devin stared at her for a long moment, her eyes intense, the frown line in her forehead pronounced as she clearly considered Van's point. Finally, she nodded and held out her hand.

"Thank you for being honest with me. I see what you're saying, and if we never meet again, I hope like hell you make it through this shit-fest."

Van forced a smile. "You too, you weird combination of egghead and military beast. Good luck."

They left the room, and Karissa was standing outside it. Van wondered just how much she'd overheard, but that was Devin's problem now. They'd made their choice, and she wouldn't stand in their way, no matter what her personal feelings were.

Devin went to touch Karissa, but she turned toward Van instead, her eyes glistening with tears. "I can't figure out how I'm supposed to feel toward you. If you hadn't attacked us, we wouldn't be here.

But if you hadn't let us in, we wouldn't be alive." Karissa hesitated, then put her hand gently on Van's arm. "And what I just heard you say makes me think there's more to you than I allowed. I'm sorry for judging you."

Van had no clue how to respond. It was a backward apology that didn't make a whole lot of sense, but it was enough. She lifted Karissa's hand and kissed the back of it, and smiled slightly when Karissa snorted. "Apologies are worth about as much as a sack of rocks these days, beautiful. But no hard feelings. Just keep each other safe, and do what you need to do."

Karissa nodded, and Devin put her arm around her as they walked down the hall ahead of Van, back to the group. She had no idea what would become of these people, but she knew she wouldn't forget them. As much as she hated what they'd been made a part of, she respected their courage. The bond between the two women was also obvious, and she wondered just how long it would last under the kind of pressure they were about to experience.

She thought of her own team and the bond they shared. She'd be wrecked if she lost them, and she wasn't even sleeping with any of them.

When they got back to the room, she grabbed Devin's shoulder. "Good luck. And if you change your mind somewhere along the way to hell, make your way to the caves at Mesa Verde."

Devin nodded and shook her hand firmly. "Thanks. Good luck to you guys too. Try not to die."

Van laughed. "We'll do our best." Devin and Karissa headed back to the bunk room, and Van went to find Ray. He was in the comms room, trying to raise James. "Any luck?"

He shook his head and thumped the box on its side. "I get to a point where I can hear him, but it's garbled. I'll keep trying."

Liz came in behind them. "I've had a thought. I mean, it's a radical one, but it might work." She paused dramatically, her eyes wide. "We could actually go look outside."

Van sighed. Sometimes the most obvious things were the ones that escaped her. "Right, jerkface. Let's go."

Liz pretended to pout as she followed Van down the hall toward the banked entrance. "No need for name-calling, grumpy ass. It's not my fault you're always so used to looking at how to fix difficult situations you forget to look for the easy shit."

They splashed through ankle-high water and Van could see light from the entrance. The ground rose as it moved toward the surface, and when they stepped out of the tunnel, Van lifted her face to the warm spring sunshine. She even heard birds chirping, and her skin tingled with the feeling of life around them.

Liz sighed happily beside her. "That was a damn good idea, if I do say so myself."

Van didn't say anything. The silence and warmth were perfect. Finally, though, she opened her eyes and started planning again. "Okay. Let's pull it together and head out. We'll need to get everyone underway."

Liz stopped her when she went to head back in. "One sec, boss. We need to deal with one big thing before we go."

Van thought about it, but didn't know what Liz meant. She looked at her questioningly.

"The body, Van. We need to bury the woman."

Van winced. She hadn't even considered it. *Fucking heartless, I am.* "Yeah, of course. Let's see what's going on."

They splashed their way back, and Van headed straight into the medical room. The woman's body was covered with a sheet, her husband slumped beside her on a chair. Van knelt in front of him. "I'm so sorry for your loss."

He looked at her but didn't really seem to see her. "If you hadn't ambushed us, we would have driven straight into that tornado. We'd all be dead anyway."

She hadn't thought of it that way and was amazed he did. But then, she never really understood the way the eggheads thought. "Be that as it may, I'm sorry." She hesitated, not wanting to sound like an ass, but she didn't have a choice. The sky was clear, and in the spring they had to make that work for them any chance they had. "Can we help you bury her before you move on?"

He nodded slowly. "Thank you." He looked at her, and this time seemed to really see her. "I understand you've said we can come with you?"

She raised her eyebrows. "I was told you'd want to go find your daughter."

He shook his head slowly, tears running down his face. "I have no idea where she might be, or where she might have gone. And I can't bear the thought of telling her about her mother…" He sobbed and then visibly pulled himself together. "I don't have the faintest idea where to look. I know for certain she wouldn't have stayed there. The only people she might have gone to were headed north. But that's not exactly a starting point, is it?"

Van didn't think so either, but she'd come across plenty of people who had about as much to go on and still decided to try it.

"I'd like to come with you. For now, at least. I want to see what you've built. And then, if I get some idea of where my daughter might have gone, I'll go find her and bring her back with me. Would that work?"

Van nodded. "Sure. And we can alert our teams across the country to keep an eye out for her. We're happy to have you come along."

Van left him to sit with his wife while she went to get Ray and Liz. She also ducked into the bunkhouse to let them know they were going to bury the woman. Edward and Devin carried his wife's body outside, and the others followed them up the hill. They laid her body beneath an enormous old willow tree, where Ray, Liz, Devin, Van, and Edward took turns digging a grave. When it was deep enough, they gently put her in.

Edward's sobbing was the background to the shovels of dirt as they refilled the grave. Once again, Van was glad she didn't love someone this much, and she hated the guilt she felt in the part they'd played in the woman getting injured. Granted, like Edward said, they might all be dead thanks to the tornado anyway, but that didn't count. She'd been out of that truck and in the storm because of the raid, and Van would have to live with that. As she placed the last shovel of dirt on the grave, she accepted her part in the woman's death.

There was silence as they stood there, looking at the fresh mound of dirt.

"Does anyone want to say anything?" Liz asked softly.

"We're scientists. I don't think any of us believe in God." Devin looked around, and the others nodded their agreement.

Ray knelt and placed his hand on the dirt. "We consign Sheila's body back to the great earth mother. From where she was born, so she returns. May her spirit be at peace."

Van smiled at him gratefully when he stood and he gave her that same knowing look he always gave her when he understood something she didn't. He'd known what to say and she had floundered. Damn, she was grateful for her team.

"Thank you." Edward touched the mound, his tears dark spots in the soil. "You'll always be my reason for living, my love."

He stood, and Devin put her arm around him as they all made their way back into the bunker. Once they were all gathered around the central room again, Van broke the silence.

"Okay, folks. Sorry to say it, but it's time to move." She looked at Ray and Mac, who nodded in answer to her unasked question. "You've all been given fresh packs. You've got minor medical supplies, some fresh clothes, rain gear, and a new sleeping bag and tent. There are also dried food rations to keep you going for a while."

Liz put a map on the table and looked at John and Natasha. "You two are headed this way. We're currently here, in Atlas, Kansas. If you take this road," she traced her fingers along the route she was talking about, "to this one, you should be safe. We've had reports of a large number of people heading north along this route, and there's safety in numbers like that." They nodded and John accepted the map from Liz.

She opened another one and spoke to Devin and Karissa. "You're going the opposite way, and this isn't a great area. Not only do you have the plains to deal with, you're going to head into the lower Rockies. You'll be dealing with a lot of wild animals, both four-legged and two-legged. My suggestion would be to hit the train tracks and follow them most of the way." She took a blue marker and put two large Xs on the map. "These are where you'll find blue trees if you need them."

Devin took the map and tucked it into the pack at her feet.

"Edward has decided to come with us, and we're going to take him with us rather than leave him here to pick up after." Van made the decision spontaneously. It seemed like a better idea than leaving him alone with only his wife's fresh grave for company.

Devin turned to Edward. "That's great news. They can help you find your daughter."

He nodded and shook her hand. "Yeah." He pulled her close and gave her a hard hug. "Thank you for everything. We all would have died out there without you." He turned to Karissa and hugged her too. "Take care of her. She'll need you."

Van left them to say the rest of their good-byes. She wasn't comfortable watching such intense displays of emotion. She and her team got the facility ready for shut down, double-checked all the locks, and motioned everyone out into the sunshine.

Ray pulled the truck around from where they'd put it in a cargo hold of the silo.

Her team got in, along with Edward, and she jumped in after them. She looked at the five people about to go their own ways and waved. "Good luck, folks. Hope you all find what you're looking for."

The others waved, and Van watched them fade away in the side view mirror. God only knew what would become of them. For now, she had her own people to take care of. "Let's get the drop done and get home."

CHAPTER THIRTEEN

Devin watched the truck until it turned a corner and was gone. It was strange to think she might never see them again. *Weird how people show up on your path, change your life, and then leave.* Not like it hadn't happened before. When she felt Karissa's hand in hers she forced herself to focus. The past was gone. There was only the future.

Natasha and John shouldered their packs. Karissa gave them both hugs and Devin shook their hands. She'd never been much of a hugger. Zeke simply smiled and hung back. He hadn't been with the group long enough to get to know them, and she could tell he didn't know what to do.

"Good luck. Be safe." Karissa held John's hand. "I hope you find your partner." She turned to Natasha. "And I hope we see you at Cheyenne one day."

Devin knew the look in Natasha's eyes. She'd seen it in soldiers' eyes when they knew they wouldn't be going home. It was resignation mixed with defeat. The trip back east would be tough. Getting back to Colorado would be practically impossible on her own, and if the convoys had begun to slow, it might be too late anyway. They all knew this was good-bye.

They waved and headed east. When they disappeared into the forest, Devin turned to Karissa and Zeke. "And that leaves us. What say we get on our way too?"

They picked up their packs. Devin missed the feel of Karissa's hand in her own but hoped they might share a tent later. Holding her in her arms all night, soothing her when nightmares had her shuddering and whimpering, had felt more right than Devin had felt in a long time. She wouldn't analyze it, and she damn sure wouldn't obsess over it. They had a hell of a long journey ahead, and adding emotional turmoil to it wasn't going to help anything.

The walk was pleasant enough. The town of Atlas had probably been abandoned long before the climate migrations began. The few buildings they passed were already nothing more than a few broken walls covered in jade green ivy and tufts of tough grass. They stopped on the dirt road to let an old-fashioned horse and cart pass. The cart was filled with several adults and children, all of whom looked solemn and tired. The adults nodded, the children looked wary, and Devin wondered what kind of world they were growing up in.

They walked for a few hours, and Devin became aware of Zeke humming behind her. When he began to sing softly, she recognized the old song and began to sing along. Soon they were in full voice, and though Karissa didn't join in, she was smiling as they made their way along the railroad tracks, past fields of wind turbines waving them by.

When they stopped for lunch, Devin had a look around while they ate the small sandwiches they'd been given. The area looked like something out of an old sepia photograph. The dry wheat poking up between the train tracks, the parched earth all around it, the watery sky…it was like color had been washed away, replaced by a muted version of lives that had once been. She sat next to Zeke, wanting something to take her attention off the feeling of time slipping away. "Have you always liked to sing?"

He nodded enthusiastically. "Always. My mom used to say I came out singing. Even when I was a toddler I'd figured out how to turn on the radio, and she'd come in and find me dancing and ranting along to the music, even though I didn't even know how to speak yet. In another world I would have loved to be a singer."

Karissa passed him a bottle of water. "But you turned to science instead?"

"Computer science. Deep space navigation. The reason is pretty stupid." He blushed and Devin laughed.

"Go on. Now you have to tell us."

"The music of the spheres."

Karissa smiled. "Ancient philosophy isn't ever a stupid reason. And Pythagoras was right, kind of. Everything is connected in a mathematical way. We just have to search for it."

"Yeah, but the planets don't hum." Zeke shrugged. "Still, I loved the idea that even the cosmos could sing. I want to hear that music someday."

"That's why you're coming with us. So you can go to space and hear the universe sing." Devin thought it was one of the purest things she'd ever heard, and her respect for Zeke doubled.

"Stupid, huh?" He hunched forward, and Karissa moved so she could put her arm around him.

"Wonderful. Beautiful." She looked at Devin. "Why are you going?"

She looked at Karissa, sunlight creating trails of gold in her hair, her eyes questioning. She owed her honesty. "There's nothing here for me to lose. I love adventure, and space…wow. I mean, it's the ultimate adventure, right? To colonize another planet, to watch it grow and change and figure out how to make life work somewhere out there. It's an amazing chance, and I want to take it."

Karissa's smile was tinged with sadness. "I understand that, definitely. My dad pretty much said the same thing."

They finished their lunches in silence, and Devin knew the other two were thinking not just of what was ahead, but what they were leaving behind. It wasn't a burden she could help them carry, but she could help them forward. She picked up her pack and spread her arms. "Adventure awaits. Shall we?"

They walked for a while in silence, only the cawing of crows and the piercing call of an occasional hawk to keep them company. This time when Zeke began to sing, his voice surprisingly low and mellow, Devin simply listened. It was a good thing his voice was so nice to listen to. She'd hate to think of being on this kind of trek with someone who sounded like a dying cat.

By nightfall, they'd made it as far as Emporia, and Devin estimated they'd managed nearly thirty miles. Karissa was limping slightly, and Zeke looked like his pack was weighing him down. The town was still alive, and Devin was glad they wouldn't have to pitch their tents tonight. They found a hotel still open on the old university grounds, and when the clerk asked how many rooms they needed, she looked at Karissa, asking a silent question. When Karissa slipped her hand into Devin's, she told the clerk two.

They went upstairs and Devin told Zeke they'd see him in the morning. He barely mumbled good night before slipping into his room. She had no doubt he'd be out cold within minutes. Karissa flopped facedown on the bed, not even removing her pack. Whatever she said was muffled by her face in the comforter.

Devin gladly put her pack down and carefully removed Karissa's. "Sorry, I didn't hear that."

Karissa turned her face to the side. "My legs feel like electrified rubber, and my feet feel like shredded glass."

Devin pulled off Karissa's boots. "Yeah, that sounds about right." She set them aside and then headed into the bathroom. She started the bathwater running and went back into the other room. "How about a nice hot bath while I go downstairs and grab us some food."

Karissa struggled to roll over and stared up at Devin from her position on the bed. "How are you not dead on your feet, too?"

"Once military, always military. Even when I took up science instead of war I made sure to keep training. It calms my mind and helps keep me centered." She nudged Karissa's foot. "Unlike the rest of you science geeks, I'm in my element."

She took Karissa's hands and pulled her upright, laughing as she groaned dramatically. "Go, you wuss. Relax in the bath. I'll be right back."

Karissa sighed. "Call Van back. Tell her I changed my mind and it turns out walking five hundred miles was a stupid idea."

Devin shook her head and opened the door. "Too late for that. We're all in now, gorgeous." She managed to get the door closed before the pillow Karissa half-heartedly flung at her hit her. Once downstairs, she ordered them soup with thick slices of rye bread, a vegetable stew, and apples covered in some kind of sweet syrup for dessert. Whatever farm was supplying them must be well guarded and well run to have rye and apples. It would be a raiders dream. A server followed her with a second tray and set it up in the room.

She looked into the bathroom, and her heart stuttered in her chest. Karissa's hair floated around her in the tub, her eyes closed, her cheeks pink from the heat of the water. She was a goddess, an apparition, something from the sexiest dream Devin hadn't even managed to have yet. Her dark nipples peeked through the thin layer of bubbles, and Devin desperately wanted to wrap her mouth around each one as Karissa bucked beneath her. She must have made some sound, because Karissa's eyes opened and she looked directly at her. Their gazes locked for a moment before Devin ducked her head and said, "Dinner's here, if you're ready." She could barely get the words out, and she turned to get some water before she embarrassed herself any further.

Karissa was unbelievably beautiful. She was also kind, funny, sweet, and had a temper Devin found both sexy and adorable. She was a stunning package, and that kind of thing could be deadly when it came to matters of the heart. Maybe she needed to slow down, give them time to breathe. But then, time wasn't on their side. Sheila's death had certainly proven that.

Karissa came out wrapped in a towel, her skin damp, her eyes bright. "That smells divine." She moved straight to the food and dunked a chunk of bread into the soup. She moaned as she munched and before she just sat on the floor next to the tray, Devin took her arm and led her to the bed.

"Sit. Relax. The food isn't going anywhere." To prove her point she picked up the tray and put it on Karissa's lap. She went to move away but stopped when Karissa put her hand over Devin's.

"Thank you."

The kiss that followed was soft, just a whisper of a promise, but it sent shivers down Devin's spine and made her knees weak. She pulled away and grabbed a tray of her own before settling next to Karissa on the bed.

They both ate everything Devin had brought up, and as Karissa licked the final bite of syrup from her fork, Devin could tell she could barely keep her eyes open. She got off the bed, put their trays outside their room in the hallway, and by the time she turned back around, Karissa's breathing was slow and steady, her neck at an awkward angle.

So much for a bit of romance. She grinned to herself. She'd known full well that wasn't in the cards. This kind of trek was going to push all of them, but especially Karissa and Zeke. She could only hope to catch a convoy, or a ride of any kind, along the way. If they only cleared thirty miles a day, it was going to take a hell of a long time to get to Colorado. She pulled the blanket down and gently rolled Karissa into bed. The towel slipped away, and Devin took the opportunity to really look at her. Her petite body was all curves and smooth skin. *Perfect. Just fucking perfect.* Devin swallowed against the desire to run her hands over Karissa's hip, to feel the curve of her waist. Instead she pulled the blanket up over her and headed off to take a cold shower.

Karissa drifted awake slowly, the soft comforter and pillow a direct contrast to the heavy, hard arm wrapped around her waist. It was the delicious kind of feeling she'd dreamt about, and she wiggled her butt slightly against the hard body behind her. The arm pulled her closer and she sighed happily. Just as she began to drift back to sleep, reality crept in and she froze.

"You fell asleep."

Devin's murmur made Karissa flush and smile. "You must not have been that good."

"Believe me, if you'd gotten a piece of me, you wouldn't have slept at all." Devin squeezed her and then let go.

Karissa turned to watch as Devin rolled off the bed. Her tight white tank top outlined a beautifully muscled back, and the loose boxer shorts hung low on her slim hips. *She sure as hell doesn't look like a scientist.* "We could stay in bed…"

Devin looked over her shoulder as she slid her jeans on. "You had your chance. You keep falling asleep, which means I'm not nearly enticing enough."

Karissa started to protest and Devin laughed.

"Kidding. I know how irresistible I am. But we need to get on the road and cover as much ground as possible." She pulled on a T-shirt and turned back to Karissa. "Before we go, I want to see if there are any leftover cars. Hell, I'd even take a few horses."

Karissa held the bedsheet over her chest. She almost never slept naked, and right now she was extremely aware of her decided lack of clothing. "I have to admit, I'm feeling a little superfluous these days. You seem to think of every step before I have a chance to jump in."

Devin frowned slightly and sat on the end of the bed. "Hey, I'm just glad I don't have to take this trip on my own. It's way more interesting with you and Zeke along." She glanced down at the sheet over Karissa's chest. "Although he'd be far less fun to cuddle at night." She laughed when Karissa kicked at her from beneath the comforter. "But if we get sick it's all up to you. Deal?"

Karissa leaned forward and kissed Devin's cheek. "Deal."

Devin jumped up and grabbed her jacket as she headed for the door. "I'm going to knock on Zeke's door and wake him up too. I'll be back as soon as I've asked around about transport."

She was gone with a smile, and Karissa flopped back onto the pillows. She couldn't believe she kept falling asleep on her. But then, it wasn't like they were spending their days lying on a beach and relaxing. Yesterday's march had been exhausting, and she knew they were in for plenty more where that came from. As she moved to get out of bed she groaned at the aching in her thighs, and when her feet touched the floor it made her eyes water. A close inspection showed her blisters on the balls and heels of both feet. She hobbled to the bathroom and pulled the first aid kit from her pack. When all the blisters were dressed and covered with thicker socks, she was able to stand properly. They'd numb out, eventually, and hopefully she'd only feel them when they stopped for the night.

She finished dressing and was grateful for the night's sleep in a real bed. Daunting was the right word for the amount of ground they still had to cover. But as Devin said, at least they were traveling together. Reminded of what she'd said about feeling like an extra wheel, she headed downstairs. She ordered breakfast for all three of them, as well as some treats for later. Devin might take care of all the practical stuff, but that didn't mean Karissa couldn't find a way to be useful too.

When she got back to the room, Devin and Zeke were waiting. She handed Devin the tray and tucked the sack into her backpack before sitting with them to eat.

"There aren't any horses to rent or buy around here. They've all become service animals. There's a great horse and cart boom in the area, but none for sale." Devin looked into her bowl like she was sorry it was empty. "But the owner said there's a junkyard about ten miles up the road, and they might have something to look at." She shrugged and set her bowl aside, taking up the coffee and sniffing it appreciatively. "It's on our route anyway, so it won't hurt to stop and ask."

"Did he say there's another place we can stay at the end of the day?" Zeke looked hopeful.

"I didn't ask, to be honest." Devin piled their dishes on the tray and stood. "I figure we'll see what's there when we get wherever there is."

He nodded, looking resigned, and stood with her. Karissa gladly took his hand to pull her to her feet. They grabbed their packs and followed Devin out into the warm morning sunshine. There wasn't a cloud in the sky, but the air felt wet and heavy. Devin stopped and inhaled. "If I had to guess, we'll see a storm by afternoon. There are a lot of waterways around here, so we'll need to watch for flooding. Find high ground to pitch our tents, if we need to."

"I really hate the idea of running through another storm." Karissa kicked at the loose rocks under her feet. She wouldn't be able to get Sheila out of her mind for a long, long time.

Devin took her hand. "Hopefully, we'll find something at the junkyard that will move us a little faster. If we do, we might be able to get to a city instead of having to pitch up."

She felt better with Devin's hand in hers, and as they set off, she allowed herself time to think about what they were walking toward.

In one sense, she agreed with Devin. It was an adventure, and the idea that she could be one of the first humans to help colonize another planet was exhilarating. But the ethics of it bothered her. Van had a point; who had the right to say who was special enough to leave, and who had to stay behind? But wasn't it like any job qualification? If you had the knowledge and experience, you got the job. She knew it wasn't that simple. The poor, the marginalized, the outcasts…they didn't have the opportunity to get the experience, so they'd be left behind almost by default. And that concept made her feel ill.

She was pulled from her confusing circular thoughts by Devin squeezing her hand. "That right there is called hairy grama," she said, pointing at a tall grass that looked like it had stems of eyelashes growing off it.

"It doesn't look anything like my grandma." Zeke bent over to examine it but didn't touch it.

Devin laughed. "I have no idea why it's called that. But it's one of the only grasses in the area that adapted to climate change. I like that something with such a weird name is still with us."

Karissa couldn't help but smile at Devin's enthusiasm. "What else do you know about this area?"

"I know there are whole beds of fossils in the upper region that are now once again under water. I got to study them early in my career, and it was pretty terrific. I know back in the twentieth century there were fifty thousand streams running through the state. I would have loved to see that."

She sounded so wistful Karissa wished she could conjure up some of those streams right now, just to see her smile. They walked in silence, and it wasn't too long before Devin pointed.

"Hey! There's the junkyard. Keep your fingers crossed."

She pushed open the heavy metal gate, and the three of them wandered past the rows and rows of rusted, torn metal. Abandoned cars, trucks, and bikes stared blindly across at one another. Even some boats lined the muddy pathways. They came to a metal shed with a crooked sign painted with "office" hanging from a chain on the door. Devin grinned, and Karissa looked at Zeke doubtfully, but they followed her in.

A man in overalls sat hunched over a sandwich, a big-eyed beagle at his feet that barely looked at them before settling once more. "Help you?"

"We've got a long journey ahead of us, and we were hoping you might have a faster way for us to get there than on foot." Devin leaned on the counter.

He clearly took in the three of them. "Money?"

"Some. Probably enough."

With a sigh and a longing look at his lunch, he pushed away from the table and waved them to follow. Down one row and along the next they followed him to a line of cars that didn't look quite as worse for wear as those by the front gate. He stopped in front of an ancient looking van.

"Runs, but just. Half a tank, and I can give you a can." He wiped grime from the windshield and peered inside, wiping the dirt on his jeans. "Get you some way. Save your feet. Leave it where it dies. Might be shelter for someone, some day. Don't think the authorities are much on watching for vehicles anymore, so you shouldn't have any legal problems before she gives out on you."

Devin looked at Karissa and Zeke and raised her eyebrows in question. Karissa pulled open the door and looked inside. It smelled like the bottom of a sickly lake bed, and the upholstery was nearly nonexistent. Moss was actually growing on the inside passenger floorboard. But it was roomy, and if it ran like the man said, it was better than walking. She liked his idea that someone might take shelter in it, too.

She held out her hand and he shook it. "We'll take it."

CHAPTER FOURTEEN

"Only a quarter tank. Plus what he's given us in the container. It might save us a good hundred miles on foot, if we're lucky." Devin ground the gears and winced, but managed to chug the old thing out of the junk yard. "I'm guessing. I have no idea how big a tank this thing has, or how much gas it uses. It could be closer to fifty, for all I know."

Karissa waved to the owner as they passed, and he gave her a nod as he continued to eat his sandwich, the beagle lying across his feet. "I'll gladly take those numbers. And if we come across a convoy on the way, we can flag it and drop the van."

Zeke was lying along the back seat, his feet up and his pack under his head. "Hell yeah. This is the way to travel. Good thing you learned to drive, Dev."

She looked at him in the rearview and grinned. Thanks to her time in the military she'd learned to drive trucks and even a tank. Civilians hadn't been allowed to drive since before she and Karissa had been born, so Zeke was right. If it hadn't been for Devin's knowledge the van wouldn't have been any good, and everyone would be footsore again tonight. When Karissa pulled off her boots and propped her feet on the dash, Devin wished she could turn on the radio and pretend this was a road trip like people used to take in times gone by.

"This is wonderful." Karissa leaned her head against the door, her hand moving in the wind. "I totally understand why these were outlawed, but it must have been amazing to just get in and go anywhere."

"Right? I mean, the freedom." Zeke sat up and looked outside. "I wish I'd been born before all the regulations."

"And before the weather disasters began." Karissa pulled her hand back inside and turned to speak to him. "Imagine never worrying about summer drought or spring floods."

"I'd like to have seen New York before the canals were built. I've seen photos of huge crowds of people on the streets on New Year's Eve, and they used to take the subway everywhere."

Zeke shuddered dramatically in the back seat. "The thought of being shut in a train tunnel miles underground makes me want to hurl. I'm glad I never had to ride one. I bet plenty of people are glad they flooded. It would be wild to dive those tunnels though. All those trains, sunken in tunnels people will never see again."

Devin felt Karissa's energy change. She went from relaxed and thoughtful to contemplative and stiff. "Hey. You okay?"

Karissa's smile wasn't believable. "Sure. It just occurred to me to wonder what people hundreds of years from now will think when they unearth things like Zeke is talking about." She shrugged and looked out the window. "But we'll never know. Even our ancestors won't know, because they won't be on this planet anymore."

Devin wasn't entirely sure why that was problematic. She'd come to realize she and Karissa saw what lay ahead of them differently, but she hadn't wanted to get into a big discussion about it and potentially ruin their time together. She was sticking her head in the sand, but so be it. She'd have plenty of time to mess things up later, the way she always did. She didn't need to jump into quicksand now.

Devin took it easy, not forcing the ancient vehicle to go too fast, in the hopes she could get every last mile out of it. Her worries about how quickly they could travel were massively eased, but this would only buy them an extra day, maybe two. Still, that was better than nothing. Zeke fell asleep in the back seat, and Karissa looked lost in thought. When they crested a ridge and Devin saw a lake off to the right, she made a quick decision to make a pit stop. It would be good to stretch, and the smell in the van, though lessened by having all the windows down, was still all rot and decay.

She pulled up in the parking lot of the deserted old reservoir. Karissa jumped out, her feet still bare, and ran onto the grass at the edge of the water. She looked so carefree, and Devin wanted to capture that moment in her memory forever. After a moment, sighing, she reached back and tugged at Zeke's shoe. "Wakey, wakey. Time for lunch."

She grabbed her pack and joined Karissa by the water. She had her eyes closed, her face turned toward the sky, and sunlight slid over her hair, making it into liquid gold. *Exquisite. Like the most beautiful statue ever created.* Zeke puffed up behind them and dropped his pack on the ground, breaking the surreal moment. Karissa turned and smiled before she loped back to the van to grab her own pack.

Grinning, Karissa took a sack out of her pack and handed it to Devin. "Surprise!"

Devin opened the bag and began to laugh. "Wow. This is quite a spread." She took out the loaf of fresh rye bread, an actual avocado, and a container of spiced soy cake. Strict regulations meant that animals such as cows and pigs, who'd been bred primarily for meat production, were no longer farmed thanks to the amount of methane they'd produced and the energy it took to feed and kill them. The development of soy crops in the US, thanks to all the rain, meant soy cakes had replaced meat almost entirely. As long as they were spiced right, they could be really good.

And this one looked like it was perfectly cooked. Devin couldn't wait to dig in, but Karissa stopped her. "There's one more."

Devin dug to the bottom of the bag and pulled out a small, red glazed cake. She looked at Karissa. "What's this?"

"Strawberry cake. The real thing."

"Wow." Zeke leaned forward and stared at it intently. "That's like finding a unicorn in your cereal box."

Karissa looked so utterly pleased Devin couldn't help herself. She leaned over and kissed her soundly. "Thank you. It's a fantastic surprise."

Karissa's eyes were wide, and she looked speechless. Devin laughed and started opening the packages. "Let's dig in."

Once they'd eaten their fill, they all lay on the grass relaxing. When a shadow passed over her, Devin opened her eyes. Thick clouds were rolling in fast.

"Shit. Come on, guys. We'd better get on the road before this hits. Maybe we can outrun it."

They packed up quickly and jumped back in the van. Lines showed around Karissa's eyes, and Zeke looked equally worried. The last storm they'd been in had killed one of their group. She threw the van in gear and got back on the road. Fortunately, it was still in pretty good shape, an offshoot of the major highway to the north of them, and she didn't have to dodge too many potholes or piles of debris. Still, she couldn't push the van too hard. When the first huge raindrops hit, her stomach dropped. The windshield wipers mostly just smeared years of muck into muddy stripes, making it hard to see. Soon, though, it was raining hard enough to wash away some of that dirt, and if she strained she could see the road.

And then she couldn't see anything. The rain fell in hard, heavy sheets, obliterating any view of the road ahead. "I need you to tell me how close we are to the side of the road," Devin said to Karissa, while keeping her focus on the road. "We need to pull over and ride this out. I can't see anymore."

Karissa helped Devin negotiate to the roadside, where an old metal rail marked the edge. Devin turned off the engine and finally breathed normally again. She lowered her shoulders and tried to shake away the stress knots. Karissa took her hand and massaged it, and Devin realized she'd been holding the steering wheel so tightly her fingers had cramped. She murmured appreciation as Karissa worked her way over each finger and palm.

Thunder shook the van and Devin flinched as lightning struck far too close, blinding her. Zeke swore, and she heard Karissa gasp quietly.

"Did either of you notice what's around us?"

"There were trees about a mile or two back." Zeke motioned to the left of the car.

"I only saw hills in front of us. I didn't really notice anything else." Karissa sounded thoughtful rather than panicky, and Devin appreciated that, when things got crazy, she seemed to ground herself in a course of action rather than emotion.

"Okay. I say we stay in the van as long as we can. But if it starts to flood, we're going to have to make a run for higher ground." She looked back at Zeke. "Can you pass me my pack? We should all be ready to move, just in case."

Zeke tossed her pack over first, then Karissa's, and quickly strapped his to his back. Karissa took out her rain slicker and put it on before lashing on her pack. At Devin's questioning look, she said, "Hey, there's no reason to get soaked to the skin if I don't have to."

"True enough. I'm sure it will be fine—"

The van rocked violently and water surged over the hood.

"What the fuck is that?" Devin leaned past Karissa and looked out the passenger window. "Shit. We need to go. Now." She tried the engine, but it was already flooded. "Get out my side."

Neither of them asked what she'd seen; they both just scrambled out after her into knee-high water. Devin held her hands over her eyes to try to block the rain. But what she saw made her wish she hadn't. She thought fast, turning in every direction to find a way out. She moved between Karissa and Zeke. "We stopped on a fucking bridge that's about to wash out. We're closer to the end of it than the beginning, so hold on. Wrap one hand around my pack strap, and one around each other's. We'll move slow and steady until we're off the bridge, and then we'll head into the trees there on the left. Ready?"

She felt the grip on her pack straps and waded away from the van. The swirling, frigid water pushed against her and she braced herself against the onslaught. *So much for covering a lot more ground.* Just as she wondered if they would have been better off staying inside it, she heard the screeching and thumping of the van being dragged away. She planted her feet hard against the rushing current and felt the other two do the same. Slowly, exhaustingly, they moved forward foot by foot.

They were nearly to the end when she heard Karissa shout, but it was too late.

The tree branch slammed into Devin's leg before spinning away in the current, and bile rose in her throat. Swallowing the scream of pain, she tried to take another step forward, but the injured leg buckled and she slipped into the water.

Karissa and Zeke's combined force kept her from going under altogether, but the pain was sucking away her ability to stay conscious. She fought it, knowing she needed to help them get across the bridge before she passed out. If she didn't, she could very well drag them under with her, and they'd all drown.

She waited, bobbing in the water like a demented buoy, and felt Karissa moving behind her. A rope slid over her chest and she hooked it under her arms. It pulled tight, and she managed to get one foot under her.

"Float!" Karissa screamed over the raging river and lashing rain. "Lean back against me. If you pass out, I've still got the rope!"

Devin turned, carefully moving her leg; the water slamming against it was agony. She leaned back and let Karissa take her weight as she lifted her legs in the water. She didn't know where Zeke was, but she bet he was tied to Karissa at the front.

Her feet touched the ground and she knew they were at the end of the flood zone. There wasn't enough water to float in now, and she groaned at the pressure of her injured leg touching the road. *Fuck. Fuck, fuck, fuck.* She was the one trained in survival. She was responsible for them. What good was she if she couldn't protect them?

Karissa turned to lift her and her bad leg twisted. She heard the scream from a distance, barely registering that it was her own, before the world went blessedly black.

CHAPTER FIFTEEN

Van wiped sweat from her forehead and then threw a final bag to the person on the ground. She jumped from the back of the truck and gratefully took a bottle of water. "That's the last of it. Should keep you going for a while, but be careful with it. Grow what you can as fast as you can. Convoy raids are getting scarce."

The intake officer nodded and turned away to add to the inventory list. Van and Liz headed into the base. Subtrop, an ancient limestone mine, had long ago been converted into nearly twelve hundred acres of underground business sites. Abandoned after the Third World War when the economy tanked, it had been a perfect place for the secondary EART base. It housed a small city of people, was perfectly climate controlled, and had great growing conditions. The only problem was the location. Kansas was tornado territory, and once the storms started, they could come in one on top of another for months at a time. That made supply drops hard, and meant life pretty much stayed underground for a good portion of the year. Permanent cave dwelling, even in caves that were white and had huge open spaces, wasn't for the thin-skinned.

Mac and Ray had already gone ahead to check in with their various departments, with Edward tagging along, looking like the analytical scientist he was, though Van had seen the tears continue to streak down his cheeks whenever he was left alone with his thoughts. Van and Liz had stayed behind to unload and make sure everything was accounted for. Each box had felt extra heavy as Van thought about the cost of this drop.

"Stop beating yourself up. If you want to torture yourself, sleep with Kelly again when we get back." Liz hopped into the train car that once had transported coal, and now had two bench seats to transport people through the maze ahead.

"You don't feel bad?" Van slid onto the seat opposite her and rubbed at the goose bumps on her arms. It was always too cool for her in the Subtrops.

"Of course I do. I feel like shit and I'll remember the way that woman's leg looked like ground meat for the rest of my life. I said you should stop beating yourself up. I didn't say anything about myself." Liz gave her a half-grin. "Shit happens, Van. We've been through enough to know that. We move on. Hell, her husband chose to come with us. That must say something."

"Yeah. I guess." In truth, she didn't want to talk about it anymore. She wanted to put it behind her and concentrate on getting back. The train stopped at level four, nearly a hundred and sixty feet underground, and they jumped off. Van rapped at the door to the chief's office and smiled when she heard his deep voice. When she walked in he jumped up and crushed her in a tight hug.

"Van, you grizzly old bitch!" He set her down and turned to Liz. "And there's my flower of desert thrush." He hugged her as tightly and laughed when Liz slapped at him to get him to put her down.

"Hey, Elin. Good to see you too." Van watched as he went to grab them a few beers. Elin Maque had been a top scientist in his day, and he'd been hiding from the government for nearly fifteen years. He'd been the one to develop the first plans to colonize another planet, but when those plans had been realized, and he understood the ramifications of what was going on, he'd taken his plans and gone into hiding. Unfortunately, there'd been plenty of other people to pick up where he'd left off. Still, he'd made the decision to stay behind, and for all his inability to be politically correct or politic in any way, Van appreciated and respected him immensely.

He handed them drinks and popped his own. "You brought supplies." When Van nodded he sighed with relief. "I knew you'd come through. You always do. Any trouble?"

When Van and Liz looked at each other but didn't say anything, he whistled. "That bad, eh?"

Van set down her drink, itching to get back above ground and headed home. "Yeah, that bad. Fuckfest for sure." She shrugged. "But it's done. The thing is, Elin, the convoys are slowing. We're seeing a lot less come through. I think the next phase is beginning."

He slumped into his chair and rubbed his hand through his thinning hair. "Yeah. Timing is about right. Planetary alignment isn't far off."

"That means it's time to make sure we're all as self-sufficient as possible. How are your grow centers doing?"

He lit up again, his moods as ephemeral as the skies he studied. "Awesome. You should go see them before you leave. The citrus trees look great, and the vegetable gardens are blooming exactly the way we hoped they would. I'm not sure about the berries, but we'll have a better feel for them by autumn."

That was what Van wanted to hear. Growing crops underground, using water filtered through the limestone along with artificial light brought in by the black silica solar panels bolted into the ground above meant they could sustain their communities. It also meant they could teach other communities to do it. It would have a ripple effect, eventually. *Who needs to leave the planet anyway?* She turned to Liz. "Can you head to the grow centers and talk to the agro folks? Get any paperwork you can to take back to Mesa. We'll see if we can replicate some of their results."

Liz tipped her drink at them and left without a word. Van turned back to Elin, who was staring at her with his fingers steepled under his chin.

"What happened out there?"

She wondered if he'd accept the thin version. "The raid went bad. Soldiers went down, but so did some eggheads. We made it into the silo base just ahead of a tornado, and a few of the eggheads made it in behind us. One died. One came with us, the rest split. Three headed to Cheyenne."

That was the truth, though it definitely left out the emotional depth, complexity, and anger involved.

"And you feel guilty."

It wasn't a question. Elin had known Van for a long time, and although she showed a hard ass to everyone else, she actually had a bit of a soft side. Somewhere. One Elin had seen a few times.

"I'm trying not to." Van sighed and closed her eyes. She was so damn tired. "It couldn't be helped, and the soldiers…well, they signed up. But the eggheads didn't."

"And you've always hated the innocent getting kicked." He smiled kindly. "I know. It's good that you feel guilty. At least you're still feeling. When you stop caring, it'll be time for you to step down."

She nodded but didn't say anything. They both knew that getting truly jaded was a harbinger for destructive leadership.

"Okay. What are your plans at Mesa?"

She refocused and gave him a rundown. "The thing is, I want to use the black silica solars, but with the fires raging through regularly, I can't figure out how to protect them. Any thoughts?"

He sat back and stared at the ceiling as he considered her question. He was one of the most intelligent people she'd ever known, and if anyone could work it out, he would.

"I'm picturing something to do with those heat tents firefighters use. The ones they wrap around themselves when they get trapped in a firestorm."

Van grabbed a pencil and started sketching. "If we use boulders to secure them, like tents, over the panels…"

He grabbed a pencil and sketched around her drawing. "You don't have to worry about breathable air. It's just about the convective elements that draw away the heat."

They stopped sketching and Van felt the excitement of a new viable source of survival pumping through her. Solar panels were great, but the black silica panels were far superior. They'd managed to grab a whole load of them, but she hadn't figured out a way to keep them from melting under the desert heat and brush fires. This was a simple, ingenious solution. Once again, it was the simple solution she'd overlooked, focusing instead on a complex option. The fire tents had been available to the public for decades and were easy to get hold of.

"You're a gem. I can't wait to get home and get installing."

"Yeah, well, you're going to have to wait it out. There's a nasty storm rolling in from the west. Doesn't look wide, though, so hopefully it'll pass quickly and you can make the run back to Mesa." He pulled out some files and thunked them on the desk. "In the meantime, we can go over other business."

She groaned and he laughed, but her mind was on the storm. *Rolling in from the west.* Where Devin and the others were headed. She hoped, for their sakes, they'd found shelter before it hit. If they were on foot, they probably had time to see it coming, whereas if they'd found something faster, they might have driven straight into it.

She grabbed another drink and settled across from Elin. There was no point in thinking about it. They were on their own, and that's all there was to it. *So why am I so damn worried?* She shut the thought down and got to work.

❖

"Hey." Ray sat beside Van and stretched out.

"Why don't you ever look wrinkled? I've been trying to work that out, but I just can't." It wasn't relevant, didn't really matter. But Ray looked tired, and Van wanted to see him smile.

She got her wish, though it was small and quick. "I can't help it the rest of you are sloppy and sweat a lot." He yawned. "I wanted to let you know James and that doctor got back to Mesa. She was okay pretty quick, so he called for a pickup. They made it back with no problems."

Van was glad to hear it. The attractive doctor had been a feature player in a few of her dreams, and she wondered if she'd live up to them when she got back. It felt like years, not days, since she'd last seen the two of them. It would have been good to have James with them, but she was also glad he was back at Mesa. She liked knowing someone with an even temper and logical mind was holding down the fort. "Did he say anything else?"

Ray's delay in responding made the knots in her shoulders spasm. He always chose his words carefully, believing as he did in their power to heal or harm, but she knew him well enough to know when something was bothering him. "Ray?"

"Fever."

The word made her feel sick. "How many?"

"Only five so far. They've got a containment unit up and running already. But with it being spring…"

He didn't need to explain. Spring meant damp, warm air in the caves. That meant disease spread like the wildfires that raged in the desert around them. If it didn't get under control quickly, it could have catastrophic consequences. "Do they need meds from Subtrops?"

"I asked. They said they've got what they need, as long as it can be contained."

Van wished she could kick something. Or throw something. But since it wasn't her office, she had to just sit and seethe at the injustice of it. There were good people living at Mesa, people who'd been cast aside, or, like Ray and the others on her team, people who believed in what they were doing and were trying to make a difference.

"Any news on the storm?"

"Passing fast. It'll hit us overnight, and we should be good to go in the morning. But we'll need to haul ass to get back before the big ones roll through."

She thought about the terrain they needed to cross to get back to Mesa. The worst of it was through the main pass in the Rockies. Mudslides and floods often made the trek treacherous, and the April and May rains could make the whole trip deadly. "Okay. Make sure the others are ready to go at daybreak, assuming the weather situation stays where it is. Get whatever info and supplies you want to take back to Mesa, and if we need any medical, make sure Mac brings it. We might not get back here for a while."

She didn't need to tell him what he already knew. If fever spread through Mesa, it could hit Van and the rest of the team just as easily as everyone else. They might not get back, ever.

Ray stood to leave and put Van's orders into play. "Oh, and Liz says there's a blonde in the canteen you might be interested in." He rolled his eyes before he left.

She'd never seen Ray with a love interest of any kind, and she knew very little about his back story. The past was private and wasn't meant to be shared; it was rare anyone asked someone else's story. The future was what mattered.

Filled with anxious energy, she jumped from her chair and headed to the canteen. Liz knew her type, and maybe that would be a good way to distract herself for the hours before they headed back to the home they'd worked so hard to build.

CHAPTER SIXTEEN

"Here." Karissa and Zeke slowly lowered Devin's limp body to the ground, trying to be careful of her twisted leg. "Thank God she passed out." Karissa hoped like hell she'd stay that way until she could figure out her leg.

"Aren't you a doctor?" Zeke asked, shivering. The rain had pretty much stopped as quickly as it had begun, but they were soaked through.

"Not that kind. I'm a scientist. I look at diseases under microscopes and figure out why they affect various body tissues." She stared at Devin's jeans, trying to figure out how to look at her leg without having to move her much. "I know the ins and outs of the body in theory, not in reality."

"Yeah, well, looks like you're going to have to put theory into practice, Doc, because I deal in code and space." Zeke pulled off his jacket and shirt, riffled through his bag for dry ones, and put them on.

He was right. She needed to step up the way Devin always stepped up for the people around her. The way she had the day Karissa had been taken. "Okay. We need to move fast, while she's out. Grab the scissors out of my pack, would you? We'll have to cut the jeans away so I don't have to move her."

Zeke did as asked and Karissa carefully cut away the leg of Devin's jeans. The water from Devin's jeans helped wash some of the blood from her leg.

"Jesus." Zeke turned away and retched.

Karissa swallowed the flare of panic. She could freak out later. Right now, she had to deal with the bit of bone sticking out of Devin's mangled kneecap. She closed her eyes and pictured every skeletal textbook she'd ever read. "Right. So we've got an open fracture. The question is where else the fracture may have taken place." Gently, she pressed above and below Devin's injury, but she couldn't feel anything specific. "If I had to guess, I'd say it's a patella only injury. I don't think the tibia or the femur have been broken, although from the direction of the fracture, the tibia could be in danger."

She turned to Zeke, feeling calm now that she had a plan. "We need to set up a tent. I want to move her inside, and we're going to need to boil some water. We're going to have to create a splint."

Devin moaned and Karissa stroked her head. Her eyes fluttered open and her face contorted in pain. "That doesn't feel like a good thing."

She started to sit up and Karissa pressed her shoulder to keep her in place. "It isn't, but I think it could be worse. To be honest, I was hoping you'd stay out until I could do something with it."

Devin closed her eyes. "You just wanted me to be quiet for a while."

"Yeah, well, what I need to do isn't going to keep you quiet, that's for sure." She leaned down and kissed her lightly. "But I'll reward you at some point for your bravery."

Devin grinned, the pain still clear in her eyes, but some of the fire back in them. "That sounds intriguing. What's the plan?"

"I want to press in two areas and see if they give you pain, or if it's pain that radiates to the injury itself." She pressed on her tibia, and Devin shook her head. She pressed on her femur, and although she winced, she shook her head again.

"Just my knee. How bad is it?"

"Open fracture of your patella." There wasn't any point in softening it. Devin was a soldier and had probably experienced far worse.

"Damn. Okay. Can you push the bone back in?"

Karissa looked at the wound. The piece that had come out was sharp with smooth edges. It didn't look like any other pieces had chipped off. That certainly didn't mean there weren't some floating around in her knee... "I might be able to, yeah. And that would be better, so we can close and pack the wound to prevent infection."

Zeke came back over and squatted on the other side of Devin. "Tent's up. You ready to get inside?"

Devin swallowed hard and Karissa could see her talking herself into it. She nodded sharply and held up her arms. Zeke and Karissa helped her stand and take all her weight on her good leg.

"We're too short to lift you. You're going to have to keep your leg up and put your weight on us to jump forward with your good one."

Sweat beaded on Devin's face and she looked terribly pale, but she managed to do what Karissa suggested and they made it to the tent Zeke had set up beneath a nice tree canopy a few feet away.

"If you lower me backward onto my ass, I can drag myself into the tent." Devin looked like she wasn't far from passing out again. Once she was on the ground, she slid backward, her arms shaking. She sank back onto the unzipped sleeping bag, her head on the blow-up pillow.

Karissa smiled at Zeke gratefully. He'd set it up so they'd hardly have to move her at all. "I think we need to get you out of the wet clothes and warmed up. I don't want you going into shock."

Devin nodded, but she didn't move. Zeke and Karissa got off her boots and socks, and then Zeke hesitated. "Um... Maybe, you know, I should wait outside."

"I don't think modesty is an issue in medical emergencies, but I can get her undressed on my own." Karissa thought about what she'd need. "We passed some Spanish moss. Can you cut me down a whole bunch of it, and get the hot water boiling?"

She would have laughed at how fast he scrambled out of the tent if she weren't so worried about Devin. She cut off the rest of Devin's jean leg and then rolled them off the other leg. She dug in Devin's pack and pulled out the shorts she liked to sleep in and tugged them on, managing to get them over her injured leg. She made quick work of her jacket and T-shirt and got her into a dry sweatshirt. Some color returned to Devin's face and Karissa breathed a little easier. She draped the top of the sleeping bag over Devin's torso.

"Better?"

"Much. Except for the bone protruding from my leg, I feel great." Devin's grin was forced.

"Okay, smart-ass. Here's what I'm thinking." She ticked the points off on her fingers. "We get some painkillers in you first. Then I gently push the bone back in and stitch the wound. I pack it with Spanish moss, which will absorb any leakage and also has antibacterial properties to help with infection. Then we fashion a splint and crutches of some kind."

Devin was watching her intently. "You're cute when you're uber focused. I'm not sure how we're going to cover another four hundred miles when I'm on crutches, but one thing at a time, eh?"

"Exactly." She grabbed her water bottle and a few pain pills from the medical pack the raiders had given them. Devin drank them down, her eyes never leaving Karissa's.

"You know you should leave me, right?"

Karissa rolled her eyes. "That hero bullshit is really sexy overall, but right now, shut it. We're not leaving you any more than you'd leave us."

Devin lay back again, her eyes closed. "So long as you think I'm sexy."

Karissa held Devin's hand and they sat in silence while Karissa waited for the pain pills to kick in. She couldn't fathom what they'd do once Devin's leg was taken care of. Walking a mile would be hard, let alone the hundreds ahead of them. And if they got caught in another storm... *One thing at a time. Focus.* When Devin's breathing evened out and it looked like she'd fallen asleep, Karissa figured it was time. She knelt beside Devin's knee and put her hand on her thigh. Devin opened one eye and looked at her.

"I'm going to start."

Devin's hands gripped the sleeping bag and she closed her eye again. "Do it."

Karissa slowly pushed the bit of exposed bone back under the skin and was glad when it seemed to slide into place without opposition. Devin hissed through her teeth, her face pale once again. Zeke came in with a bowl of steaming water and a bunch of moss draped over his shoulder.

"Perfect timing." Karissa took a piece of gauze from the kit, dipped it in the water, and wiped away the blood and dirt. Clean, it looked more PG movie bad than horror movie bad. She drew the antiseptic wipe over it and knew it took an insane amount of self-control for Devin not to jerk away from the sting. Zeke opened up the sewing kit, expertly threaded the needle, and handed it to her.

"When you deal with computer stuff you need good dexterity." He shrugged sheepishly at Karissa's look of surprise.

"That would have taken me ages. Well done." Karissa liked how pleased he looked at the compliment.

She bent over Devin's leg and started to stitch the wound. When Devin let out a strangled sound of pain, Zeke rolled up a shirt and offered it. "To bite down on."

Devin's laugh was hoarse. "I think it's supposed to be something hard, so you don't slam your teeth together. But I'll take it."

He rolled it up a little tighter and placed it between her teeth.

Karissa tried hard to be gentle and fast, but the two didn't go very well together. When she'd put in enough she thought it would at least keep the bone from sliding back out, she re-cleaned the wound, and then made long bandages of the moss, wrapping it from the bottom of her thigh to the middle of her shin. Zeke had brought in plenty, and once she'd put a thick patch over the knee, she wrapped it with an elastic bandage.

She sat back and surveyed it, feeling pleased with the job she'd done. When she looked at Devin's face, that feeling fled. Zeke was wiping the sweat from her face, but she'd clearly passed out again.

Zeke settled in next to Devin. "I'll stay with her. You should get dry."

Only then did Karissa realize how cold she was. "Okay. Back in a minute." She went out and grabbed her pack, but leaned against the tree when she started to feel dizzy. She slid down the trunk and let the tears come. Devin had unquestionably saved them from being washed away in the floodwaters, but she'd been injured in the process. Images of Sheila, the limb sticking out of her leg, being dragged through the storm with the tornado ravaging the skies behind her, invaded Karissa's thoughts. She was pretty sure Devin's injury wasn't life-threatening, but in this world, any injury could work against you. She cried softly as she thought of the possibility of losing this woman she'd come to depend on so fully. And to care about in ways she couldn't yet analyze.

Get a grip. She took in several long breaths and wiped the tears away. It was getting dark, and they needed to have it all together before night fell. She got up, grabbed her pack, and went behind the tent to change. The likelihood of any other soul being on this road, in this weather, was virtually nil, but she was still self-conscious about changing out in the open. The dry clothes felt heavenly and gave her a second wind. She shouldered her pack and went to grab Devin's, and noticed the spongy ground for the first time. More moss. She'd come back out for it later.

In the tent, she pushed their packs to the back and looked at Zeke. "How is she?"

He looked as exhausted as she felt, and before he could answer, Devin did.

"She probably doesn't look nearly as sexy as she feels." She opened her eyes and smiled at Karissa. "But she's really glad you're good with your hands."

"Yeah, well, you'll probably have a hell of a scar, and my stitches aren't pretty." She looked at Zeke and around the tent. "This tent is big enough for all three of us. I'm thinking we bunk together. If another storm hits, it seems like a better idea to be in the same place."

He nodded enthusiastically. "Love it." He moved carefully around Devin and unloaded his sleeping bag near the tent door. "I'll make us dinner." He rummaged in his pack and opened three bags of freeze-dried chili, then poured some hot water from a container into them. He held them aloft like prizes. "And presto! Dinner is served."

Karissa held out her arm and let Devin use her for leverage to lift herself into a sitting position before she pushed Devin's pack behind her to lean against.

"You're pretty good at this nursing stuff. Maybe you could have a backup career on our new planet."

Karissa snorted. "Not a chance. You're lucky I didn't vomit on you. But we can play nurse any time you want." She was glad when Devin grinned back at her, though she noticed she wasn't eating with any motivation. "You need to eat, babe. Your body is going to need fuel to heal."

Devin rolled her eyes. "Like I don't know that." She took another bite, pointedly licking the spoon clean.

Once they'd finished eating, Karissa took the foil packets, grabbed a knife from her kit, and headed outside. She knew Devin and Zeke would both be asleep within minutes, which gave her time to do what she wanted to. She wrapped the foil packets in the biodegradable bag that broke down whatever was inside it and buried it. Then she turned to the moss. She cut the dense stuff into large squares, which she laid on the roof of the tent. They'd be here for days, if not weeks. Moss made excellent rooftop waterproofing.

When she was finished and tired, she crawled back into the tent with her flashlight in her mouth. She was surprised to see Devin still upright, the map of their destination on her lap.

"I have to say, the fact that you knew to put moss on the roof of the tent may be the biggest turn-on of my life. You've captured this poor geologist's heart." Devin really did look impressed.

"Moss has amazing medicinal properties. I just happened to remember some of its other uses, too." Karissa gladly slid into the warm space Devin opened up for her by lifting the sleeping bag opening. She curled against her good side and tapped the map. "Are you trying to work out how many miles a day you can do on crutches?"

"Hardly. We both know I won't be able to stand at all for a few days." Devin stroked gentle circles on Karissa's back. "Actually, I had an idea and I want to know what you think."

Karissa didn't move. The caress felt so good, so comforting, she didn't ever want to move. "What's that?"

Devin traced the blue x marks the raiders had drawn to indicate their other safe spaces. "I think we may need to see if we can get help." She tapped one of the marks. "If I'm right, this one isn't even fifty miles away. Maybe a little more, but not much."

Karissa sat up. "We can't split up."

"I don't think we have a choice." Devin nodded at Zeke. "He's strong, and the two of you could easily cover that in two—"

"No." Karissa whispered it fiercely, not wanting to wake Zeke up. "I'm not leaving you here alone and injured." She poked Devin in the chest. "That's not up for discussion." When Devin held up her hands in surrender she settled against her once more. "And I don't know if it's a good idea to send Zeke on his own. What if he comes up against more raiders? Or gets hurt?"

"I know. I've thought of those things too. But if we come up against raiders now, we're still sitting ducks. Zeke could hide, but we'd be screwed." Devin kissed the top of her head. "I can't make it as far as we need to go. I'm not even sure I could make it to the safe house. Ris, we need help."

It was the first time Devin had ever called her by anything more than her real name, and Karissa found she liked the sound of it. A lot. She sighed, fully aware Devin was right. "Okay. But if Zeke doesn't want to do it on his own, we find another way."

She felt Devin nod and moved out of the way as she folded the map. Karissa pulled the pack from behind Devin's back and curled up against her under the sleeping bag again. Exhausted both emotionally and physically, she held Devin tight, listening to the strength of her heartbeat and paying attention to the way her arm moved under Karissa's head. She wanted to memorize everything about her. Life felt so terribly, scarily fragile. All she could do was hope that tomorrow brought some new idea, some new promise, to get them where they needed to go.

That made her consider where they were headed. Did this turn of events have some weird spiritual omen attached to it? Did it mean they shouldn't be headed there after all? Ever since Van had explained the situation, and after, when she'd overheard the conversation between Devin and Van in the weapons room, she'd had serious misgivings. She understood why Van was angry. Devin wanted adventure, and she was right, there was no bigger one than colonizing a new planet. But then, there was also the underlying issue. What about taking away the hope of a planet? Was humanity truly doomed to extinction? If all the people making discoveries in their fields were taken away, that certainly seemed like a possibility. But then, maybe people who never had a chance before could fill those voids, come up with new ideas and plans. Who was to say the people leaving were the be-all and end-all?

In the quiet moments of their walks, and when they'd been driving along beautiful roads, these thoughts kept Karissa from finding any real peace. The possibility that she should have gone with Van and helped her team instead haunted her. But that would have meant leaving Devin, and for whatever reason, that wasn't something she'd been about to do. Now, lying against her in a tent in the middle of nowhere, all she could do was exactly what her parents had taught her to do—keep moving forward and take care of the people who mattered to her.

She hugged Devin a little tighter and fell into an exhausted sleep.

CHAPTER SEVENTEEN

What makes you think anyone will come? Why would they make a hundred-mile round trip to pick up people they don't know?" Zeke looked slightly panicked as he picked at the threads of his sleeping bag.

"It's a gamble." Devin's leg ached fiercely, even with the pain pills she'd taken, and she struggled to rein in her short temper. "But Van marked these areas and said to tell them we were sent by Mesa if we needed help. If they wouldn't be willing to help us, she wouldn't have told us to do that."

"But what if no one is there? Do I wait? And for how long?"

Karissa put her hand on his to stop him from unthreading his sleeping bag completely. "If no one is there, you stay the night, leave a note explaining as best you can where we are, and come back to us."

Devin knew they were asking a lot. He was young, inexperienced, and frightened. It wasn't his fault he didn't want to go. "Look, Zeke, I get it. If you're not up for it, no problem. We'll figure something else out."

Karissa gave her a small smile and it made her glad she'd said it. She wanted to say whatever she needed to in order to make Karissa smile like that.

He sighed and rubbed his eyes hard. "I'll do it. Just because I'm a big chicken doesn't mean I won't go."

They'd broached the subject over morning coffee in the tent, which was warm and dry thanks to Karissa putting the moss on the tent roof. Zeke had listened intently, his expression growing more wary by the minute, until he'd started to look like he was going into a panic attack. Now, fortunately, he looked a lot calmer, if still pale.

"Do you know how to use a gun?" Devin couldn't help but think he'd probably never seen one before the raid.

"I hate them. But yeah. I can shoot a pistol and a shotgun." At her surprised look he shrugged, staring down at his coffee cup. "My dad was a farmer. When the wolves came after the livestock he'd start shooting. He taught me, too."

Devin remembered him saying he didn't have anyone to go back to, and if his expression was anything to go by, that remained true, even if his father was alive somewhere. "Okay. I'll give you one to take with you. Hopefully, you won't need it, but if you do, then you've got protection." She leaned forward over the map and pointed. "I think we're here, which means this EART base is the closest one." She traced another line. "I'd say make a straight line from here, which will take you to the main road. You'll leave that here to head to their base."

"I like the idea of being on the main road on my own better than walking through the woods." He stared at the map, tracing the various lines. "I'm going to pack up and get going."

Devin looked at Karissa and felt a flush rise in her face. "Do you think you could help me out of the tent? I could do with a visit to the little girls' room."

Karissa kissed her cheek. "Let me grab a stick for you to lean on. I'll take your weight on the other side. Be right back."

She scooted out of the tent, and Devin turned to Zeke. "You going to be okay? Honestly?"

He swallowed hard. "I think so. I mean, plenty of people are traveling on their own these days, right?" He nodded at her leg. "And it makes sense. You're not going to get very far, even if we managed to fashion you decent crutches. You could do even more damage to your leg, and it's not like we can wait it out here for six months while you heal." He nodded and started stuffing things in his bag. "And Karissa is the one with at least some medical knowledge, so she needs to stay with you. It has to be me."

Devin let him ramble. These were all reasons they'd already gone over, but if he needed to repeat them to himself to get up the courage to make the journey, so be it.

"I really appreciate you doing it, Zeke." She stopped and considered an option they hadn't broached. "You know, the other possibility is you don't come back. You find help, tell them where we are, and you keep going to the facility. There's no reason for you to backtrack fifty miles."

He looked at her contemplatively. "If it were me, or Karissa, and you had to make the trek, would you keep going? Would you leave the people back in the tent wondering if you'd made it or found help?"

Devin smiled and laughed. "No. I'd come back. But that's me. It doesn't have to be you."

He threw a sock at her, which she batted away. "Other people can be semi-heroes too, if you give them the chance."

Karissa ducked back into the tent. "I've got a big enough stick for you to lean on. Scoot this way, and I'll help you stand."

Devin moved carefully, every jar of her leg making her eyes water. When she was sitting with her legs outside the tent, Karissa reached down and pulled her up. She put all her weight on her good leg and accepted the sturdy branch to lean on. Between Karissa and the staff, she managed to hobble into the woods behind the tent and then faltered. She'd been injured plenty of times while in the military but never in a way that she couldn't take care of herself.

"Would this help?" Karissa grinned and held up the SheWee funnel and a roll of toilet paper.

"God yes." Now she wouldn't have to figure out how to squat without bending her knee. She took it and waited, but Karissa just stared innocently back at her. "Pretty sure we're not at that place in our relationship yet, babe."

Now Karissa blushed and stepped back. "Oh, right. Sorry. Call me when you need me." She moved toward the tent, leaving Devin to pee in peace.

When she was done, Devin leaned against a nearby tree and closed her eyes. Her leg hurt like a bitch, but she knew what badly injured really was, and this wasn't it. While it was true they needed help, and she sure as hell couldn't make it another four hundred miles on crutches, she also knew she'd be okay if she could get the kneecap repaired soon. But if she couldn't, it very well might mean she'd have a permanent problem. For someone who had always been able to depend on her body, that notion wasn't an option. Especially if she was going to another planet. Geologists did a lot of lab work, but her heart was in doing fieldwork. A mangled knee could mess that up. What if they didn't let her go on the space mission because of her injury?

She angrily brushed away the few tears of frustration that escaped. There wasn't any point in worrying about something beyond her control. She hobbled forward and called out for Karissa, who was there in an instant.

"The good part about this is that I keep getting to put my arm around you." Devin squeezed her to prove her point, and Karissa's laugh chased away the pity party she'd been about to throw for herself.

"Yeah, well, maybe at some point we'll get beyond cuddles and flirtation." Karissa lowered her onto the outdoor blanket she'd laid out.

Devin hoped the relief she felt at being able to sit down and take the weight off her leg didn't show. She never wanted to appear weak. "Apparently, being kidnapped, dragged across the country, running from tornados, and escaping a flashflood aren't actually foreplay. Who knew?"

Karissa nodded, looking wise. "It's not that they aren't foreplay, as much as you have to have the energy for sex after those things, which I don't."

Zeke came out of the tent, his pack ready. "I hope you don't mind, I took the handgun from your pack. Seemed stupid to make you move around if you don't have to."

Devin leaned back on her elbows and looked up at him. "No problem at all. You know your route? And you've got the map and compass?"

He tapped on his chest jacket pocket. "Yes to both." He started to say something else, and then stopped.

"What is it?" Karissa put her hand on his arm and he covered it with his own.

"What if I don't come back?"

Karissa started to protest, but Devin stopped her.

"He's right." She didn't want to give him a false sense of success, and he was right to ask the difficult question. "We'll wait here for four days. If you haven't come back by then, we'll pack up and make our own way to the main road, and we'll stick to it for as long as we can." She looked around them. "If there's a storm, we'll go farther into the trees for shelter, but we'll stay in this area."

"And if you're on the main road and a storm hits?"

She didn't have an answer to that. Without knowing the terrain of the main road, there was no way to know if there would be shelter. "Hopefully, we won't have to face that issue." She knew that with this plan in place, he could focus on his task. Knowing they wouldn't just sit there and wait for him until they got washed away would allow him some measure of comfort. She'd been there.

"Guess I better head out." He returned Karissa's hug and then held out his hand to Devin. "See you in a few days."

Once again, tears of frustration stung her eyes, and she blinked them away. She was never this emotional. *Must be the pain.* "See ya. Take care of yourself."

He turned away and quickly disappeared from view, but a few moments later, they heard his strong voice singing an old marching song in the distance. It had completely faded away before Karissa broke the silence.

"How about some oatmeal and pain pills for breakfast?"

"How could I turn down an offer like that?"

Karissa boiled water using a mini tea kettle and the foldable metal camping grill that went over the fire. In her dark jeans, a gray hooded sweatshirt with a science emblem emblazoned on the chest, and her hair swept up in a loose ponytail, she looked completely at home making breakfast over an open fire. Devin's pulse sped up the way it always did when she could watch Karissa simply being. She was naturally beautiful, and when she wasn't talking to people, her self-consciousness was replaced by graceful, thoughtful, movement.

"It's rude to stare." Karissa didn't look up from the bowl of oatmeal she was stirring over the fire.

"Not when you're in the woods with the most beautiful woman you've ever seen. In fact, I'd argue it would be rude not to." Devin knew her words came across as lighter than they felt.

"I wouldn't want you to be rude. Continue." She leaned over and handed Devin a bowl of oatmeal. "But eat while you're doing it."

They ate in companionable silence, the sounds of a light breeze ruffling the trees and birds calling to one another like an intimate conversation they were eavesdropping on.

When they were finished Karissa took their dishes. "I'm going to go look at the bridge. I'm curious to see what the damage is, and I'll use the water to clean the dishes." She set everything down, crawled into the tent, and brought out Devin's pack. She placed it behind her and kissed the back of her neck, making her shiver. "Now you can lean back if you want to get comfortable. I'll only be a few minutes."

Devin nodded, not wanting to break the peaceful moment. She enjoyed the sight of Karissa's perfect ass before she disappeared into the trees. Devin scooted down and leaned against her pack. Staring up at the hazy blue sky, she pondered their predicament but couldn't see that there were any options they hadn't considered. Her leg began to throb in earnest, and she couldn't get comfortable. Her irritation began to grow, and the longer Karissa was away the more she began to worry. It wasn't far back to the bridge, but she shouldn't have let her go alone. What if she'd run into more raiders? Or even a lone wolf preying on women traveling alone? Just as her imagination was about to get the better of her, and she was looking for a way to stand up and hobble after Karissa, she strolled back into view.

Devin's breathing slowed and she felt almost dizzy with relief. *This being helpless thing sucks ass.*

"What a mess." Karissa came over and dried the bowls and cups. "The bridge is a big bank of mud. I can barely see the roof of the van on the other side of the river, and there's debris everywhere. No one is going to come from that direction, that's for sure."

When Devin didn't respond, she looked up. "You okay?"

Devin found it hard to speak past the lump of emotion in her throat. Zeke was gone, trying to find help they didn't know was out there, and if something had happened to Karissa… "I was just a little worried about you, that's all."

Karissa's eyes narrowed as she looked at Devin searchingly. She stood and opened the tent flaps. "What say we get you high on pain pills and you get some more rest? I'll lie next to you."

Devin knew she hadn't fooled her. She was learning that Karissa seemed to have an innate sense of people's emotions, even when they didn't say anything. But she also seemed to know when to ask questions and when to let things go. She was glad this was one of the times she let things go. Devin didn't want to talk about her feelings of helplessness, of her lack of agility, or her fears for the future. Sleep was always a good way to get out of talking about things. She'd faked sleeping more than once in her life in order to get out of difficult conversations.

"That sounds perfect." She leaned forward so Karissa could take her pack back into the tent, and then did a kind of injured crab walk backward until she was in the tent herself. Once positioned on the sleeping bag, she sighed, exhausted from just that small bit of exertion. She moved her leg gingerly when Karissa bundled up her sleeping bag and put it under Devin's injured leg.

"Let's keep it elevated for a while. I remember reading something about that being a good idea." She handed Devin more pain pills and some water, and then blew up her own pillow. "I'm going to lie next to you and read. Try to sleep."

Devin gladly shut her eyes and drifted off. She'd always loved camping; the feeling of sleeping outside with only a thin bit of material between herself and nature quieted her soul. Karissa's side pressed to hers, and the soft turning of the book pages sent her to sleep.

❖

"I stink."

Karissa laughed. "I don't think anyone smells particularly good when they're camping."

Devin shook her head. "No, I mean I stink of river water and dried blood. I keep pulling leaves out of my hair. I don't suppose you'd help me get cleaned up?" She closed her eyes. "I hate to ask, but I don't think I can do it on my own."

Karissa dug through her pack and found the portable shower kit. "Let me heat up some water and get it set up in a tree. Then I'll come back and get you." She headed out and got the kettle boiling. She transferred the hot water into the soft PVC sack and found a tree to hang it from before she attached the nozzle and then quickly headed back to the tent. The entire time she did her best to not think of Devin wet and naked. It wouldn't help the situation.

Devin was sitting at the edge of the tent with her legs in front of her. Karissa held out her arm and let Devin leverage herself upright. When she was standing still, Karissa ducked in and grabbed the soap before coming out and helping Devin over to the makeshift shower.

She hesitated. Even after all they'd been through, she wasn't sure what the protocol was. "Do you want help getting undressed? Or do you want to just lean against the tree?"

Devin's eyes were dark and her small smile was sultry. "I'm good with you undressing me."

Karissa bit her lip and started with Devin's T-shirt. She pulled it off and set it aside, and it took full willpower to not trace the line of her muscled abs. She swallowed hard and slid her fingers under the band of her sports bra. Devin's skin broke out in goose bumps, and Karissa heard her breathing hitch when her small, perfect breasts were exposed to the morning air. *At least I'm not the only one being affected.* When she got to Devin's sweats, though, she forced herself to concentrate. She needed to take them off without bumping her leg. Carefully, she pulled them down and over the wound, and Devin hissed when she had to put a bit of weight on it to lift her other foot.

Karissa stepped back and averted her gaze. "I'll go heat some more water. You get started." She held out the soap and Devin's fingers closed over hers.

"Don't be too long."

Karissa hurried back to the fire and cursed the slowly boiling water. Once it was ready she ran back but stopped short when she got there.

A goddess was showering in front of her.

Devin's muscles bunched and released as she lathered soap over her wet skin. When she raised her arms to wash her hair, the tattoo on her back shifted in the light and looked like it could leap from her mountains of muscle beneath it, though Karissa couldn't quite make out what kind of animal the tribal markings created. Her legs were strong, her ass perfect. She could have been carved from marble.

"You could join me, you know. That way neither of us stink."

Devin hadn't turned around, but she must have known Karissa was watching. She didn't need a second invitation. She poured the hot water into the PVC sack, then quickly shucked off her own clothes. She pressed herself against Devin's back and reached around to take the soap from her. "You missed a spot." She ran her lathered hands over Devin's back, feeling every ridge and rise and liked the way Devin responded to her touch, pressing into it. Once she was done, Devin turned around and pressed her breasts to Karissa's.

"Your turn." Devin took the soap and washed Karissa in long, slow movements. Over her breasts, lingering on her nipples, before her hand slid down her stomach and between Karissa's legs.

Karissa moaned, but Devin moved away. "Tease." She opened her eyes to see the pain in Devin's expression.

"I'd love to finish this, believe me. But I don't think I can stand up much longer."

Karissa shook off the disappointment. "Of course." She turned and grabbed a towel from the tree trunk and handed it to Devin. "Dry off and let me finish up."

She quickly washed off and rinsed out her hair. Devin was right; it had been a good idea to get clean. Even if she wished it had been a dirtier way to go about it. She wrapped a towel around herself and let Devin lean on her back to the tent. She helped her redress, and Devin's silence told Karissa just how much pain she was in.

Once she was sitting down, resting against the log by the fire, Devin sighed. "I hate being this incompetent. Sorry."

She looked so downcast. "Hey, I love a good round of foreplay. And now you don't stink. It's a win-win."

Devin nodded. "Good to know."

Karissa got dressed and stoked the fire. "Rest. I'll make lunch."

By the time lunch was ready, Devin was asleep again. Karissa ate, enjoying the silence and thinking of how insanely good Devin's touch felt. Even if it was brief, it was still better than the way the touch of others had felt. She couldn't wait to feel it again and for a hell of a lot longer.

❖

"Tell me about your tattoo."

Devin leaned back against Karissa's chest, her legs out in front of her, her feet to the fire. The day had passed in a fog of pain pills and curling against Karissa as best she could. By the time dusk had fallen, she'd grown chilled and had put on a sweatshirt. Karissa had cooked them another bag of chili and then gathered some firewood. It had taken a while to start, but now it was burning beautifully. "Looking at me naked, were you?"

"Not as much as I wanted to." She pushed on Devin's shoulder. "Lean forward so I can see it again?"

Devin did as she was asked, pulled up her shirt to show the ink between her shoulder blades, and her skin tingled where Karissa traced the black lines. "It's a Celtic fox. It was a weird time in my life." Karissa pulled her shirt down and Devin settled back against her.

"How so?"

"I was in the military, traveling the world. I'd been promoted and had to visit our various bases in other countries. I'd fall asleep in one country, wake up in another, fall asleep in yet another. It was intense. But all I'd ever wanted was to see the world, so I was living my dream. And I was lucky enough to see a lot of the coastlines before they really changed."

"And your tattoo?"

Devin pinched Karissa's leg. "Impatient much? Do you have somewhere else to be?"

Karissa laughed and kissed the back of Devin's neck. "Sorry. Go on."

"So, I'm going from country to country, and suddenly it occurs to me I'm seeing foxes everywhere. In Belfast, in England, in India. Even in Tibet. Images of them and even the real thing a few times. It felt…"

"Fated?"

Devin remembered the fox that had stopped in front of her at the base in Japan. It looked like it had been dipped in red-orange paint, with a thick stripe of brilliant white on its chest. "Yeah. Kind of like that. And I actually had one walk up to me, put its paws on my legs, and just stare at me. It let me touch its head before it took off."

"Wow. That must have been amazing."

"It was. But it was more than that. I felt like it was trying to tell me something." She rolled her eyes. "Sounds stupid when I say it out loud. I've never told anyone this."

Karissa squeezed her. "I don't think it sounds stupid at all. Animals have always tried to communicate with us. We're just really bad at listening. Did you figure out what it was trying to say?"

"Honestly? No. But I researched it and found out all the symbolism of it." She hesitated, not sure she wanted to be so open. But then, it was just the two of them, and you never knew what tomorrow might bring… "It's a symbol of a lot of things. It sees the world as a playground and has a lot of fun. It's cunning and observant, often watching others while remaining unseen."

"So it's you in animal form."

"It's the me I want to be. Free, adventurous, paying attention. They're sociable, adaptable, and can call pretty much anywhere home."

Karissa's fingers ran slow trails back and forth on Devin's arms, and she was quiet for a long while. Devin got that Karissa was one of those people who thought before she spoke, so she let her process.

"I can see how that symbolism appeals to you."

Devin shifted so she could look at Karissa's face. "That was a non-committal statement."

"It wasn't meant to be. I really can see it." She looked thoughtful and a little troubled. "I think I might be the opposite of that. What animal likes to stay in one place? Like one of the lizards in the Galapagos Islands."

"You're still adventurous in some way, though. I mean, you're here when you could have gone with Van." The thought that Karissa might have gone with the raiders, staying true to her nature to stay put, made Devin uncomfortable.

"Yeah, I suppose." She sighed and moved the hair away from Devin's eyes. "I'm about ready to turn in. You?"

The conversation was over, and Devin tried to ignore the slightly deflated feeling settling in her. She'd shared something special, and although Karissa had certainly been open to it, she had a feeling it had opened another road they were going to have to traverse one day.

As she wrapped her arm around Karissa in what had begun to feel like a perfect sleeping arrangement, except for the throbbing leg, doubt began to grip her. She lived for today, but she couldn't help but wonder if Karissa would feature in many of her tomorrows.

CHAPTER EIGHTEEN

Karissa knelt beside the fire pit and stared into the flames while the kettle boiled. Devin was still sleeping after a fitful night, and Karissa had been careful not to wake her as she'd left the tent. She wanted a few moments to herself before they began another day of being alone together. Having plenty of alone time had always been a luxury, but since she'd moved back in to take care of her parents, that time had become scarce and precious. Being with Devin and Zeke was comfortable and easy, for the most part. But the situation they were in, along with the ethical questions bothering her, meant she needed some time in silence so she could process without outside input.

Their final conversation last night had been more profound than she'd meant it to be. An apology was called for. Devin had shared something important to her, and Karissa had over analyzed it and drawn comparisons, instead of simply appreciating the information for what it was. She felt bad about her reaction, as she often did when it came to communicating with people.

The kettle began to whistle, interrupting her train of thought, and she quickly took it off the heat and poured herself a cup of tea. Sipping slowly, she took in the crisp spring morning. The sky was clear blue, but she could smell the dampness in the air that suggested something else might be headed their way. She already knew where she'd move the tent if she needed to, and she'd stockpiled a bunch of wood under a particularly dense bit of tree canopy for the fire.

She grinned wryly at the thought of being the one in charge of their survival. Karissa the lab rat, who loved her down comforter and thick pillows, Sunday morning biscuits, and chatting with other scientists at conferences; that's who Devin was depending on, and while surreal, she couldn't help but be a little proud of herself, too. When it had come down to it, she'd stepped up the way she needed to, and that felt good. The question was, could she keep it up? And what about when they got to the facility in Colorado? What would she do then?

She heard rustling inside the tent and listened.

"Hello out there, anyone around?"

She liked the way Devin's voice made her feel like there were hundreds of butterflies in her stomach, and the way her smile made other parts tingle. She poured two cups of tea and went back to the tent. After handing Devin her cup, she crawled inside and sat cross-legged beside the sleeping bag. "Morning. How you feeling?"

Devin's smile was tired. "Fine. No problems at all." The pinched lines at the corner of her eyes said differently. "Thanks for the tea."

"No problem." Karissa decided not to mention the tossing and turning Devin had done in the night. No point in making Devin feel even more vulnerable. "I think I can smell rain in the air. We might need to move the tent later."

Devin frowned. "By we, you mean you." She pushed at the blanket in frustration. "I'm really sorry you need to do all this on your own."

"You know, I'm actually enjoying it." At Devin's raised eyebrows she hurried to clarify. "Not you being hurt, obviously. But it's good to get a reminder that I'm capable, you know?"

Devin yawned and shook her head. "I don't think anyone but you thought you weren't capable. You're a fighter. I had no doubts."

The simple statement of belief buoyed Karissa's already rising optimism. "Hey, you want to take a little walk today? Just to the riverside, before the storm surge that might come later."

Devin raised her arms dramatically. "God, yes. I'd love to get out of this tent for a while."

"Perfect." She pulled the sleeping bag from Devin's leg. "First though, I should check the wound site and clean it again. Then put on some fresh moss, if that's good with you."

"Damn. I guess you should. I don't relish the idea of moving it, though."

She did look genuinely worried, and Karissa wanted to reassure her, even if the truth was that it would hurt. "Hey, my sewing will be a work of art. I want to see what animal my stitches resemble."

Devin grinned and settled back, moving around so Karissa could take off her sweats. She tried not to focus on the cute boy shorts that hugged muscular thighs.

"Keep looking at me like that, and I'm going to ignore my injury and do what I've been wanting to do since I met you." Devin's tone was low, her voice husky.

Karissa swallowed the desire flaring inside her and started unwrapping Devin's leg. When Devin's touch stopped her, she looked at her face.

"At some point, Ris, we're going to have to deal with this fire between us. You're driving me crazy."

A strange little squeak of desire made it out of Karissa's mouth, much to her mortification. When Devin laughed, she pushed at her shoulder. "You're a terrible tease. Evil. And when the time comes that we can do...*something* about it, you'd better have enough energy to go for days."

The dark desire in Devin's eyes made Karissa's stomach do summersaults and her pussy throbbed in direct response to Devin's intensity. *Focus. Injured. Not a sex toy.* She went back to her job and Devin lay back on her elbows, her eyes never leaving Karissa's face.

When Karissa finally got all the bandages and moss off, she cleaned the wound site with antiseptic. It was a little swollen and pink, but the skin was cool to the touch, which was reassuring. Devin sat up to inspect it.

"I think it looks like a platypus."

Karissa looked at it from different angles but couldn't see it. "I think it looks like a caterpillar."

Devin nodded, looking super serious. "I agree. You win."

After Karissa had redressed it, she paused. "How do you feel about a makeshift splint? Just a sturdy branch behind your leg to keep you from bending it?"

Devin hesitated. "You're already doing so much—"

"A splint it is. Be right back." She knew full well it must be insanely frustrating for Devin to have to rely on anyone, so she'd probably just have to take charge here and there. Surprisingly, she was fine with that. It took a little longer than she'd thought it would, but she finally found a sturdy branch that was the right length and straight enough to be useful. When she got back to the tent she was surprised to see Devin outside it, sitting on the camping blanket. If the sheen on her forehead and the paleness of her skin were any indication, it hadn't been easy for her to do on her own.

"Hey. Thought I'd get air."

Stubborn goat. "Great." She brandished the branch and set it beside Devin before ducking into the tent to get another bandage from a medical kit. She crawled back out and slowly bandaged the branch to the back of Devin's leg. "This might give you some extra support, too."

Devin gave a quiet sigh of relief. The branch could take some of the weight now. Karissa had considered it at the beginning and then promptly forgot it when Devin couldn't move very far anyway. *Some go-to I am.*

"Ready to go to the river?" Karissa helped Devin to her feet. She handed her the staff, and they moved slowly and carefully to the riverside. Karissa led her to a large fallen tree trunk and lowered her onto it. She didn't miss Devin's expression of pain, even though she clearly tried to hide it. Karissa pulled out her water bottle and two pain pills. "And here's your reward for making it this far."

Devin took them gratefully. The river flowed strong and sure beside them, only a few feet below the bridge that had washed out days before. Two mallards came into view, and behind them seven little bundles of fluff and feathers. Devin took Karissa's hand as they watched the family paddle along close to the shore, staying out of the main current.

"I'm sorry." Karissa needed to get it out before the moment was too far gone to apologize properly.

Devin frowned. "For what?"

"For my reaction to your tattoo. I made it about me, instead of simply appreciating the value of you sharing it with me. And I'm sorry." She traced the veins along the top of Devin's hand. "I've never been good at reacting the way normal people do. I always seem to blunder and say the wrong thing. That's probably why I don't get a lot of second dates." She looked into Devin's eyes, pools of blue calm. "I'm really glad you shared the meaning of your tattoo with me. I love getting to know you."

Devin's head tilted, and she looked at Karissa for a long moment. "Thank you. That means a lot."

She didn't say anything else, but she didn't need to. Karissa could see the relief in her eyes, and she was glad she'd done it sooner than later. They were good at sitting quietly, neither of them needing to fill the air with chatter to avoid the silence, and Karissa was grateful for that. She wondered what Devin was thinking about but didn't want to intrude on her thoughts.

"Have you ever been in love?" Devin asked suddenly.

Taken aback by the question, Karissa didn't respond right away.

"Sorry. Too personal. Forget I asked."

Karissa lightly bumped Devin's side. "Hey, give a girl a chance to answer, would you?"

Devin grinned and held up her hands in surrender.

Karissa tried to form an answer that would make sense. Devin had been open with her, and she deserved the same courtesy. "I wouldn't say so, no. I want love. I want that kind of romantic thing you read about in books. Being swept off your feet, swung around in a circle and kissed senseless. I want the beauty of what my mom and dad have. Right to the end, they still held hands whenever they went anywhere, and couldn't imagine being without each other for more than a few hours at a time. I want that." She put the back of her hand to her head and pretended to swoon. "But I've never found it." She shrugged away the spurt of sadness. "As you may have noticed, I'm flawed. I don't communicate well, and I've got a temper. I live for my work, and I spend all my available time in the lab. That doesn't sit well with someone who wants to hang out with you. And I guess, if it was the right person, I wouldn't want to stay in the lab. I'd want to be with them, right?"

Devin poked at the rocks by the stream with her staff as Karissa talked. "Yeah. That's right. When you're in love, that person takes over your soul. You can't eat, can't sleep, can barely breathe when they aren't with you. Making them happy is everything. The only thing. And when you're together, the hours spin by so fast. You start to resent every minute you'll never get back, and the ones you've got left won't ever be enough."

The beauty of Devin's words contrasted heavily with the dejection in her voice, and her expression looked haunted.

"Want to talk about it?" Despite the uncomfortable jealousy Karissa felt lodge between her shoulder blades, she still wanted to know.

Devin shook her head, then sighed and poked hard at the rocks with her staff. "Maybe. I don't know. I've never talked about it before." She ran her hands through her hair, her frustration evident. "But when I tell you, you won't look at me the same again." She finally looked at Karissa, her eyes soft, her expression vulnerable. "And I really like the way you look at me."

Karissa cupped Devin's face in her hands. "The past is gone. Humans are fragile, flawed creatures. Mistakes don't make us any less lovable. It's the learning from mistakes that makes us who we are." She kissed her lightly, then drew back and let go of her face.

Devin swallowed hard. She closed her eyes and started talking. "I joined the military when I was seventeen. It was my only way out, and I wanted to see the world. I was a lesbian in a small town, and even though no one ever gave me any hassle over it, I still didn't have any community or dating pool. I thought the military would change that."

Karissa waited as Devin seemed to get lost in her thoughts. "And did it?"

Devin's eyes opened like she was startled back from a memory. "Yeah. Instead of being the only gay in the village, I was surrounded. Boot camp, senior officers, girls off base in nearby bars…I sowed my oats. I loved it, and I really got to understand who I was, who

I wanted to be. I moved through the ranks faster than any woman before me and made lieutenant in record time. I was seeing the world, and I was damn good at my job."

Her smile was wistful and Karissa braced herself.

"And then I met Julie. She'd been traveling the world, doing all the same stuff I'd been doing. We were wildfire together. From the moment we met, it was flames, and I knew she was it. I wasn't her supervisor, so it didn't matter that we were different ranks, and we moved in together pretty quickly. The thing was, she was frontline combat, and she could be called for duty any time." Devin wiped away a tear. "She got called out to the battle zone in the Soviet Union, and we had an argument. I kept telling her to put in for a promotion so she didn't have to walk into combat zones anymore, but she loved what she did. The morning she left I said a bunch of shit I didn't mean, because I was scared, and I felt like something bad was going to happen." She put her hands to her eyes and shuddered. "I told her I wouldn't be there when she got back, because she clearly didn't love me enough to try to stay."

Karissa's heart broke at the pain in Devin's voice. Her shoulders were hunched against the painful memories, and Karissa slid over and put her arm around her. She had a feeling she knew what was coming.

"Two days. It was only two days later that she was killed in action. The notification team showed up at my door, and I just nodded and said thanks for letting me know. But when I closed the door I lost it. I broke damn near everything in the house." She leaned into Karissa, tears falling freely. "She died thinking I didn't love her anymore. And ever since, I've known I don't deserve love. I'm not built for it, and I can't handle it."

Karissa let her cry, wondering how she'd held such terrible guilt inside for so long. When she quieted, Karissa said, "Can I say something?"

Devin shrugged slightly.

"Arguments happen. And if you burn like you say you did, then those arguments are obviously going to be more intense. I understand why you feel guilty; I can't imagine how awful that must have been." She pulled Devin tighter against her. "But even after knowing you for such a short time, I can tell you this for certain. She knew you loved her. If I can see it now, she definitely saw it then. You need to let go of the guilt and be happy for the beauty. Shutting yourself off because of a mistake is doing nothing more than killing off your future for a past you can't change."

Devin was quiet for a long time, and Karissa let her think. She might have overstepped herself, but Devin deserved to have someone say it, even if she couldn't believe it right away.

"Thank you." Devin pulled away and scrubbed at her face. "For listening and not judging. I'll think about what you've said. And incidentally, you had no problem saying exactly the right thing now." She glanced at the sky, which now had a few gray clouds slipping past. "Maybe we should head back to the tent. Just in case it starts. I'd rather not get caught in the river again." Her smile was tired but genuine.

They moved slowly back through the trees, and Karissa thought about all Devin had shared. Karissa's own reasons for putting off a relationship seemed far less real now that she was looking at them critically.

They got settled back in the tent after a quick lunch. The clouds had passed for the moment, but the air felt heavy with the promise of another dousing. She wouldn't move everything until she knew she needed to though. She put her pack at Devin's feet so she could lean back and face her.

Devin grinned. "Let's move into less soul-crushing territory, shall we? Tell me about your weirdest experience."

Karissa was happy to lighten the mood. She was still mulling over Devin's lost love and wondering if she'd ever match that kind of passion. "I went to England during my doctorate. I had to do some research, so I scheduled the flight a year ahead of time and everything. I ended up in this tiny village of about two hundred people. Every day, I'd get on the bus and take it into the nearby town. These two old women, Gladys and Iris, would get on the bus, sit behind me, and stroke my hair. Like I was a pet."

Devin looked incredulous. "What did you say?"

"What could I do? I thought maybe English people were weird and liked to pet people. So I let them do it. They said it was beautiful and they liked touching it. I couldn't be rude, so I just sat there and let them pet me."

"Okay, that's weird. You win."

Karissa shook her head and pointed at Devin. "Oh no. Your turn."

Devin covered a yawn. "Let's see. I was in the backwoods of a village in the Middle East. I was on base on my day off, and I was on the outer edges messing around with a car I was fixing up, mostly because I didn't have anything else to do. I came out from under the hood, and there's this little kid watching me from the other side of the fence. She's probably about six, and she's there alone. Now, the nearest houses are about fifteen miles away, and she's barefoot, holding a teddy bear that's seen better days. She's staring at me really intensely, like she's looking through me. I try talking to her, but she just looks at me. Then she points toward the village and looks at me again. She never speaks. So I start thinking she's lost or something. I tell her to wait, hoping she'll understand me, and I go get my car. I drive around and she gets in the passenger seat. Still doesn't say a word, but keeps pointing. I get to the village and she directs me to this tiny shack that's practically falling down. I follow her inside, and there's a woman on the floor. She's a mess, and she's obviously in labor. Totally alone. I spoke enough of the language to tell her I was there to help, and I got her in the car." Devin paused dramatically. "I looked everywhere for the little girl. She wasn't there. It was like she'd disappeared. So I figured she must be a neighbor kid or something. I took the woman back to base and got her medical attention. I went to check on her, and she asked me how I knew she needed help. When I told her the little girl came and got me, she freaked out. Started sobbing."

"And?" Karissa asked when Devin stopped.

"And…she'd had a little girl who was killed during the war. One who carried a teddy bear."

Karissa laughed. "You're making that up."

Devin shook her head. "Swear. Totally happened."

"So do you believe in an afterlife, then?" Karissa thought of Sheila's little funeral, and none of them had said anything about believing.

"Honestly? I don't know. I know what I saw that day, and I know I can't explain it. I don't think there's a wizard in the sky that makes things happen. But I do think there might be things we can't explain. Yet."

"I think that's what discovery is all about. The excitement that we don't have all the answers. That there are always questions."

"And that's why we're on our way to see what questions there are on another planet." Devin yawned again. "I'm really sorry. Between the pills and the pain, I'm wiped out. Mind if I take a nap?"

Karissa smiled, glad Devin could admit to not feeling great. "No problem. I'm going to pull things together so I can move us under shelter when you get up later."

Devin sat up and held onto Karissa's hand. "You're amazing, Ris. No matter what happens, I'm so damn glad to have met you."

Her words were so sweet, and so plainly real, that Karissa felt the air rush from her. "I feel the same." She pulled her hand away slowly. "And it doesn't hurt that you're easy on the eyes." She winked and smiled when Devin laughed. "Get some rest."

Devin moved into the only position she could really lie in and closed her eyes. "Yes, boss."

Karissa left the tent and began pulling their little campsite together. As she did she considered all they'd shared. Devin really was something special. Tender, strong, empathetic, kind. She'd skipped over it, but the fact was, she'd gone to a house in a war zone because a child had needed help, without any thought for her own safety. That spoke volumes. She'd been enjoying Devin's company and had been glad she was so handy. But they were playing in deeper waters now, and she wondered if she could swim with that current, or if it would wash over her and leave her parched.

CHAPTER NINETEEN

Devin nestled her face into Karissa's hair and pushed against her warm body. Every time she'd tried to shift in the night but had been unable to thanks to the damn leg, Karissa had woken, stroked her stomach or arm, and sent her back to sleep. Waking with Ris cuddled by her side, her long hair swept in every direction, her breathing so soft and sweet, made Devin's heart ache. She hadn't had this in so long, and telling Karissa the story about her past had been painful but strangely cathartic too. This morning she felt like she wanted to burst into some cheesy song about happy birds and flowing rivers. Karissa hadn't been sleeping well because Devin hadn't been sleeping well, and she was incredibly grateful she'd still chosen to stay in the tent with Devin rather than pitch one of her own so she could actually get some rest.

Devin closed her eyes, willing herself to drop back to sleep, and then opened them again. Her heart began to race.

"Ris, baby, wake up." She swept the hair from her face and squeezed her shoulder.

"Hmm? Are you okay?" She didn't open her eyes but began that rhythmic stroking on Devin's stomach like she had throughout the night.

"Ris, someone's coming. Listen."

Karissa's eyes opened wide, and she sat up.

The sharp thudding sound of big trucks was unmistakable. It was also getting closer.

Karissa scrambled to her knees, quickly pulled on her clothes and shoes, and helped Devin do the same. Neither spoke, and Devin knew they were both wondering what kind of people were headed their way. In the way that had become almost choreographed, Karissa helped Devin out of the tent, gave her the staff, and stood beside her.

"Do we move closer to the road?"

Devin thought about it. If help was nearby, they needed to snatch at it. If it wasn't Zeke, they'd have to make a decision—take the help and see if they could track him down and risk missing him altogether, or wait for him and potentially miss their only chance of rescue. It would be a hell of a choice to have to make. And if the trucks coming were bad guys, putting themselves directly in their path seemed like a stupid idea. But if they didn't and help passed them by because they were hiding...

"Let's go." Karissa pulled Devin's arm over her shoulder. "You're overthinking. That's my job."

Devin hobbled along beside her. She'd never been indecisive, but being injured seemed to make her more hesitant. She couldn't protect Karissa from danger. *This is why I don't get involved. It's too damn messy.* They made it to the road and stood on the side in plain sight. The trucks were loud now, their chugging echoing against the trees around them. They waited, watching, and she held Karissa tightly against her. She could feel the tension in Karissa's back, could see it in the frown lines in her forehead.

"Hey, it's going to be okay. Nothing will happen to you. I promise."

Karissa looked at her incredulously. "I'm not worried about myself, you idiot. I'm worried about protecting you if we're standing in the path of psychos."

Devin began to laugh, and soon Karissa joined her. "Great. We're worried about protecting each other. There are worse things." She looked back at the road when she saw movement from the corner of her eye.

First one, and then another military truck came around the corner. The debris over the bridge stopped them, and the driver jumped out. He saluted and yelled from where he stood.

"I hear you guys are in need of a lift?" He waved at the mud and tree covered bridge. "It looks like it might take us a bit to get to you." The other doors opened on the trucks, and soon there were soldiers spilling out onto the bridge, far more than had been with their convoy.

Devin heard the back truck's door slide up, and Zeke ran around the side of the truck. He picked his way across the bridge and then sprinted over to them. He grabbed them in a tight hug, and Devin laughed at his exuberance.

"You made it back." She patted his back, feeling slightly awkward at the long hug.

He finally let go and started talking, his rapid speech hard to keep up with.

"I was nearly to the EART trees when I came across the convoy. They were already well past you, but I explained what had happened and that you were injured. They agreed to help. But I was so worried you wouldn't be here. I mean, what if someone else had come and you'd gone with them? What if you'd been attacked? What if Devin's leg had become infected and she was dying?"

Karissa put her finger over his mouth. "Breathe, Zeke. We didn't think we'd see you for another few days. You've saved us."

His smile was like that of an adopted child being told how much he was wanted and loved. "I didn't think I could do it, but I did. When it rained I just hunkered down, and even when it was scary and lonely, I knew you were depending on me, so I did it." He looked behind him at the soldiers clearing a way across the bridge. "Want some help packing up? I bet they don't take long."

Karissa nodded and looked at Devin. "Why don't you stay here? Zeke and I will go get everything and come right back."

Devin chafed at doing nothing, but there wasn't a damn thing she could do except get in the way. "Sure, that sounds good, thanks."

Zeke and Karissa turned and started to walk away, but Zeke stopped and looked back. "Oh, and you'll never guess who's with them."

They walked away, and Devin could still hear him excitedly telling Karissa about his adventure. She'd told herself she wasn't overly worried, that he'd be fine, but deep down she'd wondered if she'd ever see him again. Seeing how excited and how proud of himself he was, she was glad he'd taken the journey. It would do great things for his self-confidence. But who was he talking about being with the convoy?

She searched the faces of the people on the bridge, and when one looked up at her and saluted, she laughed out loud and waved.

Sergeant Walker jogged over and shook her hand. "I can't tell you how glad I was to hear you'd made it, even though you were injured."

She swallowed the lump in her throat. *This emotion shit is getting ridiculous.* "Damn, Walker. I thought for sure the tornado would've gotten you. It's good to see you."

One of the other soldiers shouted, and Walker acknowledged him. "I'm riding in back with you, so I'll tell you all about it when we get on the road." He looked beyond her. "Do they need help?"

She shook her head, thinking of Karissa's desire to protect her. The knowledge warmed places in her that were dangerously close to the surface these days. "Nah. It's just our packs, and they can handle those. They're breaking down the tent and stuff, so it may take a few minutes."

"No problem. This convoy is a little ahead of schedule, even with backtracking to pick you up. We'll get the trucks across and then I'll help you up." He got back on the bridge and helped with getting it clear.

Watching the soldiers and waiting for Karissa and Zeke to get back, Devin had time to ponder. Yesterday, their journey had been nothing but questions. Today, they'd head to their final destination on this planet. She had no idea what would happen once they were there or what the time frame was. *What if they separate us?* She couldn't imagine not sleeping in Karissa's embrace. Not seeing her every day would be like losing a limb, and just the thought made her feel panicky. She thought Karissa felt the same way, but then, why would she? They were as different as coal and sandstone, something Karissa made clear when they'd talked about her tattoo. Maybe their feelings for each other were only born out of the fires of survival.

Once they were safe again, would they still feel this way? Devin knew she would, but she had no way of knowing how Karissa would react, and asking now wouldn't do any good. Devin would just have to wait until they got there to see what would happen. It was out of her control, and she had to be okay with that.

"Hey." Karissa set her pack down next to Devin and tugged at her shirt. "You're miles away. Want to share?"

Devin silently swore at the tears threatening to well up in her eyes. *What the hell is wrong with me?* "Not thinking of anything particular. All ready to go?" She motioned at the bridge. "Looks like they've nearly got it clear."

Karissa bit her lip, looking uncertain. "I think so." She looked at Devin, her expression searching. "Now that we're really going to get there, I'm nervous. What if it's awful?"

Devin took her hand and kissed it. "Then we'll bust out and run off into the sunset."

Zeke laughed. "The blazing hot, bake you to death sunset." He put his arm around Karissa. "It's going to be awesome. You'll see."

The rumble of the trucks starting up interrupted them, and they turned to watch as they slowly chugged forward. The first truck stopped and Walker jumped down from the back. "So, Lieutenant, any thoughts on how to get you up there without you busting my nose for causing you pain?"

Devin had jumped in and out of these trucks for most of her adult life, and now she couldn't even gingerly climb in. She looked around, puzzling it out. Van's comment back at the bunker came back to her. "That tree trunk, there. If you pull that over, I can use it as a kind of step. It's high enough I can stand on it, swivel around, and push myself backward into the truck."

Walker and two of the other soldiers did as she said without comment, and she was reminded again that rank still meant something, even though she'd been out of service for a long while now.

Karissa and Zeke stood on either side of her, and she held onto them for leverage as she used her good leg to step up onto the trunk. Once there, Walker helped her brace herself, and Karissa gently supported her leg as Walker pulled her into the truck. Once she was in, Karissa and Zeke threw in their packs, climbed up, and helped Devin move into a comfortable position at the back. Sitting on a bench would mean bending her leg, and she didn't want to do that until she was near medical help. She nodded at the other three people already in the truck, but none of them looked terribly friendly. *Good thing we're not far now.* This trip had taken far too long as it was, and spending a ton of time with grumpy butts wasn't on her list of fun things to do.

Walker jumped in and pulled the door shut. Devin noticed the way the other people in the van turned away from him. He ignored them, though, and sat on the floor facing her.

"Wow. I can't believe how good it is to see you." He shook his head. "After you guys headed into the trees we were going to head after you, but someone was injured and that tornado was moving way too fast. We'd never have made it. So we went the other direction toward an abandoned house. We got really lucky. There was a storm basement. The door had been ripped off, but it was a hell of a lot better than staying above ground. Three of us got inside and pushed up against the walls."

"Three?" Karissa touched Walker's leg, her eyes sad. "Who made it?"

He covered her hand with his own, and the gesture was so kind it made Devin ache again for all they'd been through.

"One other soldier and Igorovich. And me, obviously." He looked at Zeke, his expression sad. "Zeke told us about the others with you guys. I'm really sorry about Sheila and Edward. They were a great couple." He shrugged. "At least they'll rest in peace together, right?"

Devin felt Karissa stiffen beside her at the lie, and she pressed her shoulder to her. She hadn't thought about the raiders and what they'd tell the soldiers. Clearly, Zeke had. She looked at him and the expression in his eyes was shrewd as he looked back at her.

"Right. True."

Karissa remained tense, and Devin figured she knew why. By not telling the soldiers they knew who the raiders were, they were essentially protecting the people who had overturned their convoy, the ones tangentially responsible for Sheila's death. But if they told them Edward was alive, they might go searching for him. He'd made the choice not to go to the facility, and they needed to honor that. If she'd learned anything about Karissa, it was that she could see things as very black-and-white. She held her hand and rubbed her thumb across her knuckles, trying to be as soothing as Karissa had been when Devin was in pain. She felt her slowly relax and was able to let go of some of her own tension.

"How long until we get to the facility?" Devin asked, ready for the next aspect of the trip.

"You know where they're taking us?" One of the other people in the truck who'd been silent to this point leaned forward. "You know, and you still got in willingly?"

Devin winced and threw Walker an apologetic look. "The raiders told us." Walker looked like he was about to protest and she held up her hand. "We're going to be there soon. There's no point in keeping it from them now. And fear makes people do stupid things. At least with knowledge they can be ready for what's coming."

He considered her words, and then sighed and nodded.

She looked at the other people in the van, who were all looking at her expectantly. "We're going to Cheyenne Mountain. They're bringing in a ton of scientists for a super big government project they're working on." She stopped short of telling them the rest. She didn't know how much Walker knew, and the thought of him as one of the people left behind struck her as incredibly unfair. He was a good man, and he deserved better. She thought of Karissa's arguments on the subject and began to understand them a little better.

"What kind of project?" the same guy asked.

She shook her head, and both Karissa and Zeke stayed quiet, following her lead. "I don't know. But I know we're not headed into some kind of evil lair with a villain who eats the brains of smart people." She laughed, but no one laughed with her. "Wow. Tough crowd."

There was a strained silence, and Walker cleared his throat. "We're getting on the main road, and barring any sinkholes, washed out areas, or massive storms, we should be there in about eight hours. Maybe less." He patted Zeke's leg, who sat on the bench next to them. "If Zeke hadn't flagged us down, you guys would've been out of luck. We're one of the last convoys on our way in. We were lucky I grabbed a radio off our truck before the tornado hit, or they wouldn't have come for us, either."

Given the vastly daunting prospect they'd been facing of doing five hundred miles on foot when they'd set out, to be at their final destination by dinnertime felt slightly bizarre. Karissa rested her head on Devin's shoulder, and Devin wondered at how quiet she was. She knew Karissa processed before she spoke, unless she was really pissed off, then all bets were off. If Devin felt like the change of events was surreal, Karissa was probably even more struck by it. She knew she should ask the other scientists their names, be friendly, but she didn't have it in her. She'd get to know them in Colorado. Or not. At this point, all she could think about was keeping Karissa next to her. Zeke looked ready for anything that came at them, probably thanks to his successful hero routine, and she wasn't worried about him. Like her, he was in this for the adventure, and because he had nothing to lose.

I didn't have anything to lose. Now, though, she wasn't so sure. But then, she wouldn't have to worry about it. Karissa would be on the ship with her to another planet. *Interspatial dating. Who knew?* Maybe once they were off-planet, they'd have a chance to see if there was something more between them. For the first time in a very long time, she wanted the chance for something more in her life. She nearly snorted out loud, but she could tell from Karissa's breathing she'd already fallen asleep. *Something more than helping colonize a new planet. I'm getting greedy.*

Walker looked at Karissa and smiled at Devin. He moved to lean against a bench, and the back of the truck was silent. The group didn't feel like it had the kind of close-knit vibe her convoy had enjoyed, and she felt sorry for them. As briefly as she'd known the others, she'd never forget them, and she was glad they'd been on her path. From this point forward, it was all about the road ahead.

❖

"It's so beautiful, isn't it?"

Devin knew full well what Karissa meant, but with the dusk sunlight settling across her hair, gently lighting her face, Devin couldn't think of anything more beautiful. "You really are."

Karissa turned away from the view of the Colorado Rockies in the distance and grinned. "You're pretty romantic for a grizzled rock geek, you know."

"Hey, I'm not grizzled. Just well oiled." Devin smiled back, glad the tension seemed to have left Karissa's shoulders, at least for the moment.

"I'm glad we stopped. My butt's numb." Karissa rubbed at it as though to get the feeling back.

"Want some help with that?" Devin flexed her hands.

"How can you take this so lightly? What's wrong with you people?" Ivan Igorovich strode up to them, his face set in what she thought of as his perpetual look of disapproval. "Don't you know they killed the other people in our truck?"

Karissa moved in front of Devin as though to shield her, and it made her smile.

"They didn't kill the people in our convoy, Ivan. The raiders were responsible for that. Kind of."

She shrugged, and Devin could feel her lingering confusion. She gently put her hand on Karissa's back and was glad when she leaned into her touch.

"Are you still banging on about them taking you away against your will?" Devin asked.

He glared at her. "I'm sorry we're not all ex-military and willing to leave people we love behind. Some of us had people who loved us back, you know." He turned to Karissa and his tone softened slightly. "I've heard you speak at symposiums. I know you understand how I feel. These people are animals."

Karissa's expression was one Devin had come to recognize as the one that meant she was about to lay into someone. She leaned forward to see the show.

"And are you leaving someone behind?"

He crossed his arms. "You know what I mean."

"No, actually I don't. Are you leaving someone behind? Because the last I heard, you were single and without family. Not to mention the possibility of you being under review for taking credit for other people's work. So what are you really pissed off about, Ivan?"

He glared at her, his lips white from pursing them together so hard.

Karissa stepped into his personal space, much the way she had when she was defending the soldier at the abandoned house. That seemed like it had been years ago now.

"You know what's pissed you off, Ivan? That you're not in control, and these soldiers don't give a flying monkey's fart who you are. And you're pissed off that you're riding along with other scientists you think aren't on your level. You're pissed off that they've been chosen too, which makes you less special than you want to think you are." She poked him in the chest and he looked explosive. "You know what, Ivan? You're a fraud. That's why I didn't want to work with you back when you asked. And I think all this bitching is nothing more than a front, because you know when it comes down to it, we're down to the wire, and everyone is going to know you're a shit scientist with an indefensible ego."

His eyes were wide and spittle formed at the corners of his mouth. Devin was ready to lurch forward and shove him back if she had to, even though Karissa looked ready to punch him herself.

Finally, he stepped back, genuine hatred shining in his eyes. "You're wrong. About all of it. And as soon as I can, when all this is over with, I'll sue you for defamation of character."

Karissa's laugh was harsher than Devin had ever heard it. "On another planet? I doubt they'll be concerned that someone called you names on the playground when we're building a new civilization. You probably aren't going to make it across the finish line anyway." She turned her back on him, clearly dismissing him. "Moron."

Devin wanted to clap and cheer, but Ivan's tomato-red face and shaking hands made her hold back. She didn't want to be responsible for the first ever proven case of human implosion. He stomped away without another word, and Devin noticed a few smiles from people they hadn't met yet thrown Karissa's way. She held up her hand, and Karissa laughed as she high-fived her.

"That was incredibly unprofessional. But I couldn't help myself."

"I'm so glad. You're really something to watch when you take someone on. It's insanely hot. Let me make love to you right here on this bench."

Karissa stroked the bench like she was considering it. "Damn. Looks like we're getting back on the road. Too bad." She leaned down and gave Devin a lingering kiss. "But I bet there will be benches in the facility."

She moved away when Walker came up and took a seat beside Devin. His voice was quiet, and his eyes serious. "Can I ask you something?"

Devin answered cautiously. "Sure."

"You said the raiders told you about the facility. Zeke didn't mention you'd actually talked to them. He just said you'd found the place they'd told you was there." He looked between Devin and Karissa. "I didn't ask in the truck because I didn't want to put you in a bad position. But now that we're nearly there, can I ask? What else did they say?"

Karissa looked over her shoulder and nodded at Devin to say there wasn't anyone else around.

"Are you sure you want to know?"

He looked thoughtful. "We've never been told. We literally know who to pick up, where, and to bring them back to Colorado. But we don't know why. And it's been driving me crazy. I mean, what if I really am delivering people to a villain with a penchant for smart people's brains?" His smile was sad. "I just want to know."

Devin believed him, and she thought he had a right to know. She quickly filled him in on what they'd been told, and he listened without interruption. When she was done, he looked stunned.

"Wow." He blew out a long breath. "That's not what I expected. I mean, I don't know what I expected, but that wasn't it." He grabbed Devin's shoulder. "Thank you for telling me. I'll be able to sleep again. Even if I wasn't chosen like you guys." He helped her to her feet as the bell sounded to get back in the truck. "We'll be there in about three hours."

It had been a quick stop for a late lunch, and once they were back in the truck, Zeke looked ready to burst with excitement. He was chatting with a woman who hadn't had much to say before, but now they were talking like old friends. From what Devin could tell, she was another computer tech type, and she couldn't understand half of what they were saying, but she was glad he seemed so happy.

Once again, Karissa had gone into one of her thoughtful moods, though she stayed close to Devin's side.

"You okay, Ris?"

The door slid shut and the truck roared to life.

"Nervous. Scared. Wondering what it's going to be like." She took Devin's hand. "I'm glad you told Walker. But I wonder how that information will affect him?" She looked at Devin. "What will it be like to know you've been left behind?"

Devin didn't answer because she didn't have one. She hadn't considered that aspect, and once again, Karissa's multi-layered process had. She looked at Walker, who sat against the door looking lost in thought. *Left behind.* The phrase was sharp and stuck in her mind like a needle tipped with salt. Once she was inside the facility, she'd put those questions aside and look to the future. It was what she'd always done, and it had worked so far. She ignored the niggling notion that it wouldn't work anymore.

CHAPTER TWENTY

Van's shoulders relaxed the moment Mesa came into view. The drive back had been mercifully quick, with the exception of the sinkholes they'd had to go around and a fast-moving storm. Acid rain had been a particularly destructive force over the last few decades, and sinkholes could open up right in front of a truck going too fast to keep from falling into the bowels of the earth. As soon as they spotted one, they either had to off-road or backtrack. Once they got to the edge of the lower Rockies, things had gotten a little more serious. Heavy snow made for slow going as they'd taken the constant switchbacks toward their home. Low clouds obscured the mountaintops around them, and big horn sheep occasionally appeared like ghostly hallucinations, only to disappear back into the mist.

Now, looking up at the pink tinted sandstone walls of Cliff Palace, she felt like she'd been gone years instead of less than a week. She'd never felt as at home in her high-rise apartment as she did living on the cliff sides of this ancient monument. There were always lookouts posted on the mesa above the stone settlements, and she knew they'd have radioed in their approach. When they'd decided to take Mesa and make the long abandoned site a safe haven, they'd had to make some much needed adjustments. They'd built a long bridge over the valley floor below, trying to make as little impact as possible on the earth itself. The old road leading into the national park had fallen into utter disrepair, and their new one was not only better, it was far more direct.

She breathed in the scent of the juniper and spruce trees and felt the stress of the trip begin to fade. They'd left so they could deliver supplies to the Subtrop station, and that's exactly what they'd done. Maybe it hadn't gone totally according to plan, but it meant their outpost wouldn't have to worry, and that was all that mattered.

"Wow."

She looked at Edward, who was staring up at the settlement tucked safely into the cavernous rocks. "Pretty cool, huh?"

"I've seen photos of this place, but I never in a million years thought I'd see it in my lifetime." He craned his neck and then turned to her. "How do we get up there?"

She grinned. "Well, there's a one-hundred-and-seventy-foot ladder. That can make your knees go pretty weak." The truck pulled to a stop at the base of the sandstone wall far below the buildings. "Or you can get in this lovely metal beast here, and that will bring us up to the bridge."

She stopped in front of the makeshift elevator. "It runs on solar power, but we try not to use it too often. We haven't got an ESF big enough to run the elevator all day as well as keep the settlement going. So we're careful."

"You've got energy storage facilities here too?" He looked baffled but excited.

"We do. We're fully off grid and self-sufficient." Van tried not to look as proud as she felt when she said it. Humility hadn't always been her strong suit, but she tried.

Liz scoffed beside her as they made the slow journey upward. "Thanks to you." She pointed at the housing. "See the rooftops? The new plaster? The windows? That's all thanks to Van and her frankly scary ability to remodel anything she comes in contact with."

Without looking at her, he said, "You were an architect, Van?"

Perceptive. But he was an egghead, after all. "I was. Among other things. I like puzzles, and this is the best puzzle of all."

The elevator stopped and they filed off. They all carried gear bags, and Van couldn't wait to drop hers and climb into bed. But there were things she had to see to first.

"Hand it over." Liz held out her hand and took Van's pack. "I'll drop it in your room. Let me know if you need anything. I'll go check in with the other departments."

Van waved her off, as always glad that she often didn't even have to speak for Liz to know what she wanted. She turned to Mac, but he was already steering Edward away.

"Let's find you a bunk and get you settled down." He waved overhead, as though he knew Van would be watching them leave.

She smiled and looked at Ray. "And you?"

"I'm going to drop my pack and check in with section twelve. I want to know how the restorations are going." He gave her arm a squeeze as he went past.

And then she was alone. For the first time in days, she was surrounded by the beautiful, saturating silence that filled the canyons and mesas around them. Hawks cried overhead and laughter echoed quietly off the far end of the cave walls. It was the kind of peace she'd never been able to find while living the high life, and now it was all she craved. Making it work, helping these people not only live, but thrive, had become her sole focus.

After a few more deep breaths to bring her fully home, she headed to the medical department. Located at the far end of the complex in one of the underground circular rooms known as kivas, it was only big enough for a few patients at a time, but it was connected to another kiva via a tunnel they used for overflow. She climbed down the ladder into the cool room and blanched.

It smelled of sickness and resignation.

"Hey, boss. Welcome back." Sinclair, their chief medical officer, got up from his seat against the wall.

"I hear we've got a problem." Van looked at the seven occupied beds and kept her voice low. "Thoughts?"

Sinclair beckoned her to follow him into the kiva next door, and he closed the door behind him. "It's confirmed fever. So far these are the only cases. There's a new doctor here, the egghead John brought back while you were gone. She's got some great ideas on medications. No cure, obviously, but she knows a lot about herbal medications that can ease the pain and…" He sighed, clearly looking for the right word. "Transitions."

Van thought back to the dirty, confused woman they'd saved at the beginning of the trip. It was hard to imagine her in a lab. *She was cute though. I'll have to go see her.* "Okay. Let me know if you need anything and when the symptoms begin to worsen. Any idea where it began?"

"No idea. The first one down has been living here for months. But that doesn't mean he wasn't in contact with a carrier who isn't symptomatic, maybe a newbie. Sorry. If I figure out any connections I'll let you know." He stopped her before she could turn to leave. "I wanted to pass something by you. What if we moved the sick to Balcony?"

"Do you think that's necessary? It's not airborne." She disliked the thought of moving the sick away from the living, as though they were tainted and destined only for death. *Which is true. But still.*

"We've seen the way diseases mutate over the last two decades. I think we should move them so there's less chance of spread. I'll go with them, obviously, and Mac can hold down the fort here. But the air circulation in the kivas is better at Balcony, and they could sit outside in the sun without worrying about other people."

He was right, the air at Balcony *was* better. It was a smaller settlement, and the fires were only in a few kivas. Plus, the beautiful open space the settlement was named for really would be good for the infected. At least they could look out over the beauty of the land before the fever took them completely.

"Let me talk to Ray and see how the refurb is going. I think it was close to ready before I left. If it's in good shape, we'll get you over there." She held up her hand when he started to talk. "But I don't want you going alone. I want you to take an assistant. If you fall ill, we'll need to know right away."

"I get that. But I've treated a ton of people with fever now, and I've never had a trace. I seem to be immune. I take your point, though. I'll get someone to come with me. I'll need help looking after them when it progresses."

She could tell the thought made him as ill at ease as it did Van. They rarely had to deal with disease here, and she couldn't imagine who had brought it in with them. They were usually so careful about who they brought back, and if they came across someone with fever on the road, they were on their own. It wasn't that Van lacked compassion, but she was responsible for too many lives to let compassion for one person put the rest in jeopardy. "All right. Give me a list of names, would you? I'll check to see if they have friends or family on site we need to keep a watch on."

He turned to the desk and picked up a piece of paper. "Already done. We've got eyes on two partners and one child."

Only three of the seven had someone to care for them. It seemed like a commonality these days to have to face the world alone. "Thanks, Sin. I'll let you know about Balcony as soon as I can." She climbed out of the kiva and back to the surface. She knew she should go to her office and check in with the various departments, but she was exhausted. Ray would know if Balcony was a viable option after he checked in with section twelve, which meant Van could wait and get the information from him.

She needed sleep. The days spent dodging storms, dealing with raids, and worrying about what she'd find when she got back to Mesa had taken their toll. The spring storms had put out the early brush fires, and though the landscape above and beyond their valley looked like something out of a science fiction movie, with all the blackened trees and charred land, the spring rains would bring the land to life again. If there weren't more fires brought on by lightning to ground strikes through the summer, they could end the year with greenery and maybe even a crop or two to harvest. It wasn't likely, but she could hope.

She headed to the north tower and began climbing the four flights of stairs to her apartment at the top. Initially she'd felt a little guilty taking three rooms in the tower, when most other people only had one, but given the time and effort she put in, as well as the many meetings she had, she'd gotten over it. At the second floor, she moved to the side as she heard someone racing down the stairs above her, but it was too late. The woman crashed into her, and Van braced hard against the wall, closing the woman in her arms to keep them both from tumbling backward.

"Hey now. Stone steps can break bones, you know." Van's heart raced. The last thing she needed was an injury that put her out of commission.

"God, I'm so sorry." The woman pulled back, and then smiled when she looked at Van. "Hello again. I was hoping I'd run into my knight in black jeans soon. I didn't mean to do it literally, but it works. I'm Susan Sandish."

Damn. It was the egghead John had brought back. And cleaned up, she was intoxicatingly beautiful. Her light brown hair barely touched her shoulders, and her green eyes sparkled with excitement. A smattering of freckles covered the bridge of her nose and cheeks, and Van wanted to trace them with her thumb.

"I'm not sure knocking me down the stairs would have been a good way to treat a knight." She winced internally at the light rebuke. Sometimes she couldn't help the boss side of her coming out. "But since I hear you're making waves around here with your medical knowledge, I'll forgive you."

Susan looked suitably chastised, but the excitement in her eyes didn't dim. "I was actually on my way to the medical kiva. I think I've found a remedy that could help with some of the symptoms." She waved a little bag filled with plant matter. "I wanted to see if Dr. Sinclair might try it."

"Human experimentation?" Van grinned to show she was kidding. When people got fever, it was time to try damn near anything.

"That's right." Susan grinned back. "I'd love to talk to you when you have a chance."

Van didn't ask whether the talk would be personal or professional. She didn't care if she got to look into those eyes a little longer. "Tomorrow would be good. I need some sleep, and then I've got to check in with everyone. If you meet me in my office we can head to breakfast together."

Susan edged past Van on the narrow steps, her breasts lightly skimming Van's. "It's a date. Sleep well." She turned and raced off down the stairs, taking them two at a time, until the light from the opening and closing of the door told Van she was gone.

She shook her head as she climbed the remaining stairs without incident. There wasn't always a lot of excitement from the people who came here. They had lives to mourn, family to miss. But Susan had hardly been here any time at all, and she was already digging in like a true member of the group. It was contagious and Van wanted to be infected. Susan's desire to help could remind Van why she was doing what she was, even in the face of disease and daily stress.

Finally in her apartment, she noted that Liz had dropped her bag inside the front door, but she'd deal with it later. She stripped down and climbed into bed, sighing with pleasure at the clean sheets and thick mattress. Images of Susan's green eyes stayed with her until she fell into an exhausted, dreamless sleep.

CHAPTER TWENTY-ONE

Karissa's nerves sang with nervous anticipation. Thanks to Walker, the convoy had stopped and let everyone out right before they'd entered the Cheyenne Facility. He said they should see where they were going, and she wondered if the new information had made him feel like the chosen deserved some too.

The yawning tunnel mouth beneath the words Cheyenne Mountain Complex was forbidding. Gray metal extended from the granite rock face, an uninviting, almost subtle entrance into the underground facility. She turned and looked behind her at the beauty of Pikes Peak in the distance, and then turned back to the hole into which they were about to enter the earth. She took Devin's hand and kept looking at the tunnel entrance. "I'd rather stay out here."

Devin's look of sympathy was undermined by the eager anticipation in her eyes. "I get that. I'm glad they stopped to let us take a last look outside."

Karissa smiled at Devin's attempt to hide how she was really feeling. "But you can't wait to see what's going on in there, can you?"

"I'm so excited." She laughed. "We're about to enter one of the most heavily guarded sites in the world, to get involved in a project to explore space. I think it's incredible."

Karissa wished she could feel as giddy, but the ethics of it continued to bother her. Maybe once she was involved fully in the project she'd feel differently. She thought back to her father's words and steeled herself. She turned to Walker. "Let's do it."

Once they were back in the trucks and headed inside the mountain, the small windows did nothing to illuminate the back. After they'd driven for several minutes, Walker lifted the back door. "Might as well see where you are. We're deep enough now…"

He didn't finish the sentence, and Karissa heard someone's intake of breath at what he'd left unsaid. *There's nowhere to run even if you wanted to.* She watched the two-lane road fall away behind them. It must have been at least sixty feet wide, and the scale of such a road carved into a cave was a head rush. It was another twenty minutes or so before the convoy pulled to a stop and everyone was ushered out.

An enormous metal door stood open before a narrow white hallway. Military men with long, heavy looking guns flanked the door, but they looked bored, which Karissa took as a good sign. A man with a clipboard and a PID reader like the one Walker used stood at the entrance. He was smiling, but it didn't reach his eyes. She took an instant dislike to him and wished she was still outside looking at the peaks in the distance.

"Welcome, ladies and gentlemen, to the CMC. We know you have a million questions. Please hold on to them until we get you inside and checked in. Once you've dropped your bags in your rooms, you'll be taken to a conference room where you'll be fully briefed on the situation that brings you here. Any remaining questions after the briefing will be dealt with then." He held up the PID machine. "Please step forward, hand over your PID disc, and put your finger on the monitor. After you're checked in, step inside. Once everyone is checked in, we'll be on our way."

"You okay?" Devin whispered in her ear as they got in line with everyone else.

"No. I hate it. Getting in line to go somewhere you don't want to go because someone has told you that you have to…" Karissa shuddered. "We know what's going on, and I still hate the feel of it."

Devin's arm slid around Karissa's waist, and she moved her weight to the staff she was still using. "I know what you mean. Just think of it as a normal military thing. I've been through this kind of thing a hundred times, and it's common protocol. And I'm right beside you." She squeezed her tightly to underscore her words.

Karissa leaned into her but didn't respond. She watched the others ahead of her filing inside. Everyone looked tired, worn out, and distrustful. For the most part, anyway. Devin and Zeke both looked like they were about to get special gifts, as did the woman Zeke had been talking to. Karissa wondered if he'd shared the information only the three of them had and figured by the woman's relaxed demeanor that he had. *Amazing what happens when you just tell people what's going on.*

It was her turn to hand over her PID, and her hand shook as she held it out. He barely glanced at her before reading her name and taking her blood sample. Devin didn't let go of her, and when he realized two people were in front of him, his irritated expression changed when he looked at Devin.

He saluted. "Lieutenant Rossi. We heard you were coming and it's an honor to meet you. Great to have you here. We'll get your injury seen to right away."

She saluted back, though hers wasn't quite as crisp. She handed him her PID, still not taking her arm from around Karissa. "Thanks, glad to be here. My leg will be okay until after the briefing."

He practically fawned over her, and Karissa wondered what piece of information Devin hadn't bothered to share about her time in the military. There must be something of note, given the way the other soldiers seemed in awe of her. Once they were through the check-in and inside, she tugged on Devin's shirt.

"What heroic thing did you do that makes all these people look at you like you're a comic book superhero?"

Devin blanched slightly and looked away. "I just did my time, and I did it well. No big deal."

Karissa raised an eyebrow but didn't have a chance to ask a follow-up question. Walker tapped her on the shoulder.

"Find me in the mess hall, and I'll tell you all about it."

Devin gave him a warning look, but he just smiled sweetly at her.

"Okay, everyone. Follow me."

The group filed after the officer who'd checked them in, down long, fluorescent lit halls that made the white walls and polished floor look jaundiced. Small booths with thick windows and a wooden bench were like empty eyes watching them pass.

He climbed the utilitarian metal steps to another entrance. This one, covered by an awning that said, "Welcome to Cheyenne Mountain Complex," was obviously meant to be less forbidding than the rest of the entrances, but Karissa still couldn't help but think of Dante's entrance to hell. How many levels were here? And how did they determine who went on what level? Her stomach turned, and she wiped her sweaty palms on her jeans.

After another long corridor that had several hallways shooting off it, he turned down one that had a green stripe on the floor. "These are the dormitories." He read a list of names from his clipboard. "Those people are in this dorm. Please find a bed, drop your things, and meet back here in ten minutes." He moved to the next doorway and read more names. This time Karissa's was on it, but Devin's name wasn't called at all. "Please drop your things, and meet back here in ten minutes."

Karissa looked at Devin, her eyes wide and her heart racing. She'd had a feeling they'd be separated, but she didn't think it would happen this soon. Devin was still injured, still vulnerable. *Like they'd let anything happen to her here. I just want her with me.*

Devin slowly let go of her waist. "Give me a second." She went to the guy with the clipboard and spoke with him in low tones.

Karissa couldn't hear what she was saying, but the frown line in her forehead deepened. She finally nodded and clapped him on the shoulder as he hastily scribbled something on his clipboard. She came back to Karissa smiling.

"Because of my military status, I've been given a private room down the hall. I explained that I wasn't going to leave you, so you've been cleared to come stay in my room." She looked uncertain for a moment. "If you want to. Obviously."

Karissa let out the breath she'd been holding. "Obviously." She slid her hand into Devin's. "Thank you."

Walker, who'd been carrying Devin's pack, stepped up beside them. "I've got your room number, Lieutenant. You good for me to drop your bag? That way you don't have to walk there and back."

She smiled at him, and Karissa could see her affection for him was real.

"That would be awesome, Walker, thanks. Ris is going to be staying in my room too. Would you mind dropping her bag as well?"

He motioned and Karissa handed him her pack, feeling slightly guilty. The packs were heavy enough on their own, let alone when carrying two.

"No problem at all. See you later."

"Walker?" Devin asked.

"Yeah?"

"I thought you didn't come into the complex?"

He looked down the hall and then back at them. "I didn't. That was the last convoy pickup. We really were lucky. There are a few more coming in today and tomorrow, but there aren't any more pickups being made. So I'm here until they send me somewhere else."

Karissa smiled at him before he walked off down the hall, but her thoughts were miles away. *The last convoy.* If they hadn't been picked up, there'd be a good chance they'd still be out in the woods. *Would that be so bad?* The time alone with Devin had been precious, even if she'd been injured. What if they'd missed the convoy and had to simply go north, like everyone else? What if they'd started some kind of normal life together, that didn't include intrigue and other planets? What if they'd stayed behind...

Devin shifted her weight to lean on Karissa's shoulder and brought her back to the moment. None of those questions mattered now. All that mattered was what was ahead of them. She held on to Devin's waist, and they followed the soldier down one hall after another. Various thick colored lines ran down different hallways, just as the green line ran from the dormitories. They disappeared halfway down the halls, though, and Karissa wondered where they picked up again. And how far the halls went.

They finally entered a large room with seats facing the screen. Devin's step was faltering and Karissa could feel her fighting the pain. They hadn't offered her a wheelchair or anything, and Karissa figured it was probably some kind of military code. Some shit about not showing weakness or something like that. After this, she'd insist Devin get medical help. They'd made it this far; it would be beyond absurdity for her to get an infection now.

She helped her sit in an aisle seat and then sat beside her. It wasn't just the group from their convoy. There were probably about seventy other people in the room; they all looked as unnerved as Karissa felt. The lights flickered and then went out as the screen came to life.

A friendly looking woman in a lab coat stood next to a woman in a military uniform.

Lab coat lady started talking. "Welcome to the Cheyenne Military Complex, or CMC. We know you have a lot of questions. Hopefully, we'll answer some of them now."

They turned and Lab Coat pointed at the screen behind them, which lit up with a satellite image of Earth.

"As you all know, the planet has been in a steady decline for the last one hundred and fifty years. When the industrial revolution began, it paved the way for truly spectacular inventions and innovation. However, it also began the catastrophic decline of human existence, though there was no way to know it."

The image of the Earth changed and brightened, the coastlines shifting and population growth clear by the pinpricks of light all over it. The date and population, as well as the rise in temperature, were shown across the top.

"But in the nineteen seventies some scientists saw down the tunnel of time, and they predicted what was coming at us. Fortunately, they were able to convince certain government bodies about the path that lay ahead, and scientific teams came together with military teams to develop a worst-case scenario plan."

The military woman, who reminded Karissa of the Cheshire Cat because of her wide smile, took over.

"And that's when we brought the Space Surveillance Center to Cheyenne. First, a little bit about CMC." The screen changed to a color-coded blueprint. "We're two thousand feet underground. There are twenty-five three-story buildings on the site. NORAD and Northcom are both based here, as is a central aspect of North American government. Ten of the twenty-five buildings were added in the last twelve years, as we developed the project you're here to help with today."

Karissa heard grumblings behind her, and Ivan's clear voice saying, "As if we had a choice."

Military lady kept speaking. "The facility is an underground city, and it has all you need. A gym, pool, shopping area, restaurants, and plenty of TVs, as you may have noticed."

Both women laughed, but Karissa didn't see the funny part. There *were* a lot of TVs, but that hadn't been her biggest question.

"The TVs are so you know what's going on outside," Lab Coat continued. "We don't want you to feel completely isolated from the world. But as you know, it's not a pretty picture." The screen showed images of coastlines underwater, houses with red Xs painted on doorways and rooftops to say there were bodies inside, areas scorched by drought, and climate refugees all over the world heading somewhere other than where they'd been. "And this is why you've been brought to CMC today. We need your help."

Military lady took over. "Our planet is dying. The human race is on the verge of extinction. As scientists at the top of your fields, you know this. Viruses are incurable and deadly. Last year, two million people were killed by fever. This year, we've already lost nearly a million." Pictures of bodies in grotesque piles flashed across the screen. "This ends with us as extinct as all the animals we sent to extinction before us. Drought, famine, floods…we're running out of time. The planet can no longer sustain us."

Back to Lab Coat, who was smiling again. "But there's hope. You, and space. When exoplanet Ross 128B was discovered in the early twenty-first century, it was a major leap ahead in astronomical understanding. It also brought about hope. Over the years, the SSC has been aggressively studying the exoplanets surrounding Ross

128B's star, and we've found that Ross 128D can, in fact, support life. Not as we've lived it here, but in new and exciting ways." A picture of a planet, gray and rocky, appeared on the screen. "At two and a half times the size of Earth, there's no question it can sustain the comparatively small group"—she paused dramatically, her eyes wide—"we will be taking to live there."

The planet turned on screen and overlays of domed cities appeared on it. Everyone was silent, and Karissa felt the buzz of disbelief, delayed excitement, and fear course through the room. Or maybe that's just what she felt.

Lab Coat continued. "That's why you've been chosen. You're the elite. Your specialized skills mean that we can not only save the human race, we can start fresh. We can learn from the terrible destructiveness of our ways here and develop a new society.

"From this point forward, you'll be tested against your peers. Other scientists with specialties the same as yours will join you in a testing phase to see who can come up with the most plausible answers to the questions we'll be facing on 128D. Technicians from every field will be doing the same kind of testing, as they'll be needed to actually build the things the science teams come up with. Those from each field who come up with those answers will be asked to join the journey to the next stage of human evolution. You'll fly to the new international space station first, where you'll get your space footing and meet the other scientists who are undergoing the same process on each of the other continents. From there, you'll be launched in highly specialized ships toward your new home. Most everyone will remain in cryogenic sleep for the majority of the trip, which, thanks to the development of warp speed travel, reduces the time it takes to journey eleven light years down to only thirty years. When you wake up from your cryogenic sleep, your new life awaits. Scientific advancement of the kind every scientist dreams about will begin." Military lady pointed at the image of the new planet. "You will keep us from extinction and help us become so much more."

They moved together again, and the planet behind them continued to spin. "We hope you're ready."

The lights flashed on and the screen went black. Stunned silence filled the room. The soldier who'd met them at the door walked to the middle of the room. "There are two remaining groups to arrive between today and tomorrow. Other groups have been testing for several months, which means you're going to be testing against the best of your fields. You have three weeks to undergo mental, emotional, and physical testing. Fail any of these, and you won't be part of the team to ship out. There is a leaderboard updated daily to let you know where you stand. Anyone below the red line is in danger of staying behind."

There were murmurs of disagreement, and someone behind Karissa spoke up. "You mean you could have ripped us away from our families, from our homes, only to leave us behind? For none of it to have mattered?"

Ripples of dissent rose like waves through the room, and Karissa's anger rose with it. "Why didn't you just tell us this? So we could make our own decisions and come here prepared?" She stood and glared at Soldier Clipboard, ignoring Devin's quiet warning.

He glared back at her. "Would you have come?" He looked around the room, his distaste all but palpable. "Would you have given up your cozy labs and come running in order to save the human race?" He shook his head, looking disgusted. The façade he'd been wearing cracked easily. "No. You wouldn't have. You'd have selfishly refused, and then you would have told other people and caused worldwide panic." He pointed at Karissa but backed down when Devin slowly stood beside her. "We did what we had to do. Now, you'll do what you need to do." He looked pointedly around the room. "Trust me when I tell you that if we believe you're intentionally failing the tests, there will be consequences. And you *will* end up taking them and doing your best. I assure you, that's not a path you want to take."

He looked at the soldiers by the door and nodded. "These soldiers are going to show you back to your dormitories and explain the layout. Dinner is at seven o'clock in the main mess hall. Testing begins at eight o'clock tomorrow morning, and someone will arrive at your dormitory to take you to your testing facilities. The daily schedules are on the back of each dormitory door."

He walked away without another word, and Karissa turned to Devin. "I don't even know what to say. I can't... How can they just..."

Devin took her hand. "Let's go to our room and talk."

Walker came into the room and waved at them. "Hey. I hope you don't mind, but I've asked to be your liaison while you're here." He shrugged and looked almost shy. "I haven't made a whole lot of friends along the way. I like you guys."

Spontaneously, Karissa hugged him tightly. He was refreshingly honest in a place that felt distinctly questionable. "I'm so glad." She handed Devin her walking stick. "But first, we need to get Devin to medical."

He nodded and leaned forward. "I figured you'd say that. I borrowed a cart that's out in the hallway. I didn't think you'd be up for a chair." He moved back and grinned when Devin laughed.

"Damn right. But I'll take the cart."

They headed into the hall and helped Devin onto the back of the modified golf cart. Eventually, Karissa noticed they were following a striped line that intercepted and crossed other lines. The walls alternated between rough-hewn granite that left no question they were in caves, and regular tiled walls and floors that could have been in any office building above ground. Twenty-foot doors that were four feet thick stood open at all intersections, and Karissa could imagine how the facility would feel if they were shut in case of a nuclear emergency.

Walker stopped outside a normal door with red and white stripes across it. He buzzed, gave his name and clearance, and was admitted. Karissa helped Devin off the cart and noticed her skin was hot and she was sweating. Fear surged through her. Had infection settled in after all? Had the open wound admitted the fever virus?

As if she could sense Karissa's worry, Devin kissed her cheek and whispered, "Relax. It's just hot down here. I'll be fine."

Looking into Devin's eyes, Karissa could almost believe it. But then, she really wanted to, and denial was an addictive drug.

"Hello there." A woman with long blond hair, startling blue eyes, and a figure no doctor outside of sex movies should have, walked up to them. "What have we got here?"

Karissa wanted to step in front of Devin and say they'd find someone else but got control of her absurd jealousy. *Jesus. I'm not an animal in heat.* When she looked at Devin to talk about her injury, she didn't miss the amusement in her eyes. *Busted.*

Karissa decided to answer. "Open fracture patella injury. I cleaned it with antiseptic from our medical kit and managed to close the open wound. I then wrapped it with Spanish moss. But it hasn't been rewrapped or cleaned in more than twelve hours."

The doctor looked impressed and it mollified Karissa's ire somewhat.

"Great. The moss would keep out infection too. Good thinking." She shined a penlight in Devin's eyes and felt the pulse in her wrist. "Still, I'd like to run some tests, and let's X-ray the knee and see what we're looking at." She looked at Walker and Karissa. "Are either of you family? Or legal partners?"

Karissa didn't miss the word legal. Neither did Devin, who frowned.

"Legal doesn't matter. I want Karissa with me."

The doctor shook her head and brought over a wheelchair. Gently pushing on Devin's shoulder, she said, "I get it, but I'm sorry. Policy in this installation is legal or family only. But I promise I'll call you as soon as we're done here."

Devin sighed and shook her head when Karissa was about to argue. "Babe, military policy can't be argued with. Have Walker take you back to the room, and as soon as I'm able I'll call you guys to come get me. Okay?"

Frustration made Karissa want to kick Dr. Barbie in the shins. Logically, though, she knew she didn't have any right. Hell, they'd known each other for less time than she'd known her last dentist. "Fine. But call me as soon as you're done."

Karissa kissed her softly, letting it linger until she heard someone cough discreetly behind her. *Let Barbie chew on that.* "See you soon."

Devin's smile was for her alone, and she could see the desire in it.

"Damn right you will."

Karissa followed Walker from the room, her heart aching at leaving Devin behind.

"It's just her knee, Ris."

She looked at Walker at the use of the nickname Devin had given her.

He grinned. "Hey, I said you were friends. It gives me rights." He put his arm around her shoulders and they walked down the hall. "It's not heart surgery or anything. She'll be fine. And this way you can unpack before she gets back."

Karissa knew he was right, and she was insanely glad to have a friend there to lean on. She couldn't imagine how much harder it would have been without Walker. To be completely alone, feeling as conflicted as she did, would have been awful. She straightened, determined to be the brave person she'd been in the woods. It would give her time to think, and that was always good. And she'd be there when Devin got out. *But for how long?*

CHAPTER TWENTY-TWO

I'll be honest with you, Devin. The break was clean, and thanks to your friend's quick thinking, there wasn't any infection. It wasn't happy about not being cleaned for so long, but it's fine. That said, we need to surgically fix it. Throw in a few screws and wires. That means you're looking at recovery time of three to six weeks."

Devin's heart sank. She knew what the doctor was saying. Still, she needed to hear it out loud. "And that means?"

"That means your physical is going to be tough to pass." The doctor leaned against the bed, her expression sympathetic. "But that doesn't mean you won't pass. It's just a knee injury, and you're otherwise healthy. If you clear your other tests with flying colors, it might not work against you."

Devin felt like she could breathe again. To have gone through all they had to get here, only for it to be for nothing, would have been heartbreaking. At least she still had a chance. "Thanks. When is the surgery?"

"I can do it tomorrow morning. Go get settled and relax." She ducked into another room and brought out a wheelchair. She forestalled Devin's protest by shaking her head. "We need the swelling down as much as possible. So do me a favor and stay off it until tomorrow morning."

Devin sighed and got in the chair. Knowing it was temporary helped, but she still gritted her teeth against the feeling of helplessness she felt as the doctor wheeled her out of the med unit. "You can just call my friends. They'll come get me."

"It's no problem, really. I like getting out of the unit for a while."

Devin couldn't see her face, but if she had to guess, she'd think the doctor almost sounded mischievous. Had she noticed Karissa's less than subtle possessiveness? Was she playing a game? Devin tilted her head back so she could see the doctor's face. When she looked down at Devin and winked, Devin laughed.

"Not enough drama for you around here, Doc?"

"It's good for a patient to see how much she's wanted."

The noncommittal answer made Devin laugh again. When they got to the officer's quarters, the doctor gave a guard Devin's name and was directed to the third door on the left. She knocked and Karissa answered, looking anxious. When she saw Devin in the chair she nearly pushed the doctor out of the way to get to her. *Good for a patient indeed.*

"Are you okay? How are you feeling? What's the prognosis?" Karissa felt Devin's forehead with the back of her hand.

Devin gently took Karissa's hand in her own. "I'm fine. I feel fine. I'm only in the chair to take the swelling down. I'll have surgery tomorrow. You probably saved my leg." She kissed Karissa's palm. "Thanks for that."

The doctor broke in. "Well, I'll be going now."

Karissa turned and looked at her, and Devin could see her contemplating a response. She loved the way Karissa could be so kind and gentle one minute, and then full of righteous fire the next.

"Thank you for bringing her back. What time do you want her in surgery tomorrow?"

"I'll send Walker to get her. You begin testing in the morning, and you'll definitely want to be there on time." The doctor patted Devin on the shoulder. "Stay off it. See you in the morning."

Karissa harrumphed as she pushed Devin's chair into their room. It was bigger than the bunk rooms, with a double bed in the middle and a small kitchenette on the side.

"Not too shabby. Better than bunk beds, for sure." Devin moved from the wheelchair to the bed and Karissa sat down beside her. When she put her head on Devin's shoulder, she felt the tension in Karissa's body. "Hey, what's going on, beautiful?"

"Now that we're here, it's real. The testing thing has me freaked out. What if I fail? What if you don't? What if… I don't know. What if I get something wrong and they think I did it on purpose, and I end up in some waterboarding situation? Oh God, I'm going to have to be in a testing situation with Ivan. Surely that in itself is a test. What if it all goes to hell, in one direction or another?" She sighed heavily.

"Slow down. We take it one step at a time. We do our best, and we see what happens."

"What about your physical? Did the doctor say anything about that?"

Devin hesitated for only a second. "She said not to worry about it. I'll be fine because it's not a major thing." It was a white lie, but she didn't want Karissa throwing away her chance at space exploration just because Devin might not make the grade. Not that they had that kind of relationship, or any relationship to speak of that would speak to that kind of sacrifice… *Wow. Getting a little ahead of myself.* Still, she didn't change her answer.

Karissa got up and Devin could feel her nervous energy. She watched as she finished unpacking, moving things from one pile to another in an obvious attempt to busy herself. Devin couldn't think of anything else to say to calm her down. When she'd moved a shirt to two different piles, she finally said, "Hey, I'm hungry and it's about dinnertime. What say you chauffer me to the mess hall? We're bound to get lost a few hundred times."

Karissa looked relieved to have something to do. "Perfect. Let's go."

Devin had meant it as a joke, but the number of wrong turns they took before they finally found the canteen was ludicrous. They ended up laughing nearly hysterically at the eighth or ninth wrong turn, and even though they asked for directions, everyone seemed to offer different ways to the same place. When they got there, Devin raised her arms in victory. "Take that, starvation! Not today, you bastard."

They moved through the line, and Devin let Karissa put things on her tray. As strange as it was to be incapacitated, she had to admit it was pretty nice being fussed over. The large canteen was filled with the normal sounds of people chatting, laughing, and discussing all manner of science type things. It wasn't so different from her time in the military, and it made her momentarily nostalgic for the old days. But then, those days had been full of blood and screaming, so this was infinitely better.

Karissa parked them at an empty table and they dug in. Soon, Walker joined them.

"This is way better than MREs." Walker ate with gusto. "I'm so damn glad to be off Humpty duty."

Karissa spluttered on her bite of mashed potatoes.

Devin laughed. "Humpty duty? As in eggheads?"

He nodded and smiled as he chewed. "And just as fragile. If you guys break, it's hard to put you back together again." He tapped Devin's tray with his fork. "Unless you're a special type of Humpty."

They finished their meals quickly, and Devin knew they were enjoying the real food as much as she was. By the time she made it to the cake, she was pleasantly full.

Karissa sat back and yawned. "That was good." She stirred powdered creamer into her coffee and then looked at Walker inquisitively. "This seems like a good time for you to tell me that story you promised."

Devin groaned. "Don't you dare."

He smiled at her sweetly. "Can if I want to." He leaned forward and spoke softly. "It was in the third Western Territory conflict. Things had always been bad there, but desperation made it worse. You couldn't always tell who was friendly and who wasn't."

Devin snorted. "You talk like you were there. You're about a decade too young." She knew the story, having lived it, but to have someone else tell it was odd. She wasn't sure she wanted those memories spoken aloud.

"Hey, that kind of thing becomes legend. From the moment I hit boot camp, this was my bedtime story." He turned back to Karissa. "The place is all dust and heat. There's no shade anywhere, but the landscape can hide wide ditches where the enemy can lie in wait or plant IEDs."

Devin pretended to yawn loudly. In reality, she wanted to ward off the rising memories. She could still smell and taste that red dust, feel the grit on her skin and the sweat running down her back under the fifty pounds of gear she'd been wearing.

He ignored her, but Karissa took her hand under the table.

"There's this special battalion made up of soldiers and scientists. They're on a research and supply mission when they get a call about another squad taking heavy fire nearby. They're not really equipped to help, but they're the only ones close enough, so they head straight into the fray."

Memories long buried began to swarm and sting like angry insects, and Devin squeezed Karissa's hand to ground herself.

"When they get there, it's a shit storm. Everyone is pinned down, and then the lieutenant sees two soldiers get hit. She breaks cover and heads straight for them. Bullets hitting the dirt all around her, she drops beside one, sees that he's alive, and then checks the other. Both are seriously wounded but alive. So she drags them *both* back to cover. No one knows how she didn't get shot, but she made it back with both of them in tow."

"Did they live?" Karissa looked completely enthralled.

"Yup. But that's not the end of the story." His expression showed just how determined he was to finish the tale. "Once she's got them back under cover, she lights up the drone vid. She does a full recon on the zone, then feeds info back to command. She gives exact coordinates, and two minutes later, there's a targeted air attack. Her quick thinking and expertise saved the lives of twenty-two people that day. The fact that she could give coordinates via drone, even with the wind and dust blowing everywhere, is the stuff myths are made of." He sat back, looking extremely satisfied and at Devin like she was a hero.

Karissa turned to her. "How did you know what to tell them?"

Devin tried not to let it show that her hands were shaking as the day replayed in her memory, though she knew Karissa could probably feel it. "I took a swag and it came out all right in the end."

"A swag?"

"A scientific wild-ass guess." She grinned and felt the vivid images begin to fade. "I got lucky."

She could see the empathy in Karissa's eyes. She'd never been comfortable letting other people see her emotions, but for whatever reason, it was different with Ris.

"She was awarded the Distinguished Service Cross. First ever woman to get one."

Devin didn't tell him she'd left that medal behind in New York. She just smiled and let him have his moment. If he wanted to think of her that way, she wouldn't disabuse him. People needed their heroes and gods to give hope to otherwise hard and often tragic lives. He believed in a mythic version of her, and she could live with that if it made him happy. Not everyone had to carry demons of the past in their souls.

Karissa pushed back from the table. "I'm beat, you guys. And I can't wait to sleep in a real bed." She looked at Devin and winked. "What about you?"

"So ready."

Walker stood and saluted her. "You may not see it, and you may not want to hear it. But you're a hero, and you'll never be forgotten. Even when you leave this planet, we'll remember you." He grabbed a handful of grapes and smiled as he popped one in his mouth. "I'll see you bright and early to take you to surgery."

He sauntered off to join another table, and Devin didn't miss the looks and whispers of the others he sat with, who looked over his shoulder at her.

"Can you get me out of the zoo, please?"

Karissa pushed her chair and laughed. "Gladly. It's a lot of pressure to be a superhero's girlfriend, you know. No one ever thinks about how hard she has it."

Although Ris's words were lighthearted, Devin's stomach flipped at her using the word girlfriend. She liked the sound of it, but the reminder of her time in the military soured the idea of relationships. It took her back to when she'd met Karissa. All she'd wanted was some fun and someone to chat with. When had that become something meaningful?

They made it back to their room with only one wrong turn, and Karissa helped Devin onto the bed. She knelt in front of her and took her hands in her own.

"Talk to me."

Devin didn't play dumb. There wasn't any point in pretense with Ris. "They see the act. They see what they want to see. But they don't hear the screams. They don't know that the strike killed people. Enemy combatants, yeah. But people just the same." She let the tears roll down her face unchecked, something that hadn't happened in a very long time. "It's a lot of blood to have on your hands. They say I saved twenty people. But I killed thirty. What does that make me?"

Karissa wiped the tears from Devin's face and got her a tissue. Sitting beside her on the bed, she did that thinking thing Devin had grown used to, even as she slowly rubbed Devin's back in soothing motions.

"It makes you a product of our times." She moved to take off Devin's shoes and socks, then helped her take off her jeans and shirt. She pulled back the covers and helped Devin into bed, all the while looking lost in thought. "It makes you someone who did what you had to do, in an environment no human being should ever be in. It makes you someone who saved the people she needed to save in a brave and committed way."

Devin watched through tear-blurred eyes as Karissa quickly got out of her clothes and into the shorts and tank top she slept in. She wished like hell their third time in a real bed could be under far better circumstances. But when Karissa got into bed next to her and pulled her close, she closed her eyes and drank in the serenity she found in Karissa's arms.

"It makes you a soldier, one who did her job and continues to pay the price for doing so. And that you pay the price and still manage to be the person you are makes you a hero in my book."

Years of nightmares, of self-loathing and trying desperately to make up for all she'd done, melted away like snow at the first hint of summer sun. She'd never talked about the experience, never admitted what she thought would be seen as weakness. But then, she'd never felt as safe as she did right now, in an underground bunker with a questionable future. And it was all due to Karissa.

They lay quietly and Devin felt Karissa's breathing change to the slow, even cadence of sleep. Pulling her tight, she let herself drift off, lost in thoughts of a future that held more promise than the brightest sunrise.

CHAPTER TWENTY-THREE

Van rubbed her temples and scraped for any tidbit of information she might have forgotten. She'd managed to get two areas up and running without any issue. Why should Balcony be so different? The restorations on the other areas were going well too, according to Ray. But the walls at Balcony kept crumbling every time they attempted new plaster, and there was no logical reason for it. It was nearly the same age as the other sections and made of the same rock. It had looked well preserved, but the moment they'd started work on it the problems had tripled. Edward, the egghead who'd decided to come with them after the disastrous raid, had been working on different possibilities to do with the ecology and atmospheric pressure, but so far hadn't been able to come up with an answer either.

Liz sat across from her, staring at the wall map but not saying anything.

"We've had two more come down with fever. I want to get all the infected out of Cliff as soon as we can." She'd told Sinclair she wasn't happy about the idea, but the ugly truth was that she needed to protect the rest of the community, and if moving the sick to another location worked, then it was all for the better.

"Why don't we move them to Spruce until we can get them settled at Balcony?" Liz threw a cracker at the map. "Spruce is nearly ready."

Van stared at the map, following the lines in and out of the area. Finally, she shook her head. "I don't want them that far away if they need help. And although we've got the rock falls under control there, I wouldn't want to put the sick and helpless in a situation where they were trapped." She tapped her head on the desk hoping to knock the answers into it.

"Too bad they didn't leave any records behind." Liz tilted her head back, threw a cracker in the air, and grunted when it hit her cheek instead of going into her mouth.

Van looked up, struck by a solution. "The Ute tribes. They might know."

Liz held up her hands. "Not me, boss. I've got my projects up and running again."

"See if you can raise Ray on the comms, would you?"

Liz did as asked, and Van got up to trace the road to the Ute territory. It wasn't too far, and if anyone might have answers, it would be them. The knowledge was ancient, but it was the only option she had.

Ray came in a few minutes later and ducked the cracker Liz threw at him when he entered. "I've missed you too." He pulled up a chair and looked at Van expectantly, as usual a man of few words.

"I want to know if you'll go to the Ute Nation and see if they have an answer to our Balcony problem." Everyone knew Van didn't expect anyone to blindly follow orders, and Ray was one of those who knew that best. She really was *asking*, not ordering.

He looked at the map and then got up to study it closer. "Tribal HQ?"

She tapped on another area of the map. "Not necessarily. There are villages all along here, and you may find the answers there without having to travel all the way to HQ."

"If the villages are still there. I know they were hard hit by fever." He took a handful of Liz's fish crackers and ignored her when she tried to bat his hand away. "Even if I have to go to their headquarters I'd be back by tomorrow night, assuming no storms roll in." He held up one of the crackers. "Do we have more of these somewhere?"

Liz glared at Van. "No. None. Anywhere."

Van smiled at Ray. "I know where she's stashed them. You go to the Ute for me, and I'll get you a box when you get back."

He stuck out his hand and she shook it. "Deal. See you tomorrow. I'll take comms."

He left, and Van felt a smidgeon of hope. The knowledge might have been lost long ago, but the tribe's oral history lived on through their dwindling numbers. That they'd managed to keep their tribe going at all was astounding, given the odds against them.

"What do we do in the meantime?" Liz chomped on her crackers as though to make a point. "And I'm hiding my stash."

"I want to talk to Dr. Sandish, Sinclair, and Mac. See what they've come up with. And I want to check on the solar panel protection team to see if they think it will work." She'd taken the designs from Subtrop and given them to the architectural climate team, and they'd been eager to start rigging options. Though the last fire had cleared a vast area of new growth, which meant they were safe from new fires for a few months, she wanted to be prepared when the autumn fire season hit for real.

"I think you'd gladly play doctor with Dr. Sandish." Liz wiggled her eyebrows and made a kissy face. "You've been spending a lot of time together."

"We haven't been back long, so that's an exaggeration. And shut up." After their breakfast the morning after Van had returned, she'd found any excuse to seek Susan out. And if she wasn't mistaken, Susan was doing the same. Van would be sweating outside, trying to work through new designs, and Susan would appear at her side with a cold drink or an offer of food. She liked the attention. Probably too much.

"Whatever. You'll settle down and have babies like all the other lesbians. Just you watch." Liz stood and stretched. "I'm heading to the canteen. I want to check food stores and see what the garden looks like. See you later."

Van mock saluted. When the door closed, she was grateful for the moment alone. Things had been going full tilt in the few days she'd been back, and she'd hardly had a moment to herself except when she finally fell into bed at night, only to wake far too soon in the morning. She smiled at the thought of Susan's tough attitude, and she knew that was what had gotten her to the safe house that day they'd gone on the raid. At breakfast that first morning after they'd gotten back, she'd told Susan all about the Cheyenne facility. After all, the knowledge might mean she'd want to get there as soon as possible. But her attitude hadn't wavered. She wasn't going to be a pawn for anyone, and she'd already fallen in love with Mesa. The words had warmed Van's heart, and other places, and she'd been under Susan's spell ever since. She pushed those thoughts aside and dedicated the next hour to paperwork and making sure everything was up to date, and then she took the back tunnels down to the medical kiva.

She could hear Susan's voice before she even entered the kiva. It was like a hammer covered in silk. Soft, but determined.

"I want to try this. I think we stand a damn good chance."

"And I think it's too soon. We don't know the side effects."

Van entered to see Susan and Sinclair facing off. "Looks like I've arrived at just the right time. Or the wrong one. Depending on your moods."

Susan held up a vial with a cloudy tinted liquid in it. "I think I've found a way to ease the pain and to potentially slow the fever."

"But she doesn't know, and human trial is the only way to find out. It's made from a toxic plant, so it could potentially kill them." Sinclair stood with his arms crossed, glaring at Susan.

"Okay, let's slow down." Van pulled a chair up to a desk littered with drawings and lists. "Tell me what you've got."

Susan dug through the papers and pulled out several sheets. "It's a distillation of several different flowers and herbs. Willow bark to ease pain, joe-pye weed, which was used to help with typhus fevers in the nineteen hundreds, and borage, which has been used both topically and internally for everything from eczema to irritable bowl."

"And it's toxic if you've got the wrong dosage." Sinclair pointed at the drawing of the offending flower. "If the person can't stomach it, or if they're allergic to it…"

Van glanced at him as she picked up the papers to read them. "I thought you were of the opinion that anything was better than what they're going through, Sin?"

He sighed and dropped his arms from his chest. "I know. I said that. But when it comes to actually doing it, I don't know. It feels like a deadly game of chance."

Van scanned the papers, though most of it was in medical jargon that was like reading a foreign language. "I get that. So here's my question. Have you asked the patients what they'd want?"

By the chagrined look on both their faces, she guessed the answer.

"Right. In that case, that's my suggestion." She nodded at the vial in Susan's hand. "Sin, we all know where they're headed, unless you two come up with some kind of miracle cure. But if this gives them some relief, then I say go for it." She winced. "And if it doesn't, and it ends up making them decline faster," she closed her eyes, saddened to say it, "well, then their suffering from the fever doesn't last as long. But ultimately, let them have the final say. It's their lives, so give them the option."

"I'm ninety percent certain it will have a restorative effect." Susan took Sinclair's hand. "Take the leap with me."

Van was glad to see Sinclair soften. His heart was in the right place. So was Susan's. They'd make it work, even if there were some growing pains.

His shrug was barely noticeable. "Okay. Let's start with the ones who came down with it first, though. Then work backward to the most recently infected. We'll ask Mac to help."

Susan nodded, looking satisfied. She turned to Van. "Any news about Balcony?"

"I've asked Ray to go to the Ute and see if they have any suggestions. Any more indication of fever anywhere?" She wasn't sure she wanted the answer. A true outbreak here would be disastrous.

"None so far. But we're having trouble figuring out the spread. The last two to come down didn't seem to be around those already infected. That could mean it's airborne."

"Or it could mean they touched areas the infected touched." Susan looked baffled. "We don't know, and all we can do is watch."

"Let me know if anything changes or if you need anything."

Susan stopped her with a gentle touch. "Actually, do you think Ray would mind if I went to the Ute with him?"

Van didn't answer, stunned that Susan would be willing to go beyond Mesa knowing what she did about how hard it was out there.

Clearly sensing Van's hesitation, Susan hurried on. "They may know of herbal remedies or combinations I haven't thought of, or that I haven't got books on. It could help not just with fever but with anything else we might face."

"Sure. But do you need to be here to administer the cocktail you came up with?" That wasn't the real reason Van didn't want Susan to go. But she wouldn't voice the truth. Emotional stuff wasn't her thing.

"Sinclair and Mac can do it, especially if we're just starting with a few test cases."

He nodded, looking between the two of them. His expression held some bit of understanding Van wasn't sure she wanted him to have.

"Sure, no problem. I'll get Ray on the comms and tell him to wait for you, if he isn't already gone." She headed for the ladder, ignoring the worried cramp in her gut. She was in no position to tell Susan she couldn't do anything, especially when it could help the community.

"I'll come up with you." Susan followed her up the ladder and at the top, took Van's hand in hers. "I'll be careful."

Jesus. Am I that transparent? "I'm not worried."

Susan smiled, and it lit her eyes. "Yes, you are. And I'm glad." She gave Van a lingering kiss on the cheek.

When she pulled away, Van stared at her, tongue-tied for perhaps the first time in her life.

Susan laughed and started to climb back down the ladder. "Call Ray, boss lady. I've got to gather some things before I go." She blew Van a kiss just before she disappeared below into the kiva.

Van touched her cheek and walked back to her office in a daze. *For fuck's sake. It was just a kiss on the cheek. What will I do if she kisses me for real? Dissolve into a puddle?* The thought seemed entirely plausible.

CHAPTER TWENTY-FOUR

Karissa fell onto the bed, mentally and emotionally exhausted. She curled into a ball and thought of home. It seemed almost as far away as the space station they'd be arriving at in just a few weeks.

If I pass the tests. The days had begun to meld into one another. TV screens with scenery of forests and beaches were meant to be soothing reminders of the world above them, and as she passed them she tried to pay attention to the way the sun stroked the leaves, or the way the shadows crawled up their limbs. But seeing something on a screen wasn't anything like being out in the open air, something she missed more and more as the days fled by.

Each day, the alarm was followed by getting ready and helping Devin get ready. Then breakfast in the canteen, followed by a long walk to her testing zone, which was in a separate building from Devin's testing area. Ivan would come into the test room late, throw some rude comment or strange, backhanded compliment at her, and then take his seat directly behind her. He'd saunter past when he was finished, and she was sure he'd actually leaned over to sniff her hair once, which definitely put her off.

Discussion over lunch consisted of talking over what the day's tests had been and against whom. They were getting to know their competition, and Karissa was glad she wasn't one of the ones who'd been there since the beginning. There were many scientists on site who were below the red line on the leaderboard, and were unlikely to rise above it. They'd be unable to take part in one of the greatest adventures in human history, but they still showed up for obligatory testing, knowing it was probably futile. Although there was plenty of bitterness, Karissa also recognized an element of relief in some people. Aside from meal times, there wasn't a lot of time for basic socializing, so she hadn't gotten to know many people's stories.

That doesn't stop Devin. Karissa smiled when she thought of Devin's enthusiasm. She loved the challenges, and the daily tests energized her. She'd also never had a lack of people willing to push her chair through the halls. She and Walker had already gotten in trouble for racing another pair down the long corridor, nearly taking out a group of soldiers. Her surgery had gone perfectly, and she was determined to heal as quickly as possible.

While Karissa enjoyed thinking of new ways to look at potential problems, the pressure of *why* she was doing it never left her alone. And that pressure was growing. Even with the daily afternoon lectures on what to expect at the space station, and then what to expect on the new planet, she couldn't seem to find the same enthusiasm Devin had. When she was faced with a genetically altered virus and the test included finding treatments using a strange option of variables, she enjoyed the challenge, but couldn't help wonder why she wasn't doing that to help the people who *already* needed that help. The ones who'd become climate refugees. The ones like her parents, who'd died in the home they'd raised her in, because the government had given up looking for a cure in order to look toward the stars instead.

The door opened and closed again, but she didn't uncurl. She felt Devin's weight on the bed as she transferred out of the wheelchair, and she relaxed into her when she lay against her and wrapped an arm around her.

"Want to talk about it?"

Unbidden, the tears began to flow. "I don't know what to say."

Devin let her cry and didn't pressure her to talk, which was exactly what Karissa needed. Eventually, she stopped and rolled over to face Devin.

"Do you have any doubts?" she asked.

"About the project?" She wiped away Karissa's tears. "Or about us?"

"Either. Both. Yes." *Us.* That was a topic they'd stayed away from. Neither had broached it, and Karissa had been glad to let it lie, especially when she was as confused as she was. But if they were going to share, maybe now was the time.

"Yes. And no." At Karissa's frown, Devin laughed. "Yes. I've got reservations about the project. Let's start there."

Karissa sat up, startled. "You do? But you seem so excited. I didn't want to rain on your parade."

Devin struggled to sit up and get her leg in a comfortable position. "I am excited. I think what's happening is amazing. I love the testing that's forcing me to really think about options and contingencies. And to be able to go to another planet…that's just crazy. But." She moved hair off Karissa's face. "I don't like the way it's being done. I don't like that there's going to be an elite class of people who get to leave. I don't like the secrecy, and I don't like the backstabbing."

Devin was referring to the rumor that a scientist had managed to mess up another scientist's test, nearly putting them out of the running. As the date to leave got closer, the stakes were higher and tensions were getting out of control. Pressure was mounting and it showed.

"I can't tell you how relieved I am to hear it. I thought I must be crazy and the only one who's…"

"Confused about whether or not you want to go?" Devin's smile was sad but understanding.

"Yeah. That." Karissa laid her head on Devin's shoulder. "As much as I can see the adventure in it and how incredible it would be, I can't get over the ethical issue of being chosen, while so many others weren't."

"I know what you mean. But you're not alone, babe. There are a lot of people who feel that way. You're not terribly social, so you don't hear it. But the ethical question is being talked about plenty." She seemed to search for the right words. "I guess the final question is one only you can answer. Is staying behind more important to you than going to space and starting fresh? Which one do you want, in the depths of your soul?"

Karissa couldn't answer the question, and she wondered if Devin could. But she couldn't bring herself to ask. She wasn't ready for a definitive answer, and she wasn't sure Devin had one to give, anyway.

"And what about us?" That wasn't an easy question to ask, either, but it felt less loaded.

Devin kissed the top of her head. "You know, since Julie, the idea of being a part of an 'us' again seemed impossible. But getting to sleep next to you every night, and being able to wake up next to you in the morning, is just about the best thing in the world. On any planet. You're really special, Ris. Our time together has made my life complete in ways I couldn't imagine before."

Karissa lifted her head and watched Devin's expression. She looked contemplative rather than emotional, something Karissa could identify with. "I feel the same way."

"So what has you worried?"

Voicing it would make it real, but she owed them both that. "My doubts about leaving the planet. What if one of us passes all the tests and one of us doesn't? What if we both do, but we don't want to go? What if we do go, and when we get up there," Karissa pointed upward, "things go sideways and we don't end up together? It will be awkward and horrible to see you every day and know you don't want me—"

"Whoa, babe. Slow down." Devin lifted Karissa's chin so she could look into her eyes. "What-ifs are an opium road trip to Wonderland. They'll confuse things and get you not knowing which way is up."

She stroked Karissa's hair and her fingers lightly ran over the back of Karissa's neck. She shivered under Devin's touch, much the way she had back in the woods. They'd been too busy, and Devin too injured, to have much in the way of sexual interaction. That didn't mean Karissa didn't appreciate the contours of Devin's hard body every time she helped her dress, or that she didn't feel every muscle that tensed and relaxed against her when they were sleeping at night.

She raised her eyes to look at Devin and saw her own desire reflected back at her. Devin lowered her head and Karissa gladly met her halfway. The kiss was like that of their first but sharper. It held more promise, more questions, more need. Devin's hands slid under her shirt, and she raised her arms so she could pull it off. She unfastened her bra and broke out in goose bumps as Devin slid the straps slowly off her arms. Her nipples were achingly hard, and when Devin took one in her mouth she cried out and pushed forward into the warm heat of Devin's mouth.

"Please."

Her whispered plea was all it took. Devin's sound of desire amped up Karissa's and they fell back together on the bed. Fierce, desperate kisses were accompanied by their almost frantic caresses. Devin pulled at Karissa's jeans and pushed them open to get inside. At the firm touch of Devin's thumb on her clit, Karissa arched and cried out. She needed this. She needed to give in to nothing but the physical sensation of being wanted. She needed to feel. She needed Devin.

Devin's fingers slid into her and she moaned, clutching at Devin's shoulder, feeling the muscles ripple beneath her fingers. She pushed against Devin's hand, felt her go deeper and closed her eyes as Devin plunged into her, fucking her with the ferocity of delayed gratification and questions unanswered. She came, and came again, and then a third time before she put her hand on Devin's arm to stop her.

"Wait. Let me breathe."

Devin chuckled and lay beside her, holding her close.

When she could speak again, Karissa moved off the bed. She quickly took off the rest of her clothes, and then made quick work of taking off Devin's. Looking at the body that might as well be carved out of marble, she was once again taken aback by how perfect she found Devin's body. Reminded of their time in the forest, she wanted to feel Devin's skin under her hands again.

"Scoot up."

Devin obligingly slid up the bed. Now that she had a full brace on, they didn't have to be quite as careful about not twisting it or accidently hitting it. Still, Karissa was cautious as she joined Devin on the bed.

"I think you're most comfortable on your back." Karissa gave her a lopsided grin and moved so she was between Devin's legs.

"I think you're right." Devin's voice was husky, her eyes dark.

Karissa breathed in the scent of Devin's arousal and slowly began to lick delicate circles around her clit. Gratified when Devin moaned and clutched at the sheets, she kept the slow pace, only quickening it when Devin thrust against her mouth. She pulled Devin's clit into her mouth, sucking and licking, before entering her with one finger and fucking her in time to her sucking.

"Fuck. Fuck, baby. Fucking don't stop."

Devin's pleas were an aphrodisiac, and Karissa felt herself grow wet again. When Devin came, bucking and swearing, Karissa was on the edge herself. As soon as Devin's orgasm passed, Karissa moved next to her, took her hand, and put it against her aching center. Devin pushed into her, and within seconds, Karissa came yet again.

They collapsed together and Karissa curled against Devin's side, her head on her chest.

In the ensuing silence, Karissa felt like the world had settled. All the questions, all the worries, were kept at bay because she was in Devin's arms. For now, that was good enough. Tomorrow could wait.

She woke discombobulated, unable to figure out where she was. When she felt the weight of Devin's arm across her stomach, she remembered and her pulse slowed. She'd been having some terrible nightmare about being chased but unable to get more than a few steps ahead of the predator. A knock on the door pulled her all the way from the dream, and she slid from under Devin's arm. She pulled a towel around her and opened the door enough to peek around it.

"Hey there. You guys missed the afternoon lecture series. Just wanted to check and make sure you were okay." Walker glanced at her obviously bare shoulders and quickly looked away.

"Thanks for checking. Is it dinnertime?"

"Yeah. You want help with Devin's chair, or…um, shall I meet you at the canteen?"

She grinned at his discomfort. He knew they were together, but faced with evidence, he was clearly out of his element. "Good idea. We'll see you there in fifteen."

He waved and loped off down the hall. *Sweet.* For all that he was a soldier, he was still young, and moments like this made her want to tease him like a big sister would. She closed the door and went back to the bed.

"Hey, sleepyhead. It's time for dinner."

Devin stirred and smiled up at her sleepily. "Hey, beautiful. I'm not sure you left me any energy to get out of bed."

Karissa felt herself blush and was glad Devin couldn't see it in the dark. "Then we'd better feed you so you have more energy for later."

Devin's eyes flashed and she sat up. "I like the sound of that. Let's go so we can get back."

They laughed and joked as they got dressed and Karissa left their room feeling more lighthearted than she had in weeks. When they turned down the final corridor to the canteen, Zeke ran up next to them.

Karissa gave him a hug. "We've hardly seen you since we got here. Join us for dinner?"

He looked around the canteen. "Let me get Gemma. She's the one on the convoy with us, and we'll come sit with you."

Karissa left Devin parked at a table while she went to get their meals. She accepted a scoop of potatoes just as she heard a familiar voice behind her, one that made her grind her teeth.

"You know they're not going to allow lesbians up there, right?" Ivan nonchalantly put some food on his tray. "What would be the point?"

Though she told herself not to rise to the bait, she couldn't help it. "The point would be to have a group of extraordinary people to build a planet. There will be enough heterosexual people to propagate. I think we've learned there's no need to rush to grow a population."

"Extraordinary, yes. But being extraordinary means being able to do everything." He leered at her and looked her over. "And you're hardly going to do *everything*, are you?"

He strolled off, whistling, and she picked up a piece of cheesecake. Just as she was taking aim, Walker grabbed her arm.

"That would be a waste of a really good dessert. And you'd probably be considered a troublemaker, which you don't want when you're heading into the final stages of testing." He took the cake from her and put it on his own tray.

"Who does he think he is? How dare he?"

Walker pushed Devin's tray between theirs and shrugged. "People can be assholes. Being brilliant doesn't mean you're not one. It just usually means you use bigger words to prove you're a dick."

Karissa laughed, jerked out of her outrage in the face of his charm. "True."

They got back to the table to find Zeke and his friend Gemma having an animated conversation with Devin. They were discussing that afternoon's lecture about the topographic views of the planet, and Devin's tests to determine different ways of building accommodation.

Karissa loved listening to Devin's ideas and the way she broke down the jargon of her profession made it easy to follow. The others were equally enthralled, and Karissa found her enthusiasm for the project growing. *It really is an amazing chance.*

The others convinced Devin and Karissa to go to the movies with them after dinner, and Karissa liked the easy camaraderie they shared. It was like having real friends, something she hadn't had for a long while. Sitting in the dark, holding Devin's hand as they watched an old movie of comic book heroes saving the world, she almost felt like life was normal. And in this moment, for tonight, she could pretend that it was. As Devin had said, she'd deal with tomorrow, tomorrow.

CHAPTER TWENTY-FIVE

Devin wheeled herself to her morning test. Walker had finally been given duties to attend to, and Ris had needed to get to her own test. But she was okay with having a moment alone. She smiled and nodded at people as they passed on their way to their own daily routines, but her thoughts were far away.

Karissa's doubts about the project, and about the two of them, weren't unfounded. The ethics of the project could easily be called into question, and Devin was battling her own issues there. She *wanted* to go to space. She wanted that adventure, but she was pissed off with herself for wanting it. She wished she had Karissa's passionate devotion to ideals; maybe that would make it easier. Devin truly believed in right and wrong, and that was causing her all kinds of stress too. She couldn't find that black-and-white line this time, even though it seemed like it should be clear. Were her own desires getting in the way? Was she stubbornly refusing to see what was right in front of her? She didn't think so, but if that was the case, surely she'd have a better idea of where she stood on the ethics question.

She got to her training room and rolled up to the desk that had been put in to accommodate the chair. She could technically get out of the chair now and walk with crutches, but the doc had said it'd be best to keep the pressure off it for at least a week, and if that meant better chances of passing her physical, she'd do whatever it took. Fortunately, most of the facility was wheelchair accessible, and she had a whole new empathy for people who'd had to deal with that issue their entire lives. Especially in a world that had become less tolerant as living became about pure survival.

Today's test was handed out by the same person who'd handed out all the other tests. Someone tall and thin who wore a creepy blank mask over their face and a hat that obscured their hair. She knew all the test handlers dressed the same. It was so they couldn't be identified outside the testing zones and pressured into providing test information in any way. It was a simple safeguard, but it did lend an air of the peculiar to the testing process. Three other geologists were in the room. She'd been testing against all of them, and she recognized the signs of stress fatigue in two. Sweating, bags under their eyes, tremors in their hands. If they didn't fail the written test, they'd damn sure fail the physical. Taking tests here wouldn't be anything compared to having to do it for real in a life and death situation on another planet. Better they drop out now than when people were depending on them for their lives.

"Begin," the mechanical voice announced over the intercom.

Devin relegated thoughts of the others to the back of her mind. This moment wasn't about them. It was about testing her knowledge, her imagination, her limitations. And she loved it. The thought of using those things to help build a new civilization was exhilarating and kept her focused. Today's test felt like it had been made for her. It was all about using the geological makeup of the land to create shelters. Essentially, living *in* the land as a way to be protected from it. It was something she'd already done, albeit with a vastly different landscape and weather system in a climate zone that had become uninhabitable. She worked furiously, her thoughts on fire with plans and variables. She could picture it in its totality, and when the buzzer rang to signify the testing was over, she sat back and reveled in the possibilities. Energized, she wanted to race through the halls, climb mountains, leap off waterfalls.

She was brought back to earth by a clanging thud behind her. She turned to see one of the other scientists on the floor. Staff raced into the room and were helping him instantly. A medical team showed up with a gurney, and Devin wondered if they'd been on standby. The staff likely saw the same physical markers she had and had prepared for it. *How many people literally collapse?* She knew that the extreme dangers they could face meant that psychological strength counted for as much, if not more, than physical strength. If they collapsed during testing, they didn't belong in space. In that way, it was a lot like the military. When other people were counting on you for their lives, there wasn't room for weakness of any kind.

She wondered how Karissa would feel at the thought. She'd let her talk out her fears, but Devin hadn't been as willing to share. She wanted Ris to feel safe. She felt things intensely, and Devin knew she needed to let out some of the pressure. Devin's internal pressure came from the gray area, a place she'd never been comfortable. When the raiders had first told them about the reason they'd been chosen, she'd felt like an orphan getting a Christmas gift. She'd been given exactly the adventure she'd been ready for the day she'd been picked up by the convoy. But spending time with Karissa had made her look harder at that gift, and she saw the flaws and cracks in it. She couldn't help but feel that beneath the shiny promise lay a tarnished lie.

She rolled to the canteen, the buzz from the testing diminished by the heavy thoughts. But when she got there, there was an entirely different buzz running through the room. Excited chatter filled the air, but she couldn't make out what it was about. When she got to their usual table Zeke launched in.

"Did you hear?" He was practically vibrating with excitement.

"Hear what? I've been in testing." Devin looked around for Karissa. Hearing important news felt wrong without her there.

"The most recent satellite imagery has sent back evidence of running water on the surface of 128D, which will obviously make beginning life there way easier. They've given 128 a name."

Zeke paused dramatically and Devin laughed.

"Go on. I'm listening."

"Neo Phos."

Karissa sat down next to Devin, her hand gentle on Devin's back. "New light. That doesn't seem hugely imaginative."

Zeke rolled his eyes. "It's metaphorical and all that, too. It's *our* new light. And there's double the amount of light available to the planet, but not so much it will fry it. But enough to warm it." He hugged Gemma close, who also looked as excited as he was.

Devin kissed Karissa, glad she was there. She looked tired, though, and it put Devin in mind of the collapsed scientist in her test zone. "You okay?"

"Someone kept me up late." She grinned and the fire from the night before shone in her eyes.

They'd gone back to their room after the movie and made love again several times throughout the night. Devin couldn't seem to get enough of her, and if she believed in magic, this would have been the spell to beat all spells. "That was naughty of them, seeing as how you had testing today." She kissed Karissa's fingertips and enjoyed the way she shivered in response. "How did it go?"

The light faded from Karissa's expression. "How about I go get lunch and then we talk about it?"

Devin nodded, searching Karissa's eyes for answers. She thought of Karissa's question about what if one of them passed testing and one didn't, which was quickly followed by a sick feeling. She watched as Karissa moved to the lunch line. Watching from a distance, it looked like Karissa was terribly alone. She smiled at a few people, but no one stopped to chat. Even with the big news circulating, she seemed apart from everything rather than in the thick of it. Devin's heart ached for her. Karissa lived so much in her own head that when she wanted out, there wasn't anyone there to talk to. She was Devin's opposite that way, and she wished she could help. But then, that's who Karissa was, and maybe it was just Devin's projection of how she'd feel in the same situation.

She joined in the conversation around her but kept watch on Karissa. She saw Ivan glowering at her and wondered what his problem was. She nearly laughed out loud when she remembered Karissa standing up to him on the journey there. *That's his beef. He doesn't like that she doesn't kowtow to him.* The more she watched him, the more she realized it wasn't just that Karissa didn't back down. He was attracted to her, and she was a lesbian. *He must feel like someone pissed in his cereal.* When Karissa made it back to her, with Ivan still watching in the distance, Devin pulled her down for a long, slow kiss.

"Wow. Not that I'm complaining, but what was that for?" Karissa set their trays on the table, smiling.

"Because you're the most beautiful woman here, and I'm lucky you chose me." She didn't need to tell her Ivan looked utterly enraged, which was simply a side benefit of getting to kiss Karissa the way she wanted to. "So, tell me about your day."

Karissa took a bite of her soy pasta before starting. "I'm not sure if I passed today's test. I couldn't concentrate, and when I did, I kept trying to place the details into this planet's needs rather than the new planet's possibilities."

That could nail Karissa's test to the wall. "That doesn't mean you didn't put in the details they need to see."

She sighed. "I know. And I tried to clarify at the end. But I hadn't even finished by the time the buzzer went off."

Zeke chimed in, leaving off his conversation with others at the end of the table. "That doesn't mean anything, Karissa. I haven't completed a test yet, and I'm still in the running."

She smiled at him, but Devin could see her heart wasn't in it. Conversation flowed around them, and Devin kept one hand on Karissa's leg while they ate, wanting to make sure she knew she wasn't alone. She barely touched her food and Devin's worry increased.

"Want to head back to the room before the afternoon lecture? I've heard it's compulsory, but we still have some time before it starts."

Karissa pushed her tray away. "That sounds perfect."

They were quiet as Karissa pushed Devin's chair back to their room. Once inside, Devin grabbed her crutches and moved to the bed. "Talk to me." She opened her arms and Karissa moved into them. She said something, but with her face pressed to Devin's chest, she couldn't make it out. "What was that, babe?"

Karissa turned her head, and there were tears tracking down her face. "I didn't care."

"About?"

"About the test. I didn't care that I was doing it, and I didn't care if I failed it. I barely looked at the questions."

Devin quelled the immediate panic that rose tsunami-like in her chest. If Karissa simply gave up, then there was no question about them going to space together, and there was a chance she'd be taken away to be "convinced" to try harder. The notion was sickening. "Is it because you were overtired?"

Her shoulders slumped. She pulled away and put her head in her hands. "No. I don't think so. It just feels so…so…" She waved her hands in a circle. "Like I'm in a storm. Like I don't have any say over which way the wind takes me."

Devin searched for an answer, one that would convince Karissa to keep going. "Because you're out of control. Since this began you haven't had a say in what happens, and even now, you're being tested, but you don't have the option to simply say you don't want that."

Karissa sniffled and nodded, that contemplative look on her face that Devin knew so well.

"But, babe, you can't just give up. You can't have made this whole journey for nothing. It's like your dad said, you have to help humanity."

As soon as the words were out of her mouth, Devin knew she'd made a mistake.

Karissa's expression went from sad to pissed off in a split second. "How dare you bring my parents into this? Maybe if I was out there, *helping humanity*, I could have come up with something to help the fever. Maybe if I could *help humanity*, I'd be doing something worthwhile. Not sitting around in a cave seeing if I'm better than the next guy. Seeing if I'm good enough to go off planet with the *special* people." She stared at Devin, her hands on her hips and her eyes flashing. "But you don't get that, do you? For all your military experience and being down on the ground with real people, you're actually an elitist."

"*I'm* an elitist? I'm a fucking *realist*. This planet is dying, Ris. This is the next stage of extinction, and yeah, that's shitty. But unlike the damn dinosaurs we have a way to keep going as a species, and I'm not going to turn that down just because I've got the skills to stay behind and watch the world burn as I build things that won't, eventually, be enough. I can be one of the people that help the human race continue. Doesn't that mean anything to you?"

They faced off, and as angry as she was, Devin wanted to grab Karissa and kiss the hell out of her. Apparently, Karissa didn't feel the same.

She grabbed her bag, threw some clothes in it, and headed for the door.

"What, you're going to just walk away?" Devin's anger flared into fear. If she left, she very well might not come back.

"I think we need some breathing room. I need to figure out what I want, and I can't do that when you're...you."

"When I'm me? What does that mean?"

Karissa slumped against the door like the air had been let out of her. "When you're the comic book hero, and I'm just the girl that never figures out who the hero behind the mask is, because she's just a regular girl." Tears began to fall again. "I'm so lost, and you know what you want. You say you're unsure too, but I think deep down you'll be fine getting on that space ship. The thing is, I don't know if I can get on it with you." She opened the door. "I'll see you at the lecture."

The door closed softly behind her. To Devin, it sounded of a terrible finality she never thought she'd have to face again.

The lecture hall was full when Devin made it in. She was late, but she'd had to make a stop along the way. The screen at the front showed the latest satellite information coming in from the probe at Neo Phos. The data was being compiled as quickly as possible, and everyone was told the information pertinent to their specialties would be disseminated within the next two days. They needed to study it, interpret it as best they could, and then use the new material on their next testing sessions, which would be delayed until the data was parsed out. That meant everyone had time off, a new concept for all those who'd been under testing conditions.

Devin searched the room for Ris but couldn't see her anywhere. *Does she truly not give a damn anymore?* Her heart raced. *She can't just give up.* Their fight had opened a chasm between them, and everything that had been said had been true, which made it that much worse. She didn't blame Karissa for leaving, but she wanted to talk things out rather than let them build into something truly insurmountable. What was ahead was going to be difficult enough without having to face it alone.

She saw Zeke and waved him over. "Have you seen Karissa?"

He pointed toward the far end of the hall. "She was over there at the beginning." He looked at Devin curiously. "She looked pretty rough. Everything okay?"

She tried to look positive but knew it wasn't convincing. "Yeah, I think so. You know, it's not easy for some people."

He clapped her on the back. "If anyone can help her, you can."

He headed back to his seat and Devin kept searching the room, hoping to catch a glimpse of her. But the lecture ended, the admonishment to keep studying and get rest following everyone out. As excited as everyone else was, Devin just wanted to find Karissa.

She was heading into the hallway when someone jostled her, and she saw a foot connect with one of her crutches. It swept the crutch forward and she lost her balance, just managing to land on her good side rather than the injured one. Before the people around her stopped to help, she caught Ivan looking back at her over his shoulder, his steely eyes hard.

Then people were helping her up, and she had to fend off offers to take her to medical. "Just getting used to the crutches, guys, no problem. But thanks."

They dispersed and she caught her breath. The guy was bad news, and if he was stooping to actual violence, it could spell trouble for Karissa. The need to find her quadrupled and she decided she needed assistance.

She found Walker in the medical zone talking to a big beefy guy. The guy touched Walker's arm and she stopped short. She'd never given a thought to Walker's sexual orientation because it hadn't mattered. Still, the fact that he was gay took her by surprise. He looked back, saw her, and waved her over.

"Hey. This is Brian. He's on the eco engineering team. He's at the top of the leaderboard in his group." His smile was sad. "He'll be leaving when the rest of you do."

Brian brushed tears from his eyes as he held out his hand. "You must be Devin. Nice to meet you. I've heard a lot about you and Karissa."

Devin smiled at him, too distracted to get into small talk. "She's actually the reason I'm here. Have you seen her?"

Walker looked confused. "No, not since yesterday. What's up?"

Step up. Don't be a coward. "We had a fight. I said some stupid shit, and I think a scientist *friend* of ours might be gunning for her."

Brian touched Walker's arm. "That's my cue. Come grab me when you're done." He gave him a quick kiss and then headed off down the hall.

Walker watched him go, and Devin could see the longing in his eyes. *Is that what I'll look like if Karissa walks away from me?* She couldn't bear the thought.

"Where would she feel safest? Other than with you?"

Relieved to not have to search this enormous facility on her own, she slowed down and thought. "A library. I'd say a lab, but with all the testing, I don't think that's where she'd go right now. Somewhere quiet where she can think."

He closed his eyes as he thought. "It's not like there are a lot of spaces you can be alone down here. I can think of two; one is the library in sector seven, and the other is the chapel, way down at the end of the East Wing."

"Sector seven is farthest away. You'll get there faster. I'll check the chapel. If you find her within thirty minutes, meet me at the chapel. After that, I'll head back to our room in case she shows up there."

He squeezed her shoulder. "Relax. We'll find her." He loped off down the hall.

Devin turned and headed for the chapel. She found it odd it was still in use and hadn't been converted to some more useful place. Fewer than ten percent of scientists believed in a higher being, and the scientists here, who were ready to go to another planet, probably weren't among that number. But then, there were plenty of non-science staff here, too.

When she got there she barely managed to push the heavy wood doors open without getting her crutches trapped in them. The small room, complete with wooden pews and a large stained-glass window, up-lit from below to simulate natural light, was empty. Except for one person, sitting two rows from the front, right in the middle.

Devin felt the weight of worry lift from her chest. She made her way up the aisle and stopped at the pew. "Mind if I join you?"

Karissa didn't look at her. "Sure."

Not promising. She maneuvered into the pew and settled next to her. But then the words escaped her, and she sat silently, unable to think of a single thing to say to break the thick tension between them.

"I was thinking about Natasha and John. I wonder where they are."

Karissa's voice was soft, her tone far away, and Devin ached to bridge the distance.

"I bet they found their way to the place where John's partner was waiting. Hell, Natasha could be on her way here." They were empty words, optimism that didn't mean anything in the here and now. And they both knew it.

Karissa rested her head on the pew in front of her. "You were right."

Devin had no idea what she might have been right about, and she moved ahead cautiously. "Was I?"

"You became a scientist because you loved the land. You loved feeling the dirt under your fingers and watching the wind create a new playground for you. You didn't have to control it. You just had to understand it."

Devin had never thought of it in those terms, but she saw the truth of it. She stayed quiet to let Karissa continue her train of thought.

"But I came to science to learn how to control disease. I wanted to learn how to heal by controlling viruses. I wanted to stop epidemics by controlling the ways they could be spread. My world was a lab—ordered, refined...controlled." Tears fell from her cheeks and onto the polished foot plinth below. "And now I have no control. I can't use science to help people. I can't study what I want to study. I have to study what they want me to, show them the knowledge I have in order to be what they want me to be, to go on some grand excursion I'm not even sure I want to be part of. Since I was chosen, none of what I want matters." She sobbed and held herself. "And I hate it."

Devin took a chance and wrapped her arm around Karissa. Gratified when she moved closer instead of pulling away, Devin relaxed and her thoughts cleared of the all-consuming fear and panic so she could think rationally again. Instead of just letting Karissa vent, she allowed herself to really consider her position. Not just in principle, but in action. Her own doubts about the project rose and combined with those Karissa voiced. Still, she didn't know what the next step was. So she did what she always did. She took it one step at a time, and she appealed to Karissa's rational, logical side.

"I understand. I really do. The question, as I see it, is how we get you feeling like you've got some control again. No matter what I think, or how I feel, or what's going on with the project. What can we do to make you feel like you've got some say in your life again?"

For all that Devin had thought the chapel must be outdated, it was in the silence of contemplation that she realized how useful it still was. Maybe not as a place to pray to a sky wizard, but definitely a place where you could allow yourself to be truly still and listen to the voice within. Hers was clamoring for attention, but now wasn't the time. She analyzed the different colors in the stained glass, looked at the grain of wood in the pews, and breathed in the calm available in the empty space, all while she gave Karissa time to think.

"How do you do it?" Karissa finally sat back and leaned against Devin. "You said you have doubts too. How do you justify the testing?"

Devin didn't care for the word justify, but she let it go. "I like testing myself. I like seeing what I can come up with." She followed the thread. "Maybe that's the answer, Ris. Maybe you should stop focusing on the why of it, and simply look at the moment. Instead of thinking ahead to space, or looking behind us at the people out there, look at this moment. Every test could teach you something new about yourself, about the way you think and interpret. If you look at it purely in the moment and take what you can from it, maybe it will take some of the pressure off." It sounded right to Devin, but she couldn't be sure what Karissa would take from it.

Karissa frowned and rubbed at her eyes. "I think that makes sense. I've always been told I worry too much about both the future and the past. I'm not sure I can let those fears go, given where we are and what's coming. But maybe I can focus more on what I'm getting out of it." She gave Devin a side-glance. "Thank you."

Though it felt like they'd come to a truce, Devin could feel things still weren't the way they should be. "Will you come back to the room tonight?"

Karissa shook her head slightly. "I'm going to sleep here tonight, I think. Just for some alone time."

Devin wanted to push, wanted to beg, but didn't. She had to respect Karissa's need for quiet, even if it meant having to be without her. "I'll miss you."

Karissa's smile was tired, sad. "I'll miss you too."

Devin got up to leave, not knowing what else to say, and needing to go before she put her foot in it again. Their ideals, the questions and worries, still stood between them, and she had no idea what to do about that. Fortunately, she could still do something nice. "We've got tomorrow off. Will you meet me after breakfast? I have something to show you."

Karissa looked mildly curious and nodded. "Of course."

Devin hesitated, waiting for something she couldn't name, but the moment passed. "Okay. Well, I'll see you in the morning. If you change your mind, you know what bed I'm in."

Karissa reached up and touched her hand. "I know. Just bear with me, okay?"

Devin swallowed the lump in her throat. "Any time. Oh, and, Ris? Ivan is being a real bastard right now. Keep an eye out, okay?" Karissa nodded, and Devin headed back down the aisle to the doors. When she got to the door she looked back at Karissa. Her head was down, and Devin could see her shoulders shaking as she cried. She desperately wanted to turn back, to hold her and reassure her, but that wasn't what Karissa wanted. She wanted to be alone in her confusion and grief, and given Devin's own state of mind, she couldn't be much help anyway. She made her way back to her room, wondering how her military hardened heart could be so damn soft.

CHAPTER TWENTY-SIX

The mid-afternoon blue sky with wispy clouds stretched as far as Van could see. The smell of warm pine and juniper filled her with the sense of home. As much as she appreciated her surroundings, she didn't look much beyond the road leading into the canyon below Cliff Palace. It was still empty.

They should have been back days ago. She'd been unable to reach Ray on the comms and had spent sleepless nights wondering if she'd been wrong to send them to the Ute Nation after all. Ray said they'd been hard hit by fever; what if he and Susan came down with it? She wouldn't forgive herself for knowingly sending them into possibly infected zones. She missed Susan's quick wit, her gentle but strong presence. Not to mention her rather perfect ass. Sinclair and Mac were holding their own, and the cocktail Susan had come up with seemed to be having some results, though the trial group was already pretty far gone, so it was hard to tell. Van could see the strain on them, though, taking care of so many patients. She needed more medical help. Maybe it was time to go on a scouting mission. Summer storms wouldn't be as bad as spring storms, and they would have a window of opportunity before the tornado season hit in earnest. They could do a run to the north and see if there were any medically trained people who wanted to relocate. She had a lot of people at Mesa, but for whatever reason, not many were doctors or nurses.

A puff of dust caught her eye just as she'd started to head for the ladder down to the caves. She shaded her eyes and watched… "Yes! Finally." There was no one to hear her relief, but she felt the need to shout it just the same. Ray's truck threw up dust in its wake as it neared the entrance to Cliff. Van hurried down the ladder to the cave top and sent the metal lift to the ground. She paced, listening for the sound of the truck doors slamming. She could hear their voices down below and Susan's low laughter made Van tingle in her happy places. The sound of the elevator rising made her bounce on her toes. When it came to the top and they stepped out, she barely restrained herself from leaping on them both.

"We've been worried sick about you guys. What happened to your comms?" Not really the welcome she wanted to give, but the pent up fear and frustration were going to come out first, apparently.

Susan raised an eyebrow and gave her that cute little half-smirk that made her look incredibly fuckable. "Good to be back."

Ray raised the comms unit. "It went dead on the second day. I took it apart and tried to figure out what was wrong with it, but I can't find the fault."

Susan moved into Van's personal space and looked up at her. "And I missed you, too."

Van breathed in Susan's scent, a heady mix of flowers and sunshine. "I was worried," she said softly, looking into Susan's beautiful eyes.

"Yeah, I got that." She leaned up and kissed her, just a swift touch. "But you'll be glad we stayed and did what we needed to do. We have a lot to tell you." She stepped back and looked at Ray, who was standing with his back to them.

"Is it okay to look now?"

Van laughed and punched his shoulder. "Tell me your news."

He turned and picked up his duffel bag. "I think a few others might want to hear this. Grab Liz and Mac, and we'll meet in your office. I need a shower."

Susan grimaced. "Me too. See you in thirty minutes? Oh, and grab Sinclair, too."

Van managed to keep from asking if she needed someone to wash her back, but barely. "See you in a few."

She watched them disappear into the caves and pulled herself together. That they had good news was great. Hopefully, it was the kind of outcome she really needed. She headed to her office to call the others for the meeting.

Thirty minutes later, Liz threw a wad of paper at her. "If you don't stop tapping your foot I'm going to have to cut it off."

She threw the paper back but stopped the tapping. "I just want to know what they found out."

"Yeah. And it's snowing on the sun. Why haven't you just made a move already? All that pent up sexual energy is going to explode and send us all skyrocketing to hell."

"You and your bizarre metaphors. I don't know what you're saying half the time. And what makes you think I haven't?" Van bypassed the question, but the door opened before Liz could follow it up.

"This conversation isn't over." Liz rocked back in her chair, glaring at Van.

"That sounds ominous. We'll have to be quick so you can get back to your love-hate relationship." Susan came in, followed by Ray, Sinclair, and Mac.

"Pure hate. Can't stand her face." Liz grinned and winked at Susan.

Susan shook her head and put her satchel on Van's desk. She looked at Ray. "Why don't you start?"

He turned a chair around and straddled it. "We headed for the northern edge of the Ute territory. I figured I'd follow the tribal borders down the line until we hit their HQ. The problem was that the first three areas we hit were deserted."

While he talked Van looked at the map, mentally marking the areas he was talking about. "Fever?"

"Lots of burial pyres, so yeah. They used to bury in caves, but once fever came, they started burning so the fever didn't get into the water and food."

Susan pitched in. "The thing was, even when we left each deserted settlement, it felt like we were being watched."

Ray nodded. "And we were. By the time we reached the fourth settlement they were waiting for us. They kept us outside the main encampment until they were sure we weren't carrying fever. But instead of taking us to their usual place, they took us into their caves."

Van leaned forward. "They're using caves?"

"Not just caves. An entire cave network. Underground running springs and everything. Amazing stuff. They've been working on it for decades, keeping it hidden from outsider eyes. They only let us in after I explained we were living in the caves at Mesa. They've had scouts see what we're doing here and they approve. We got lucky."

Van figured they'd have lookouts. The Native American population in the area was extremely protective of Mesa. She was glad they hadn't already taken over Mesa themselves. "Did you learn anything from their cave setup?"

Ray watched as Susan handed Van a large clay pot of something from the duffel bag. "That's the answer to Balcony. It's also the answer to our problems with damp walls. They make it out of clay, silt, sand—"

"I've tried all that." Deflated, Van wanted to get on with it. "Nothing new?"

He gave her a look that told her to shut up and she did.

"As I was saying. Clay, silt, sand, *and* a combination of corn husks mixed with soy paste and the ashes of the burned land after wildfires. They churn it together, and then they stomp on it. They take shifts, stomping it into a huge vat of plaster. Then they apply it by hand, which helps it stay in place better than plaster tools. And it works." His smile was one of awe. "You should see the way they've done the insides of their caves. They're waterproof, temperature regulated, and smooth as silk. And the color of the clay comes through, giving it a truly beautiful atmosphere."

That was probably the most words Van had ever heard come out of Ray in one go. His reaction to what he'd seen made it that much more impressive. "And they gave you the ratios?"

He dug through the bag and handed her a piece of paper. "All there. What's in the jar is to try on Balcony. They're certain it will work, but it makes sense to see if it will before we go stomping around making our own."

"How long will it take to dry if it works?" Hope restored, Van turned the big clay jar in her hands.

"Three days in good weather."

She handed it back to him. "Let me know how it goes, and what you need to make it happen if it does."

He smiled and placed the jar carefully at his feet. "A deal's a deal. I want my fish crackers." Liz groaned as Van opened her desk drawer and threw him a box. He cracked it open before nodding at Susan.

"Now for my news." She took several more pots out of the duffel bag. "They were hard hit by fever, like Ray said. But throughout the course of it they came up with remedies to help with the pain and confusion. Right at the end of the outbreak they were facing they found something that seemed to slow it down, and the last two people who got sick *didn't die*."

There wasn't a sound in the room as everyone looked at her. Finally, Van said, "Are you saying they found a *cure* for fever?"

"It's possible. But we know how fast fever mutates, so it could be that what worked for them then might not work now. Their last case was nearly a year ago, thanks to the fact that they've shut themselves off from the outside world and moved into the caves."

Van touched the jars on her desk. "Is this it?"

"It's the components. They've given me specifics on how to mix them and how much to give." Susan turned to Sinclair. "Have there been any new cases?"

He held up his finger. "One was brought in this morning from Kodack House. It's the first one outside Cliff, and there's no known connection between him and the others."

Susan put the jars in the bag. "They said the mixture needs to be given within twenty-four hours of the patient coming down with the disease. I need to get it mixed. Let's see if it still works on whatever variant of fever we've got here."

Van's mind spun with the implications. A cure for fever. They could save countless lives. "Whatever you need to do, do it."

Susan turned to Mac and Sinclair. "Can you help me get it mixed? It's taken orally, so we'll have to support the patients who are worse off to get it down."

They stood and Van stopped them before they left. "You guys... Damn good work. Thanks so much for doing it." It felt like a lame accolade, but she wasn't sure how else to say it.

Ray just waved as he left with his precious jar, and Susan winked at her. "See you at dinner?"

Liz coughed indiscreetly behind her hand, and Van threw her a warning look. "Yeah, I'd like that."

Once again, she and Liz were alone in the room. Van leaned against the door. "A cure for fever. Could it be that easy?"

"No." Liz shrugged when Van looked at her. "Sorry, but things are never that easy. But it's a good step. The problem is we don't know how people are getting infected. And until we figure that out, we're a step behind."

Van slid into her chair, the hope brought by Ray and Susan dimmed but not gone. "So that's the next step. Let's figure that out, or find someone who can."

CHAPTER TWENTY-SEVEN

K arissa's back ached, and her head throbbed like she'd enjoyed a night drinking jet fuel. Apparently, wood benches weren't made to be slept on, which had probably helped keep parishioners awake in the old days. She'd cried herself to sleep, only stopping her sobbing when she couldn't breathe properly anymore because her nose was so blocked. But as she sat up and stretched her aching muscles, she knew she felt a little better for having given in to the need to release all that bottled up frustration. She'd missed being in Devin's arms and had seriously considered going back to their room, but she wasn't quite ready. She knew Devin understood, at least theoretically, where she was coming from. Maybe she couldn't empathize, but she really was trying to understand and be supportive.

But that didn't help Karissa with the questions plaguing her. Devin's idea about focusing on what she could get out of the situation was a good one, and she was going to put it into motion. The bigger question, and one she hadn't brought up, was how out of control she felt when it came to their relationship. The sex wasn't just phenomenal; it was the kind of spiritual the ancient Greeks wrote about in their epic poetry. There was no question she'd fallen in love with Devin. And in the outside world, that would've been enough. But here, two thousand feet underground with departure from the planet looming, it wasn't enough. Because Karissa didn't want to leave.

In the lucid moments between bouts of crying, she'd come to realize the answer to one of Devin's earlier questions. She'd asked what was most important to her, and in the early hours of the morning, she'd found the answer. As amazing as the journey would be, as incredible as the opportunity was, Karissa didn't want to go. She wanted to use her skills to stay here, on Earth, and help make life livable. If it was true they were in a definitive extinction phase, then whatever she did might be for nothing. But that didn't matter. She just knew that she wasn't the kind of person who could leave other people to die, especially if she had the skill set to help. However, that didn't mean she was angry with those who wanted to go. She fully understood Devin's desire to go on this amazing adventure. She understood the passion that fueled those who would be starting life on a new planet and why they'd want to do such a thing. Saving the human race, which might not be savable here on Earth, was a logical position.

It just wasn't *her* position.

She heard the bell ring for breakfast and figured Devin would probably be in the canteen by the time Karissa made it back to their room. She wanted to shower and make herself feel somewhat human before she met Devin for whatever she had waiting. She wasn't sure when, or how, to tell Devin the conclusion she had come to. It was a conclusion that meant they couldn't, wouldn't, be together. Devin would be on another planet, one far, far away from the world Karissa would be living on. That meant their time together was both more heartbreaking and more precious.

She'd only taken a few steps away from the chapel when she heard footsteps coming up fast behind her. Before she could turn to see who it was, she was slammed into the wall, the air knocked from her. A pinprick to her neck made her flail in fear, but within seconds, the room faded. Nausea swamped her just before everything went black.

Karissa's body felt like molasses dipped in tar, and her vision doubled everything in front of her. She closed her eyes and willed the room to stop spinning. She tried to get to her hands and feet, but she couldn't move either. Her wrists were bound to a pipe that ran the length of the wall and her ankles were tied tightly together, effectively immobilizing her. She closed her eyes to keep the room from spinning, and once it stopped she opened her eyes again and saw the uncarved granite above her. A single light buzzed on the far wall, leaving most of the area in shadow. She tried to get a sense of where she was, and could just make out the other walls of the large granite cave. There was nothing in it but the light, her, and a few pieces of broken wood furniture thrown in a corner.

She tried to picture the maps she'd studied of the complex and couldn't remember there being a room like this. But if they hadn't been using it, they probably wouldn't have listed it. She had no idea where she was, but she had a good idea of who'd done it. When a door opened on the far wall, letting in a burst of light, she squinted against it but recognized the silhouette.

"What the hell is wrong with you?" Her voice sounded like that of a smoker, and she wondered how long she'd been knocked out for.

"Oh good, you're awake. I may have used a little too much, but I wanted to be sure you didn't cause me any trouble. And since you were finally without that jarhead you've taken up with, you gave me just the chance I needed." Ivan squatted down next to her, his eyes filled with loathing. "Comfy?"

"Do you seriously think you can get away with this?" She pulled at the ropes on her wrists, but they just grew tighter and her fingers started to tingle.

"How cliché. Yes. I know I will." He sniffed and moved away from her with a look of distaste. "You see, no one knows you're here. No one would ever think that I, a world-renowned scientist, would take issue with a slummer like you." He sighed theatrically. "But I'll admit you've gotten under my skin. You made it extremely hard to concentrate during testing, you know. With your brilliance, we would've made an excellent team on Phos. But you're clearly too stubborn to see it."

Karissa stared at him, horrified. She'd known he was an ass, but she'd never figured him for a psychopath. "Stubborn? What about the fact that I don't like you and I never have?"

He wagged a finger at her like she was a bad child. "You never got to know me, and I'm sure some of your dislike was born of intimidation." He flicked lint off his sleeve. "You'll stay here until testing is over. As soon as you've missed your first test, you'll be disqualified anyway. But my place on the leaderboard is tenuous. With you out of the running I'll go above the red line. And when I make sure the good lieutenant's knee is out of commission again, she'll miss that departure too. Not for any other reason than I despise her."

The thought that he'd hurt Devin was enraging. But tied up, she couldn't even lash out to kick him.

"Good. I can see you understand." He knelt in front of her again and moved a piece of hair away from her eye, almost tenderly. "Don't worry. After we've boarded I'll let someone know where to find you. I'm not a monster, after all. And of course by then it will be too late for them to hold me accountable for it. It's a win-win."

His hand was close enough to her face that she snapped at it, hoping to bite him. But he pulled away too quickly and stood. "And that's the thanks I get." He shrugged. "So be it. If you hadn't been so rude and abrasive, it might not have come to this." He laughed. "Or maybe it would have. Who knows." He checked his watch. "Time to go. I do love the vegetarian lasagna at lunch."

Karissa didn't bother begging. She knew it would fall on deaf ears. Her biggest fear was what would happen to Devin.

"Oh, and if you were wondering," he said before he opened the door. "Your conspirator looks like the world has fallen on her shoulders. Apparently, she had a date this morning who didn't show up, and now she's convinced you simply don't want to see her. So she's not looking for you. Pity." He quickly pulled the door open and shut it behind him.

He moved too quickly for her to yell. Obviously, he'd expected that, with how fast he'd made his exit.

She closed her eyes and breathed slowly. Just like she'd had to do when Devin was injured, she needed to keep calm and figure out what to do next. There was always an answer. She just had to find it before it was too late.

❖

"She said she'd meet me." Devin turned her glass around in her hands, turning, turning, turning, avoiding her reflection. "I guess she made her decision in the chapel."

Walker gently put his hand on hers to stop her glass mauling. "She might have overslept. She might still be working things out. You just have to wait for her to come around. I've seen how you guys are together. I can't believe you won't find a way."

She sighed and leaned back. "What about you and your guy? No way around that?"

He winced. "Touché. The difference is that I'm not some brilliant egghead. And while we've got a connection, it isn't one he'd give up space exploration for. He really wants to go, and he wouldn't be okay staying with me instead. I get it. We had what we had. And while there are some soldiers going, they've been handpicked because they have other useful skills too." He shrugged. "I'm a one-trick pony, so this is where I'll be staying."

"What will you do? Once we go?" She hadn't considered the next stage for the people left behind.

"Wait for the end?" He laughed. "I'll stay in the military. I'll protect people. I'll keep going. It's not like the world is ending tomorrow. We still have a semblance of government, and that's where I'll be. Hell, maybe I'll even go protect one of the Gateway cities. It sounds like that's what a lot of the military people are planning on." He punched her shoulder. "Don't worry about me, you softie."

Devin grinned and punched him back. "I just wanted to know if you were going out pillaging." She couldn't shake the feeling that something was wrong. Something more than Karissa needing more time. She looked at the doorway when she heard obnoxious laughter and saw Ivan with a few of his cronies. He smiled at her, and it was so full of malice it set her teeth on edge.

"I really hate that guy. I'm sorry I saved his ass after that tornado."

Devin picked at her lunch. "Yeah, it's pretty shitty we lost good people and he managed to make it through." She realized how that might sound and looked at Walker. "But you shouldn't ever feel bad for saving anyone's life. It's not your call to make, right?"

He yawned. "Yeah, I know. Look, I'm going to take a quick nap before my next shift begins. If you still haven't heard from Karissa by dinnertime, we'll go find her, okay?"

She nodded and watched him head out. He was well liked, and for good reason. *It's not your call to make.* The words bounced around in her head. They'd come out so easily, and with sudden, aching clarity, she understood where Karissa was coming from. She grabbed her crutches and moved as quickly as she could out of the canteen. Before she reached the door, there was a splash of something, the sound of ice cubes hitting the tile, and then...

"Fuck!" Devin's crutches slid out from under her and her feet couldn't get purchase on the slick flooring. Her shoulder hit the wall and then she went down on one knee. Her bad one.

Pain stabbed through her, making her gasp and struggle to move the injured leg into a better position. Two people were there to help and guided her into a sitting position on the floor. Liquid soaked through her pants as she sat in whatever had been spilled. It took every ounce of control not to throw up from the pain lancing through her.

"Goodness. How careless of me. I do hope you're okay."

She looked up into Ivan's mocking expression. "You're lucky I'm down here, asshole, or I'd wipe that smile right off your ugly plastic face."

His eyes narrowed and his false smile turned nasty. "Down there is where you belong. You and anyone like you." He backed up, the mask back in place. "As I said, I'm so sorry. I hope it heals quickly. It's not long before we leave, you know."

He sauntered away, whistling like some demented dwarf.

Someone came up with a wheelchair and Devin was helped into it. On her way to the medical unit, she pictured Ivan's face as he'd looked down at her. *The bastard meant to do it. Just like he did yesterday.* Panic began to bubble up once again. *Where is Karissa?*

The trip to medical didn't last long. The doc made quick work of checking it out, and although it was inflamed, she was lucky. It hadn't been reinjured. She'd have to stick to the wheelchair again for a while, but that was the least of her worries. There was no question in her mind now that something was wrong. The place was huge, but the area they used to get from testing to meals and bed wasn't all that spread out. She should have come across Karissa by now. She checked the chapel and even went all the way to the library in sector seven to see if she was there. No one had seen her.

On her way back to their room, she saw that the new testing schedule had gone up. Next to it, posted in massive capital letters, was a sign that made her heart race.

FIVE DAYS TO LAUNCH FROM LOCKHEED MARTIN, DENVER. BE READY 0300.

Five days until they left the planet. Forever. If the buzz when they'd named the planet had been loud, now it was out of control. New energy flooded the halls as people made their way to whatever departments they worked for and prepared for the trip of a lifetime. *Damn, Karissa, where are you?*

She saw Ivan looking at the testing schedule. He checked his watch, went into the canteen, and threw some things on a tray without really looking at them. Then he headed out again, this time with purpose. He moved through the crowds in the halls easier than she could, and by the time she cleared them, he was gone. Where was he going with a food tray? She doubted he had friends to eat with elsewhere, and the bunk rooms were the other way. She considered going to the facility police, but she had no proof Ivan was anything other than an ass. And if she tipped him off, and he really had done something to Karissa, it could put Karissa's life in jeopardy. She'd have to find a way to watch him. *And if you have hurt her, you bastard, I'll make sure it's the last thing you do.*

CHAPTER TWENTY-EIGHT

The room had finally stopped spinning, but Karissa's back ached fiercely from the unnatural position. She hadn't been able to loosen the cuffs at all, and with her ankles tied tightly together she couldn't get comfortable. The single light buzzed on faithfully, and she was grateful she hadn't been left in total darkness too. That didn't seem like a kindness on Ivan's part, so the light must be constant. That meant the room wasn't completely unknown. But for all intents and purposes, she was stuck in a cave, and the only person who would hear her voice echo off the cave walls was her.

She drifted in and out of consciousness as the drug wore off. Dreams of Devin laughing, crying, and being hurt plagued her, and she fought to stay awake. Their last words had been so fraught with fear and confusion. She hated the thought that Devin might get on a ship thinking that Karissa had just given up on them and walked away. She hated that she wouldn't get to say good-bye or hold her one last time.

Tears flowed and she shook herself. *Pull it together. She's not gone and I'm not dead.* She squinted at the jumble of furniture at the far end of the cave, and a plan started to come together. But one wrong move and Ivan would make it impossible. She had no idea how long it had been since he'd left, and she wondered just how long he planned on keeping her there. As though summoned by her thoughts, the door opened and he came in with a tray.

"How's my little supplicant doing? Coming around, I trust?" He put the tray on the floor and pushed it toward her, keeping his distance.

She kept her eyes half-lidded, her head tilted to one side as though too heavy to lift. "I think you nearly killed me with whatever you gave me. I can't keep my eyes open."

He tutted. "Just shows you wouldn't have been any good on Phos anyway. Too weak." He reached into his pocket and pulled out a handcuff key, which he dangled in front of her. "If you promise to behave, I'll uncuff your wrists so you can eat."

She barely nodded, her mind racing with possibilities. The problem was, if she made a run for it and didn't get away, he could easily leave her here to die with no food or water. She needed to be careful. Controlled. Like any experiment. *Think.*

He pulled her wrists up and undid one cuff.

With a groan, she lowered her arms and shook them to get the feeling back. She grabbed the glass of water and drank, the welcome cold running through her.

He stood watching her with an expression she couldn't read.

"It's too bad, really. If I thought there was any chance we could work things out, or that you wouldn't keep me below the line on the leaderboard, I might reconsider this little escapade. But I know I'm just being a sentimental old fool."

Karissa ate in silence, slowly. She didn't want to make herself sick, and although she didn't feel like eating, she didn't know when he'd come back with more. If she was going to make it out of here, she'd have to keep her strength up. He watched her eat every bite, creeping her out, and when she was done he pulled the tray away with his foot.

"You're welcome. Now, put your hands back up, and I'll bring you dinner later."

She stared at his feet, hoping he wouldn't see the fury in her expression. "Could you at least just cuff them behind me instead of to the metal thing?"

He seemed to consider. "I don't see why not. You see? I can be reasonable. You would've liked me, in other circumstances."

The only way I'll like you is if you're burning in hell. "Thank you."

He recuffed her wrists behind her and his hand slid over her shoulder, brushing her hair over it. She shivered and couldn't help flinching away from his touch.

"As I thought." He picked up the tray and stormed from the room, the door clanging shut behind him.

The moment he was gone, Karissa rolled onto her back. She stretched her arms as far as they would go and wiggled her butt back. She'd seen people do it in movies and had to hope like hell it was actually possible. The muscles in her arms and shoulders screamed, and the metal cut into her wrists. She twisted, contorted, rolled, and arched. With a final agonized cry, she managed to get her wrists over her feet so they were in front of her.

Karissa lay still, catching her breath, letting the fire in her muscles cool and the trembling in her arms grow still. *Control. Think.* She rose to her knees and awkwardly pulled herself along the floor toward the pile of furniture. Tears slid down her cheeks as her hands scraped along the floor and her knees protested the granite beneath them. But when she got to the furniture, it was all worth it.

The wood was sharp in places and nails stuck out haphazardly. Random pieces of bent metal were mixed in with the wood. She raised her feet over a long, sharp shard of metal and began sawing at the ropes between her ankles. Her thighs burned and she had to keep stopping, but then she'd start again. *Control. Think.* When she'd been at it for a while, and it felt like it could be time for him to come back, she slowly made her way back to where he'd left her. She'd been there only moments before he came in with another tray.

"I'm afraid I don't have time to keep you company for dinner, my dear. Our launch date has been announced, you see. You can take heart you won't be here much longer."

Karissa kept her side to him, her head resting against the wall, and didn't answer. If he thought she was beaten he'd pay far less attention to her, and that was what she needed. She just had to hope he didn't notice her arms weren't where they should be. Fortunately, he seemed distracted by his news and barely looked at her.

"Not feeling talkative, mmm? Not a problem. Sleep well." He practically skipped to the door. "Just think. This time, five days from now, I'll be on my way to a new planet. And you'll be here, watching me go." He giggled like some creepy horror movie cliché before he slipped out the door.

"Dammed if I'll be watching you do anything other than go to jail, you piece of shit." Karissa's voice murmured back at her from the cave walls as she began her trek back to the furniture. The ropes around her ankles were looser. Once they were free, she'd figure out the next step. She thought of Devin's words. *Take things one step at a time.* She started sawing at the rope again.

❖

"I'm going out of my damn mind." Devin wanted to punch something. Hard. There'd been no sign of Karissa anywhere, and Ivan was grinning like the proverbial cat who ate something it shouldn't have.

"We'll work together. If he's done something, we'll find out," Zeke whispered, leaning forward.

"He's right. You've got a team, Lieutenant. Just tell us what to do."

She nodded gratefully at Walker, who discreetly handed her a radio from his bag, and then passed one to Zeke as well. He agreed with her that they had no proof to bring against Ivan, but he also agreed that he was a damn good suspect. Testing started the next morning, and if they didn't get Karissa to her test, she'd automatically be disqualified and Ivan would go above the red line on the leaderboard. Although Devin knew how torn Ris was about the whole situation, she didn't deserve to have the choice taken away from her. It needed to be hers, not someone else's.

"Okay. I'll start following him, but he'll be watching for me. I lost him down the blue corridor at lunchtime. I lost him when he dodged down yellow after dinner." Her heart hurt at the words she had to say next. "He had food trays with him both times, and I can't help but think they weren't for him. That was lunch and dinner, which means he probably won't go back to wherever he was going again tonight. But if we spook him, he might not go back at all, and we could lose our chance to save her." The thought was sickening, and she could feel the blood rush from her head. Walker tapped the table pointedly and she focused.

"Walker, you've got free rein of this facility. I need you to see what's beyond the normal areas. What rooms don't they use? Are there storage areas? See what you can find." She took a drink of water and wondered if Karissa was eating and drinking whatever he was bringing her. After their days of survival on the trip here, hopefully, she'd be thinking of those things. "Zeke, take Gemma with you and wander the South and West halls like you're just a romantic couple looking for some privacy. See how far you can get without someone taking notice. Then we'll have a perimeter Ivan could have gone to."

"No problem. When do you want us to report back?" Walker stood, his expression intense.

"I'm taking the East and North Halls. Meet back in two hours at my room." She grabbed Zeke's hand when he stood. "Be careful. Don't put yourself in danger. He knows we're tight. And obviously, if you find anything, get on the radio so the rest of us come running."

Zeke grinned. "Aw. I knew you loved me."

She rolled her eyes and watched them leave. The wheelchair was slowing her down, but it couldn't be helped. Maybe this way she'd look less conspicuous, too. *That's a stupid thought. They'll notice me no matter what.* She'd have to take the chance and talk her way out of it if anyone got pissy. She set off down the North Hall, past the offices she knew, and then into more unfamiliar territory. Offices lined both sides, and there were lots of people busy inside them. No one gave her an extra glance as she rolled by, trying to look as though she knew exactly where she was going. When she got to the end of the hall, she pushed open a heavy door. Beyond it were some stairs leading into a storage depot. That, too, was busy. Forklifts moved massive steel boxes, bosses shouted at other non-bosses, and the whole area was tightly controlled chaos.

There's no way he'd get someone past this craziness. She turned her wheelchair and headed back the way she'd come. Again, no one stopped her. *Guess they figure if you're down here, you're not a threat.* It made sense, though it was a little disconcerting.

She made it to the East Hall and started the same routine. *Hold on, Ris. I'll find you.*

❖

Sweat ran in rivers down Karissa's face, back, and between her breasts. The cave wasn't warm, but the exertion of trying to free her ankles was exhausting. The rope was thick and knotted. But when the last thread broke, she nearly yelled with victory. She had no idea how long it had taken, but it didn't matter. She stood on shaky legs and moved to the door.

She nearly wept when she saw what was missing. There was no handle on this side of the door. Smooth metal ran from top to bottom, and there wasn't even a gap she could try to slide her fingers into. She slid down the wall and rested her head on her knees. She let the tears fall but kept herself from breaking down completely. *Control. Think.*

The pile of broken odds and ends provided an option. She dug through it and found a solid piece of wood, heavy enough to do some damage, but light enough she could lift it and bring it down with force, even with her hands still cuffed. Now she just had to wait until he brought breakfast. She moved to the other side of the door so he wouldn't see her right when he came in, giving her an element of surprise and hopefully just enough time.

She closed her eyes and thought of Devin and their last conversation. She loved Devin, there was no question. Could she give up life here to be with her? To go live Devin's dream? Other people were excited about it and couldn't wait to take that step. If Karissa could just let go, if she could let the adventure take her away, why couldn't she be like them? This was her chance, too.

The science of it was truly exceptional. The advances, the challenges. It would all be amazing. And she'd get the chance to live that adventure with Devin at her side. It was a weird kind of fairy tale, and she could give herself a happy ending. Assuming, of course, that they didn't all die the moment they landed on the other planet. *And there I go again. Worrying about the future.* But it wasn't like worrying about gaining five pounds over Christmas. It was becoming an extraterrestrial life form. Someone who lived on another planet. And that was huge.

She thought of Natasha and John. She thought of the raiders and Edward. She thought of her own parents, and all the others who had died from a virus she had been unable to find a cure for. Maybe this really was an extinction event there was no recovery from. The bottom line, though, was starting to come down to Devin. Could Karissa really watch the ship leave, knowing Devin was on it and she'd never see her again? Could she live with the knowledge she'd left the rest of humanity behind to die, unaided, because she'd gone off with the woman she loved?

The questions crashed against the walls of her mind the same way she'd crashed around in the cave. Purpose without accomplishing much of anything. She pressed her ear to the door and listened, but she couldn't hear anything. She slowly drifted to sleep, the thick wood in her hands and the comfort of answers far away.

Devin was exhausted. Rolling the damn wheelchair down corridor after corridor was tiring, as was the pain. The East Hall was far longer and more maze like than she'd anticipated. Every time she turned down one hallway, another loomed. But this was more promising, too. Beyond the chapel, she'd come across several empty rooms the farther she'd gone. Rooms they hadn't bothered transforming that remained damp, unhewn granite. She was going to be late getting back to meet the others, but it looked like she was coming to the end of the maze. When she turned the wheelchair to head back, her heart heavy and disappointment bitter, she caught the shimmer of something against the wall. Everything down here was in a state of stasis; a layer of dust lined the floors and it felt like ghosts might live in the shadows. There shouldn't be anything shiny.

When she got closer, she saw that it was a fork. One that still had uncrusted food on it. Her heart raced and she picked up the radio. "East Hall. Follow to the end." She wheeled close to the walls, following the lines of them and saw a partially hidden final corridor at the end of the hall. She would have missed it entirely if not for the fork. It looked like they'd begun digging another section and then stopped, leaving the corridor unfinished and abandoned. Just beyond the corner of it was a metal door. One with a shiny handle.

"Karissa?" She tried the door, but it was locked. "Ris? Are you in there?"

She was glad she was sitting down when she heard Karissa's faint voice answer. Her knees might have given out with relief had she been standing.

"Devin? I'm here!"

"Are you okay?" Devin kept slamming against the door handle, but with a door like the ones they had in this place, it wasn't going to budge.

"I'm fine. I'm handcuffed, and there's no door handle on this side."

Devin keyed the radio. "Bring someone with key access. Go all the way down to the end. There's a corridor beyond where you think there should be one." She listened to Walker's affirmative reply. Now she had to wait, and she wouldn't breathe okay until she had Ris back in her arms. "I've got help coming, babe. We'll have you out of there in a minute."

"Are you okay? He said he was going to hurt you."

Bastard. He'd left Karissa alone, cuffed, and worried about Devin as well. "I'm fine. He managed to trip me up, but I'm okay." There was silence for a moment, and Devin grew worried Karissa wasn't as okay as she said she was. "Babe?"

"I love you."

Devin's breath caught in her chest and she blinked back the tears that rose like a flash flood. "I—"

"Wait. Let me get this out before the door opens and other people get here."

Devin heard a scraping sound, and Karissa's voice became a little clearer. *She must be right against the door.* She put her hand against it, wishing she could see Ris's face.

"I'm in love with you. I don't want to lose you. I'm completely confused about what comes next, but I need you to know that whatever it is, I want to face it with you. And I'm sorry I've been like a livewire in water. I hate being out of control, and you already know that about me. I hope you can forgive me."

Devin rattled at the door handle, wishing she could just rip the damn thing off. She needed Karissa in her arms. Just as she was about to reply, a group of people came around the corner, Walker in front. The soldier who had met them on their first day and checked them in was right behind him.

"Lieutenant. Looks like you've got a situation to brief me on."

"Sir. The door is locked."

He took out an enormous ring of keys. "It might take a few minutes, but we'll get it open." He went to work, trying key after key.

Walker squeezed Devin's shoulder. "She all right?"

"Says so." Zeke and Gemma were staring in fascination, and she grinned at them. "Little bit of excitement before you go off-planet, huh?"

Zeke laughed. "My life has been nothing but excitement since I met you. Living on another planet will be a breeze in comparison."

The soldier grunted as the key slid into the lock and the door opened. Karissa stepped into the opening, a huge board in her hands, her eyes squinting against the light. When she saw Devin she threw the board aside and dropped to her knees beside her. She laid her head on Devin's lap and cried.

"I didn't know if I'd see you again. I thought I might actually die in there."

The soldier came out of the cave Karissa had been locked in. "God knows how he even found this place, and I definitely want to know how he got a key. You're damn lucky the lieutenant found you."

Devin stroked Karissa's hair, the relief she felt at having her safe quickly replaced by a strange combination of worry and rage. "Babe, your wrists are bloody and you've got blood on your shoes. How bad are your ankles?"

Karissa shifted and raised the legs of her pants. Where the rope had been was blistered and raw, blood trailing down in thin streams to her shoes. "Not too bad. I think it looks worse than it is, although it will probably hurt like a bitch when I shower." The soldier took out a handcuff key and carefully slid them off her.

She shuddered and put her head back down on Devin's lap.

Walker got on the radio and switched channels. "We need a med bed wheeled to the far East—"

Devin held up her hand for him to stop. "Ris, why don't you sit on my lap, and Walker can push us back to the cross tunnel? It will take them a while to find us, and I want to get you out of here as fast as possible."

Karissa smiled through her tears. "You just want me on your lap." She stood gingerly and positioned herself on Devin's lap. "I think it's a great idea."

The soldier asked her a few questions, and Karissa gave him the details he needed. He got on the radio and ordered the military police to meet him at Ivan's room. At the cross tunnel section, a med bed was waiting and Karissa climbed onto it.

He patted her shoulder awkwardly. "We'll take him into custody. No need to worry from here on out. Good luck with tomorrow's tests." He turned and strode off, barking orders on the radio.

"I think I'll head back to my station." Walker kissed Karissa's cheek and saluted Devin. "Night."

Zeke took Gemma's hand. "And that's enough excitement for me. See you tomorrow."

A medical person pushed Devin's chair so she was able to hold onto Karissa's hand. They didn't say anything on the way to the med unit, but Devin's mind was racing. There was so much to say, so many things they needed to talk through. But first she wanted Karissa all to herself, wrapped safely in her arms. She moved out of the way so the medical team could take care of Karissa's wrists and ankles, but she made sure to stay where Karissa could see her. She'd looked so small, so vulnerable when she'd appeared in the doorway. But with that board in her hands, clearly ready to defend herself, she'd also looked damned strong.

When the team finished bandaging her they gave her pain medication and released her. A medic pushed Devin's chair, and Karissa walked gingerly beside her back to their room, their hands once again intertwined. The air between them seemed weighted, like the break right before a storm.

Once they were alone, Devin sat on the bed and pulled Karissa against her. They sat that way for a while, until Devin finally said, "I still have that surprise for you. You up for one more trip?"

Karissa looked at her searchingly, and Devin could see the questions in her eyes.

"I don't have a lot of energy left, but I have some. I want to sleep for a week."

Devin picked up the internal phone and called the person she'd arranged a favor with. She took Karissa's jacket from the closet, as well as her own. A moment later, a soft knock sounded at the door. "Come on. We won't have to walk much."

She led Karissa out of their room to the wide corridor behind it, used for vehicles. A small tram car was waiting and she waved to the driver. "Hop in."

"Where are we going?" Karissa settled in beneath Devin's arm, draped around her shoulders.

"If I told you it wouldn't be much of a surprise." She kissed the top of her head and pulled her close. "You'll find out in a minute."

The air grew warmer as they headed down the long road, past the buildings to where it led to the entrance of the facility. The tram car took them just beyond the entrance, and the fresh, warm night air was intoxicating. The driver turned. "You've got an hour, tops. I'll wait just inside."

Devin nodded and helped Karissa out of the tram to the dirt path up the side. They climbed it slowly and stopped at a bench tucked against the rock.

"This is amazing. I never imagined I could miss the night sky so much." Karissa leaned against the cliff side and looked up. "Thank you. Is this even allowed?"

"Not technically. But I ran into an old friend from the service, and I assured him we wouldn't try to take off. I thought you needed some fresh air." Devin took her hand and looked up at the sky too. "I love you, too, Ris. I never thought I'd love someone again. And now I know the love I have for you is something I've never known. When I couldn't find you, when I thought he might have taken you away from me…" She swallowed hard but let the tears fall. If there was ever a time to be truly open, this was it. "I can't lose you. I wouldn't be whole without you. If you'll have me, I want to stay here, on Earth, with you at my side."

Karissa turned to her, her eyes wide. "But you wanted to go so badly. I'd never ask you to give up that kind of dream."

"You're not asking. And I've had plenty of time to think. I can see both sides of this thing. When you called me an elitist, it stunned me." She shook her head when Karissa started to speak. "Wait. You were right. The fact that I'm willing to take off without thinking of the consequences to those left behind is pretty shit. The fact is, though, we can't all go. We can't evacuate seven billion people. Someone has to go, and it makes sense that it's the people who can figure out how to make it work." She stopped to kiss Karissa's knuckles, the stark white bandage around her wrist glowing against the night. "But I don't have to be one of those people to have an awesome adventure. I can make a real difference here, and still do what I love. Because when it comes down to it, you're my adventure, and wherever we go, I'll be happy."

Karissa wiped tears from her cheeks. "I was going to tell you I'd decided to go with you."

Devin laughed. "Really?"

"I don't want to be without you, and if that means going to live on another planet, then that's what we'll do."

Devin leaned back and looked up at the zillions of sparkling dots in the night sky. Of all the ones she could see, Phos wasn't one of them. It was hard to conceptualize. "But it's not what you really want. And if you went, you'd always wonder. What if you could have done something here? Is everyone on Earth gone? Are humans extinct on the blue planet? It would drive you crazy."

Karissa sighed. "True. But will you look up there, when things are insane and hard down here, and resent the fact that you didn't go?"

Devin considered the question, owing Karissa nothing less than the truth. "I'll admit, I'll wonder how it's going. I'll wonder what they're doing and if anyone from out there will ever come back." She turned so she could face Karissa, needing her to see the honesty in her eyes. "But resent it? Not as long as I've got you by my side." She grinned. "Besides, thanks to all the testing, I've got some kick-ass new ideas I can put to the test here. We'll take things on together, no matter where we decide to go after this."

Karissa threw her arms around Devin and cried. Eventually, she pulled back and kissed her, long and hard. "I love you so much."

"And I love you. What say we spend the rest of our time lying over there on the grass? I want to show you how much I missed you last night."

CHAPTER TWENTY-NINE

Karissa woke when the alarm went off. Her body ached, and her wrists and ankles were stiff with pain. She opened her eyes and smiled when she saw Devin looking back at her. "Hey."

"Hey yourself." Devin brushed a piece of hair away from her eyes. "Sleep okay?"

Karissa grinned. "Thanks to someone tiring me out before we even made it to the bed." The time on the grass under the stars had been fleeting, but they'd made the most of it. Being out in the open after so much time underground was like being set free from a cage. The warm air was like a lover's touch and when combined with Devin's actual touch, Karissa had been in heaven. Going back into the caves had been like being stuffed back into the mouth of a lion, but she wouldn't have to wait much longer to get back into the air.

"Why set the alarm? If we miss our tests we're out of the game. We can sleep in." A shiver of fear crept in. Had Devin changed her mind?

"I totally understand if you want to do it that way. But I want to finish as the best, for no other reason than to justify my enormous ego. And like I said, I've learned a lot from these tests. I want to take as much knowledge with me as I can before we leave."

With the pressure of going off planet gone, Karissa could appreciate the idea. "I'll take mine too. If I didn't fail yesterday's."

Devin threw off the covers and swung out of bed. "Better get to it then, sweet butt."

Karissa laughed and got dressed. She felt lighter than she had since this whole thing had begun, and hope was returning rapidly. But when they headed down the corridor toward the canteen, that hope turned to confusion. People were stopping to stare and whisper. She leaned down. "What's going on?" she murmured in Devin's ear. "Why do I feel like a lab rat?"

Devin looked contemplative. "If I had to guess, word of Ivan's arrest has already gotten around. And they'll know why."

Karissa hated being the focus of attention, especially gossip. But there was no way around this, and time was short. She wouldn't have to put up with it much longer. She pushed Devin to their usual table and received hugs from Walker, Zeke, and even Gemma.

"Have you heard?" Zeke asked.

"You're like some kind of cyber wire, plugged into everything. What's up?" Devin asked.

"When they arrested Ivan, he denied it at first. Then he blamed it on Karissa, saying she'd asked him to kidnap her so she wouldn't have to go." Everyone laughed as he nodded. "Seriously. He put up a fight, saying he was the most brilliant mind here, and they couldn't keep him from going to Phos."

Walker chimed in. "The thing is, they won't just keep him from going to Phos. There are plenty of people staying here once the rest leave, and they plan on keeping him in jail for a long while. He stole the keys from someone's office, so he's the only one in custody. No trial necessary."

Karissa wanted to feel some sense of pity for Ivan, but she couldn't muster any. The man was a psycho bastard, and he deserved what he got. They could put him back in that cave he'd left her in, for all she cared.

Zeke took over. "And today is the last day of testing. Tomorrow is the physical, and then it's a rest day before we ship out." He looked at Karissa, his expression turning sad. "I don't know if you saw the leaderboard?"

She smiled at him and took his hand. "I didn't make it through?"

He shook his head. "I'm really sorry. You're below the red line, and there's someone above you. With it being the last day of testing...I wasn't sure if you knew."

He had tears in his eyes, and her heart swelled with gratitude. "I didn't know, but I had a feeling I bombed that last one. But I'm good with it. You guys are going to do awesome things up there." She turned to Devin. "Ivan didn't have to mess with me after all. He just had to wait for the results to come in, and he would have gone above me on the leaderboard. Anyway, I guess it lets me off the hook."

Devin shrugged. "It does. Now you can sleep in and kick back for the next few days."

Walker looked stunned. "I didn't check the board. I just assumed... You're not leaving, Karissa?"

Again, she was warmed by the relief in Walker's eyes. She might not have biological family anymore, but she had chosen family. "Nope. I have no idea where I'll go from here, though." She didn't mention the fact that Devin wasn't leaving either. It wasn't her place to tell others that.

"I'll look out for her, Lieutenant. I promise." Walker held Devin's shoulder in his hand.

"That won't be necessary, but thanks. I've decided to stay behind, too. We'll figure out the next steps once the others are gone."

He looked like he was about to say something when the warning bell rang.

"I'd better get to my test." She pushed away from the table but pulled Karissa back down to the bench when she stood. "Stay here. Have a cup of coffee. Relax. Zeke can push me most of the way, and I'll see you at lunch." She gave her a quick kiss, and then Zeke, Gemma, and Devin were off, chatting about the next few days.

Karissa turned back to her coffee, but stilled when she saw the expression on Walker's face. "What is it?"

He frowned and played with a rolled-up napkin. "I don't know that she's going to have a choice if she passes her final tests."

Fear flowed through Karissa's veins. "What do you mean she won't have a choice?"

He looked around and leaned closer. "You guys were *chosen*, Karissa. Do you think the government spent millions choosing the right people, tracking them down, bringing them to a secret facility, just to have them say at the very end, 'no thanks'? Once she's proven she's the best, I'd bet money they'll get her on that ship, with or without her consent."

"Jesus." Karissa should have thought of it. They both should have. They hadn't had a choice in coming, why would they have a choice in leaving? If Devin had skipped the test, if she'd shown a personality flaw that indicated she might not be dependable, maybe she'd have been out of the running, although that could have had other, more graphic, consequences. But now, with a final test ahead, the only thing she might not pass would be the physical, and that she didn't have any control over.

Now, all Karissa could do was wait. In a few days, she might be watching Devin leave for space after all.

The test was harder than any she'd previously taken. Factors involving the new information about the planet were on hand and to be taken into consideration. Wind speed, light, sun, heat, storms… there was a whole new data set, and it put Devin's knowledge to its limits. It was fantastic. She loved puzzling it out, writing down options, only to scribble them out and find another track. But now she found herself thinking along two lines. The one that included the data set, and the one that included the elements around her she was already familiar with. That meant not only was she pushing herself, she was pushing herself for a damn good reason. And that felt good.

The buzzer sounded just as she finished the final question and she stretched, feeling the muscles in her back pop and crack. Riding around in the wheelchair was messing with her body, and she couldn't wait to get back in shape. Once she and Ris figured out where to go next, she'd make it a point to get fit again.

The lights flashed and a video appeared on the monitor. "Please attend a mandatory luncheon lecture. Lunch will be provided in Canteen Two."

Another mandatory lecture. She wouldn't miss those. She wheeled past the last remaining scientist in her group, who looked like an old mannequin, his skin was so gray. Devin was grateful she hadn't taken the testing as hard as some of the others.

She wheeled quickly to the canteen, where Karissa was waiting with the others of their little family group. She kissed her and noticed the strain lines around her eyes right away. "What's wrong? Has something happened with Ivan?"

Karissa's smile was forced. "No, nothing like that. We'll talk about it in private, okay?"

The lights flickered, and they moved to a table already set up with dishes of food. Devin couldn't eat. Was Karissa having doubts about them?

Just before the lights dimmed and the screen lit, Karissa leaned over. "It's not about us, either." She kissed Devin's palm. "I love you. Now eat."

Devin relaxed, able to breathe again. She'd never been this twisted up about a woman, and she wasn't sure she was handling it very well. She looked up from her stew at the start of the presentation. The disembodied narrator talked as images flashed across the screen.

"We are about to begin the next stage of our exploration into the stars. Your testing has come to an end. Those of you who have passed your exams and who pass your final physicals tomorrow will be coming to Phos. The new light of our beginning."

The screen split into several different scenes, all showing various launch sites around the world before panning to the cities nearby with populations struggling to survive and adapt to the new climate conditions. Wind turbine farms, solar panel fields, and bio domes were shown like pots at the end of rainbows.

"Not everyone can go to Phos. You were chosen as the best of the best, and those who go to Phos will be the ones who are most likely to help create a new civilization. A question we'd like to answer for you now is one many have been asking: what about those of you who don't go to Phos?"

Devin felt Karissa's hand tremble in hers. *Is she worried about what we'll do after this?* She shifted so she could put her arm against Karissa's, just to let her know she was there.

"Once the convoys to the launch sites have left, you have several options. One is to stay right here in the comfort of Cheyenne Mountain. As top scientists, you can use this as your base of

operations. It's safe, you're protected from the elements, and you can continue your work using our state-of-the-art facilities." The screen panned around the facility they'd already come to know well. *"Should you choose to leave the facility, you're free to do so. Survival packs will be provided to anyone who wishes to return to their home states, or go to a Gateway city. Finally, for those young enough, you're welcome to put your name on the waiting list. Assuming all goes well, and there's no reason not to, our intention is to send another ship to Phos after we've settled on the ground there. You'd leave Earth after we get to Phos, joining us there twenty years after we have settled."*

The scene changed again, this time to the interior of the ship they'd be taking to Phos. Devin's attention drifted. They could stay here in Cheyenne. That wasn't something she'd considered. It was safe, they'd have their own place, and they wouldn't have to worry about the weather. But was there food and water enough to keep them going? It didn't mention that part. Who would be running the facility? There were an awful lot of questions for those who'd be staying. She didn't like the feeling of it.

The film finally ended and the lights flickered back on. The room erupted in noisy conversation, and Devin turned to the others at her table. "Who the hell wants to sleep for twenty years? Can you imagine the state of your ass by the time you got out of the capsule?"

Zeke grinned. "I don't care about the state of my ass when I get there. As long as I get to see it."

Devin understood his enthusiasm, but the concept really had lost its shine for her. "Yeah, well, find a way to write and let me know all about it, huh?"

Karissa stood, looking unsteady on her feet. "I'd like to go lie down. Can we go back to the room?"

Devin saw the tremor in her hands, the worry in her eyes. "Of course."

They made their way through the throngs of people standing around talking. Though a few looks were still thrown their way, there were far fewer already. There were more important things to think about. Back in their room, Karissa flopped backward on the bed and rubbed at her temple.

"I'm so tired of this roller coaster." She turned on her side and curled into a ball, facing Devin.

"What's going on? Talk to me."

Karissa hesitated. "I don't know if I should tell you. What if I do—"

"Babe, stop. No whatifs. We deal with the facts at hand and work things through."

"You're right." Karissa told Devin about her conversation with Walker. "What if you pass that last test and your physical?" Tears slid down her cheeks unchecked. "What if they force you to go?"

Devin couldn't believe they hadn't considered that possibility. It was asinine that she'd thought she'd be able to just walk away. "When my physical comes up tomorrow I'll make it clear my knee is torched, that it's too bad to get around on. I'll tell them I'm all messed up in the head. I'll lay it on thick so there's no way they can pass me through."

Karissa nodded slowly, her eyes narrowed in thought. "That might work. Maybe. After all we've been through here, it wouldn't be a stretch."

Devin smiled, hoping it looked more genuine than it felt. It wasn't easy tricking medical personnel, and it was even harder to trick military trained medical staff. She'd just have to give it everything she had.

"In the meantime…" Devin crawled onto the bed next to Karissa. "Let's see if I could pass a physical from you." She wanted to keep it lighthearted, even if it felt like the world could fall from under her feet at any second. For Karissa, who'd already been through so much, she needed to be strong. She could fall apart when this was all over, wherever she ended up.

Chapter Thirty

Devin did everything she could. She groaned when they moved her knee, she talked about nightmares and hallucinations. She worked up tears by thinking about Karissa being held in that cave and used them to talk about how afraid of going to space she was. She gave it her best performance, and she hoped it was enough.

Karissa was in the movie theater with Zeke, who had already passed his physical with flying colors. Devin didn't want to bother her. She'd get her results within the hour, and she wanted them in hand before she saw Karissa again. They hadn't talked about a plan beyond today. The hangman's noose was tightening, and there was no way to know if there'd be a last-minute reprieve. Karissa had tossed and turned all night, crying out until Devin stroked her back and helped her go back to sleep.

She was in the chapel, thinking, when the door opened. Walker came in and joined her. Without looking at her, he handed her the white envelope. She tore it open, read it, and set it on the wood seat beside her.

"So that's it."

Walker shrugged. "Guess so. I heard you played it hard, but they didn't fall for it. Everyone here knows you're with Ris, and everyone knows what happened with Ivan. They'd expect you to want to stay."

• 261 •

Welcome to the new light expedition. Be ready at 0300 hours to take your place on the next journey of the human race. There wasn't any ambiguity in the letter. There wasn't any room for negotiation. "I don't suppose you know of someone I can talk to. Someone to get me out of sight."

He shook his head. "Orders are strict now. Tensions are high. No one is going to do anything to piss anyone else off." He finally looked at her and his dark cheeks were stained with tears. "I'm so sorry, Devin."

She wondered how sacrilegious it would be to throw up in a chapel. Her whole body hurt, containing as it did the impotent rage. "And if I snuck out?"

Again, he shook his head. "They're guarding every exit with double teams. They're on the lookout. When you leave here you'll see what I mean. Armed guards are everywhere."

"Well, fuck." She didn't know what else to say. The dreams she'd just started allowing to filter in, the hope she had for a totally different adventure than the one she'd planned on, was dashed against the rocks like a seashell.

❖

Karissa sobbed until her ribs ached. She held Devin close, wishing she could crawl under her skin, wishing she'd passed that last stupid test. Wishing for time, so much more time. But there wasn't any. They spent their last day together in bed, not even leaving for meals. Karissa traced every inch of Devin's body, trying to memorize every curve, the way every muscle tensed, the way her jaw tensed when she came. She stared into her eyes, searching out every color change and wondering if it would look like any of the cosmic colors they'd pass in space. She listened to her breathe, and they shared special memories of childhood and embarrassments of their teenage years. It was like trying to fit an entire relationship into twenty-four hours.

"What will you do? After we go?" Devin stroked Karissa's back.

"I can't think beyond you leaving tomorrow. I'll stay here and figure out what to do next." Her breathing was ragged, like sorrow was sitting on her chest. "It's not like there's any hurry."

When the alarm went off, they stayed locked together.

"Maybe if I just don't show up they won't notice." Devin's words were soft and filled with pain.

Before Karissa could respond, there was a knock at the door. "Lieutenant, we're here to escort you to the bus."

Devin slowly climbed out of bed and opened the door. "I'm not even dressed yet, guys."

The soldier saluted. "Yes, ma'am. We'll wait until you're ready, but we're on a tight schedule."

She closed the door without saying anything. Karissa got out of bed and helped her dress, letting her hands linger as she pulled her shoes and socks on. Her world was crumbling, and there was no way to stop it. When Devin was dressed, her packed duffel bag in hand, they stood holding each other until there was another knock on the door, this one more urgent.

"Ma'am, we really need to go."

"Why are there soldiers here to escort you?" Karissa asked, her voice muffled by Devin's shirt, but she didn't want to move away from the scent of her.

"Probably because I tried so hard to blow my physical. It likely sent up flags, and they're making sure I don't try to hide."

Karissa didn't respond. It made sense, and she wished they'd run…somewhere in the night. Somewhere they wouldn't be found.

The door opened and the soldier moved into the doorway. "I'm sorry, Lieutenant, but we need to go. Now."

Karissa could see Devin's jaw working, could see her ready to put up a fight. She touched her face, cupping it in her hand. "Remember what you told me when I was fighting the convoy pickup? You told me not to let my parents have a last image of me being dragged away…"

Devin squeezed her eyes shut and kissed Karissa's forehead. "You're right. As usual." She slowly let go of Karissa and picked up her bag. The soldier held the door open for her. She was on her crutches now, her bag slung over her shoulder.

Karissa followed them into the corridor. She couldn't breathe. Her whole body trembled, and her heart was shattering into a million pieces of poisoned glass. But she stayed upright, let the tears fall, and didn't collapse. She didn't want the last image of her Devin saw to be her crumpled in a heap like a ragdoll.

Devin stopped and turned around, and the soldier on her left took her arm, as though to keep her from going back. She shot him a look and he relented, but he didn't step away. She waved before they turned the corner.

And then she was gone.

Karissa gave in and fell to her knees. She wrapped her arms around herself and sobbed. She curled into a ball and cried for the happiness she'd had, and lost. She cried for the woman she'd love until the last star faded away.

CHAPTER THIRTY-ONE

Devin couldn't swallow past the lump of emotion in her throat. The early morning air still had a spring chill, and the cloudless sky was dotted with stars. The same stars she and Karissa had watched that night after Devin's injury. The pain in Karissa's expression had very nearly made Devin fight the soldiers beside her, just so she could run back and hold her for one more minute.

But one minute wouldn't be enough, and she wasn't physically fit enough to take on one soldier, let alone two. The tram ride to the entrance seemed to take forever and to go too fast. Every moment took her away from Karissa, and she didn't give a damn what adventure was in front of her. The one she wanted was crying in a hallway behind her. The crutches weighed as much as lead when she stepped out of the tram toward the entrance to the facility. The sight ahead was daunting. A long line of fully armed military trucks was already chugging out steam into the damp morning air. Each truck had a line of people boarding, and Devin joined the final truck. Numb, she grabbed someone's hand as they helped her into the truck but didn't notice who it was. She took a seat and cradled her crutches, the image of Karissa's beautiful tear-stained face all she could see.

The doors closed, the click of the lock final. She wanted to stand up, to pound on the door, to demand to be let out. But as the truck rolled out with the others, she knew there was no point.

There were thirty other people in the truck with her, but there was no conversation. She wondered how many others were leaving loved ones behind. *A month ago, I didn't have a reason to stay. Now that I do, I can't.* The injustice of it flooded her and she had to white knuckle her duffel bag to keep from screaming.

The journey to the air force base was far too short. Thirty minutes after they'd boarded the truck, it stopped. Devin let everyone else file past and had to be tugged on by a soldier before she could bring herself to grab her crutches and bag and move off the truck. Floodlights made it look like daytime and she was momentarily stunned at the number of people ahead of her.

Hundreds of military trucks were letting off their passengers. She heard someone near her say, "They've brought in some of the overseas people to leave from here instead of from the Africa or Asia bases."

She remembered the lectures. That their ship wouldn't be the only one heading for the space station. There were five others coming from other bases and continents. Six ships, carrying thousands of people to a new planet. Before Karissa, she would have been exhilarated. Now, she thought of the people being left behind. Of the woman she loved, left behind.

She was on the edge of a throng slowly moving forward when someone jostled her, causing her to lose her grip on one of her crutches. She leaned down to grab it but stopped when there was a firm hand on her shoulder, holding her down.

"Here, let me help."

She gave Walker a puzzled look when he bent to "help." He was in civilian clothes and a ball cap, giving her a startling vision of what he'd looked like as a normal person.

His mouth was nearly touching her ear. "We've got one chance. When the commotion starts, move into the shadows. Get under truck twenty-two and wait for me." He stood, handed her the crutch, and moved off into the crowd.

Her heart raced and her palms grew sweaty on the handles of her crutches. *One chance.* If it failed, the worst they could do would be to drag her unconscious onto the ship. Karissa wasn't here to see it, so that wouldn't be the end of the world. But if it worked... She had no idea what they'd planned, but she trusted Walker and he had good instincts. If he had a plan, she'd take it. She had to hope it wouldn't land him in the shit if it failed. Anticipation made it so she could hear everything, see the different colored clothing in every hue, and smell the fear and excitement emanating from the crowd like a confused cologne.

A shout rose from ahead of her and the crowd scattered in a circular pattern, voices raised in dismay. The guard's attention moved to the disturbance, and she slipped back into the shadows just far enough behind a guard to be out of his peripheral vision, then pretended to be fixing her crutch as other guards moved forward to see what the problem was. Once they were beyond her, and the rear guard was watching the back of the line, she slid around the front of the truck and looked at the number. Twenty. She stayed low and moved carefully between the trucks until she made it to twenty-two. She put her crutches down and crawled beneath it to lie on her stomach, her leg bent slightly to accommodate her knee.

The voices seemed far away, and the longer she waited the more she worried. What would happen if she didn't check in on the ship? Would they come looking for her? Or would they give her up as a loss and keep to the schedule? The latter seemed more likely. All she had to do was wait it out. But she had a feeling that wasn't all Walker had in mind.

A pair of sneakers crunched in the gravel next to her, and she held her breath. When he dropped down next to her and waved, she grew dizzy with relief.

"Come on out. We've got about fifteen minutes to get you out of here." He pulled her crutches out and gave her a hand up. "Come on." He helped her into the back of the truck and pulled up the heavy black tarp shielding now empty boxes. One large one was on the floor. "Get into that one." He pointed to one on top of others as he shrugged into a military uniform shirt. "I'm going to put this one on the floor on top of you, so it just looks like a stack of empties we're returning to base. I'm driving, so if I step on it and things get bumpy, you'll know things have gone to hell."

She climbed into the box and winced with the angle she had to get her knee into. He set her crutches on top of her, then moved the larger box on top to cover her. There was no lid on hers, so it wasn't as bad as it could have been.

"See you soon. Hang in there."

She heard the truck door come down, and it went completely dark. The rumbling of the engine reverberated in the boxes around her, and she closed her eyes. There was no question in her mind she was doing the right thing; she just prayed it meant she'd be back in Karissa's arms sooner than later.

Karissa dragged herself to a sitting position and leaned against the wall. A few people walked by, but no one stopped. *How many other people are feeling the way I am right now?* If the lack of attention was anything to go by, plenty. How could the world just keep going? How could it give up thousands of people to a new planet and not even stutter-step? It wasn't right, and it wasn't fair. She took in a long, shaky breath. She had no idea what to do next, or where to start. She could get off the hallway floor. That would be a good start. Maybe tomorrow she'd see if she could find Walker. He'd said he would stay working for the military. She had no one and nowhere to go. So maybe she'd see if she could get work where he was. Then she'd still have one friend in the world, one last tie to Devin.

Is she already on board? Is her knee okay? The look on Devin's face had mirrored the way Karissa felt, and she hated that she couldn't take her pain away. She used the wall for leverage and managed to stand, even though her body felt like a black hole—empty and dark. She went back into their room and hugged Devin's pillow to her, which started another flood of tears. The loss of her parents had left her bereft. Losing Devin felt like more than she could live with. People lived with the grief of loss all over the world; she'd learn. But right now, she couldn't fathom a world without Devin in it. She cried herself to sleep, wondering how she was going to keep moving forward.

When she woke she was terribly thirsty. She made her way to the canteen and saw a wall clock. Allowing for two hours to get everyone on board and situated, and an hour to launch, she figured they'd have set off around seven a.m. It was after nine now, which meant Devin, Zeke, Gemma, and thousands of others were already in orbit around the Earth. By lunchtime, they could have docked with the space station, the first stop in their extraordinary journey. When she got to the canteen, all the TVs showed the motion of the shuttle, which was indeed in orbit. Sound turned low explained how the mission was going so far. Karissa watched the huge vessel and let the tears flow once more. There were a few others in the canteen, also watching the TV, but conversation was muted, and more than a few people looked the way Karissa felt. In that, anyway, she wasn't alone.

She made herself a piece of toast to try to quell the queasy tumbling of her stomach and sat with a cup of tea away from the TV. She couldn't watch as Devin moved farther from her every minute. She looked up, startled, when someone put a hand on her shoulder.

"Hey. You holding up?"

She stood and hugged Walker close. "Not really."

"Me either." He hugged her back. "Did you watch the launch?"

"I couldn't. I cried myself to sleep instead. Did you watch it? Did you see her?"

He sat with her on the bench and pushed her tea in front of her. "You're pale as a ghost. We rolled out before the launch, but we stopped on the road to watch it go. It really was something. And I did see her, and she was fine."

Karissa held his hand. "Devin told me about your partner. I'm so sorry."

He swallowed and his eyes were glassy. "Just means I know what you're going through." He motioned at her cup. "I'm going to get some coffee. Want another?"

She nodded and watched him, so grateful she still had a friend around. She couldn't bring herself to ask more about Devin when Walker was hurting over his own loss. When he came back he set their cups down and faced her.

"Any idea what you're going to do next?"

She bit her lip, hoping he'd be okay with her suggestion. "I don't know about you, but I don't have anyone else now. I was thinking maybe I'd find out where you were going and tag along."

His smile was genuine and relieved. "That's awesome. I was going to stay in the military, but I've given it a lot of thought, and I want something else. But I was going to stay here for a while until I figured out where to go. Now we can do that together." He looked at her over his coffee cup. "Are you good with hanging out for a while? I want to know what the options are before I make a decision."

The tea tasted extra bitter and she put it aside. "Definitely. I'm not ready to leave the last place I was with Devin. Not yet."

"Cool. Look, I have to go on duty for a while. Meet me here for dinner?"

She nodded and smiled as he headed out. Now though, she was at a loss. No testing, no job, no Devin. No family to return to. She felt the lump rise in her throat once more and hurried back to their room. There was no point in sobbing in front of everyone. Again.

By the time she made it to the canteen for dinner she was sick to death of her own company. She'd berated herself for blowing the last test, she'd yelled at herself for not finding a way to help Devin escape. She'd played the what-if game until she wanted to scream. Nothing would bring Devin back.

Walker was waiting by a table in the back, far from their usual one. He waved and she grabbed a dinner tray. She didn't feel like eating but going through the routine was blankly satisfying.

"Needed more space?" She set her tray down and looked around at the practically empty room.

His expression was unreadable, an unusual aspect for him. "I wanted to talk to you about something serious."

She pushed aside the possibility there could be something wrong with Devin. He wouldn't know it if there was. "Is something wrong?"

"Maybe. You know how they said you eggheads were free to come or go after they left? Now there's whispers on the wind that they're going to keep you here. At least, those who were close to passing, in order to chew up the data still being sent from the satellites and feed it to the space station. Then, when they start their journey to Phos, there will still be scientists down here working on the project, getting things ready for their arrival, so to speak."

It made perfect sense. Just because they hadn't been the brightest of the bright didn't mean they weren't still useful. It might even give her some purpose, to be working on things Devin would find useful one day. "But this bothers you."

He looked around as though to make sure no one was listening. "It's the choice thing. You didn't have a choice to come here, and now they're saying you might not have the choice to leave. I think that's shitty."

Put that way, it did get Karissa's ire up.

"I wanted to know if you'd consider leaving with me, tonight. We'll head out for one of the raiders camps, I think. I've heard there's one not too far from here. I think we should go while we have the chance. If we decide to go to a Gateway city later, we can. But I don't think we can wait any longer to make a run for it."

She studied him. There was no question he was in earnest, and she knew full well he was genuine. But she couldn't help but feel he wasn't telling her something. His eye contact wasn't quite right…he looked to the side of her, instead of at her. "Is there more?"

He shook his head. "Kind of. But I'd rather tell you on the road."

She shrugged. She'd go with him no matter what, so she'd be content to wait for more information. "Okay. What time and where?"

"I'll come by your room around eleven. I'll take care of provisions and a vehicle. You just be ready to go."

He kissed her cheek and was gone in a flash. She still didn't feel like she could breathe, but he was right. If she stayed here she wanted it to be her choice. She had no intention of living underground for the rest of her life and having to ask permission just to look up at the night sky. She headed to her room to pack.

At eleven, she was waiting anxiously for Walker to knock. But when he did she nearly jumped out of her skin. She slung her bag over her shoulder and gave the room one last look. She'd fallen in love here, and she'd lost that love here. It would always be sacred space. She opened the door and fell in beside Walker, who moved quickly and quietly through the various corridors until he got to the back road. The very one they'd come in on. A smaller than usual army truck was waiting and she jumped into the passenger seat. As they headed down the road leading to the outside she felt some of the weight come off her shoulders. She'd never wanted to be there and without Devin there didn't seem much point in staying. She was glad Walker had come up with a different plan.

She settled back against the seat and let the warm night air flow past her hand. When Walker pulled over about a mile beyond the facility she looked at him questioningly.

"Just need to pick something up real quick. Be right back."

She closed her eyes and sighed. When the passenger door opened she looked up in alarm, and then nearly cried out.

"Hey, beautiful. I don't suppose I could ride with you?"

Karissa scrambled out of the truck and threw herself into Devin's arms. She kissed her cheeks, lips, eyes. "How? How did you get away?"

Devin's eyes sparkled as she held Karissa close. "It's a long story. What do you say we get on the road and we put some distance between us and this place? I don't want to get locked up for desertion if they decide they need something to do." She gave Karissa a lingering kiss. "We've got plenty of time to fill you in."

Karissa climbed back into the truck and gave Walker a huge kiss on the cheek. "Why didn't you tell me?"

"I needed you to keep looking like your world had ended, so no one got suspicious. Sorry."

Devin climbed up beside Karissa and draped her arm around her shoulders. "Let's get out of here."

Karissa snuggled in against Devin, breathing her in, willing herself to believe she wasn't an apparition. "Don't ever leave me again."

Devin kissed the top of her head. "Not for all the planets in the universe."

CHAPTER THIRTY-TWO

The days were growing hotter, and even at seven in the morning, warm winds blew Karissa's hair into a frenzy around her face. She quickly tied it up and climbed back into the truck Walker had "borrowed" from the Cheyenne facility.

"Five hours down, one to go, if we're lucky." Devin kissed Karissa's cheek from her position in the middle of the bench seat.

"Skies are clear. I think we'll be fine." Walker threw it into drive and the truck rumbled to life.

Devin tugged on Karissa's hand. "Whatcha thinking about?"

"About Zeke. I wonder how he's doing. I still can't believe he did what he did to help."

Walker laughed. "You should have seen the faces of everyone around him. That old medicine we found in storage didn't just make him vomit. It was like something out of a horror film. He was like a cannon of puke."

"Well, it certainly drew attention away from me." Devin grimaced. "Even if it was a gross solution."

"As soon as it got out of his system he would've been fine. He was going to say it was just nerves so it wouldn't be a real problem. And now that he's looking down at Earth from the space station, I bet he's happy he helped." Walker dropped down a gear as the elevation decreased on the highway.

"I can't wait to see what they've got going at Mesa." Karissa was still ambivalent about the raiders, but when she'd really asked herself what she wanted, it was to help people, and that's what Van had said they were doing.

The ride was easy, and as they headed into what was once a national park, Devin leaned across Karissa to get a better view, until Karissa finally told Walker to pull over for a second to let them switch places. Devin gave her a big grin and kept her head out the window as they traversed the long road with a sharp drop-off on one side and magnificent cliffs on the other. Copper lines like finger paint ran through buff stone dotted by dark green pine and juniper. Hawks circled lazily overhead, and a coyote ran across the road in front of them, making Walker brake suddenly.

It was pristine and the most beautifully natural place Karissa had ever been. She felt as free as the hawk and as grounded as the trees. She knew she'd love it there, and if the look on Devin's face was any indication, so would she.

The truck slowed and Karissa looked at Walker. "Something wrong?"

"Not exactly. This road keeps going, but you see that marker there, on the trunk of that tree? There's a road leading off it, and it's been used recently. I wonder if that's the way we should go."

Devin leaned across them to look where he was indicating. Karissa laughed when she pushed her chest harder into Karissa's arm than necessary.

"I think you're right. If it doesn't go anywhere, then we'll just come back to this road. But I bet they created a faster route than the one that leads around the park."

He put the truck in gear and slowly turned onto the dirt road. Within fifty feet, it was clear it had been built with one-way traffic in mind, but it was in perfect condition. Much of it was a purpose-built bridge, keeping it above the valley floor.

"Fascinating. They've created a bridge that won't block the flow of the river in the spring but that can still be used year-round." Devin was hanging out the window, looking at the road below them.

"Look." Karissa pointed. "That's incredible. And it looks like we've got a welcoming party."

The cliff dwellings above them were perfectly nestled inside an enormous cave opening. She could see people moving from building to building, climbing ladders, and even some gathered in a circular area. On the road in front of them was a truck with several people standing in front of it. One of them had a very large gun slung over his shoulder.

Walker stopped the truck and they all got out. Karissa took Devin's hand as they walked toward the group. She didn't think there was any danger, but Van had made it clear she took the safety of her settlement seriously.

"Well, well. Look what the cat dragged in." Van stepped forward and held out her hand. "Good to see you looking so alive."

Devin shook her hand. "Good to be alive. We thought we'd take you up on your offer of hospitality."

"You made it! I knew you wouldn't go." Edward ducked around Van and grabbed Karissa in a huge hug.

She hugged him back, feeling like she'd regained a brother. "You look fantastic."

He turned and hugged Devin and nodded at Walker. "I can't believe you're really here. I can't wait to hear all about it."

Karissa took Devin's hand again, wanting the sense of grounding she always gave her. This was all a little overwhelming now that she was here. "We were hoping we'd still be welcome."

"You're more than welcome. We were doing a patrol and checking for an ingredient we need. Edward was helping us locate areas we might find it." Van looked at Walker and tilted her head. "Weren't you a soldier?"

He nodded. "I was. Now I'm…" He looked at Devin and shrugged.

"A security consultant." She grinned and raised her eyebrows. "He's got good tactical skills and he's great at survival. And he's a damn good man."

Van held out her hand. "Always glad to have good men here, too." She turned and pointed at the buildings above them. "That's Cliff Palace. We generally just call it Cliff. We've also got several other places we'll show you, although we've got plenty of space at Cliff if that's where you want to stay. Remind me what your specialties are again?"

Devin was staring at Cliff, her eyes moving constantly as she took it all in. "I'm a geologist with an interest in terrestrial development."

Van put her hands together like she was praying. "Thank fuck. Just what we've needed. We're having some problems you may be able to help us with."

Karissa smiled at the look of avid excitement in Devin's eyes. She'd found her adventure after all. "I work in infectious disease studies."

Van turned and looked at the woman behind her. "Hear that, Liz? A builder and a doctor. It's like there's a god answering our prayers."

Liz smiled and gave Karissa a nod. Karissa remembered her from the raid. She wasn't much of a talker, but she'd seemed all right. It looked like they'd have plenty of time to get to know her. "I'm not a doctor, doctor. Just to be clear."

Van held up her hand to stop her. "Around here, we adapt our skills to do what we have to. And we've got fever."

Devin's attention snapped back to her. "How bad?"

"Not too bad, and we've killed a mosquito population we think was the cause. We've got a medicine that seems to be doing wonders, but it could always mutate."

"Hey, boss, maybe we could have this little reunion in the shade?" Liz said from where she was leaning against the truck.

"Sorry. Let's go. Follow us."

Walker, Devin, and Karissa got back in their truck and followed Van's vehicle down the road. Edward kept looking back at them like a kid making sure his present wasn't going to be taken away. Karissa smiled at him and waved, and laughed when he waved back.

"You okay?" Devin asked, holding her hand.

"Because of the fever thing?" Karissa didn't want to admit the word itself made her feel ill, and the thought of facing it here, where she'd thought they'd find sanctuary, was even worse. "I admit it threw me. But maybe this is my chance to do something about the disease that took my parents. Maybe it's my chance to make a difference." It didn't stop the slight tremor she felt inside, but she knew the words were true.

"I'm right beside you, okay? And if it becomes too much, we'll find somewhere else to go."

Karissa didn't want to find somewhere else. She wanted this to be their home; she'd get over her past so she could have a future. They parked behind Van's truck and Karissa looked up. The dwellings were stunning and perfectly protected from the elements. It was obvious why they'd held out for so long. They grabbed their duffel bags, and Van said she'd send someone down to grab the extra supplies they'd brought with them. They took the little metal elevator to the top.

When they stepped out of it, Van turned to them and said proudly, "Welcome to Mesa."

By nightfall Devin and Karissa were settled into an upper room in the building Van had called the Tower. It was comfortable and the handmade furniture was beautiful. Devin lay on the bed with Karissa in her arms, listening to the sound of an owl in the distance.

Karissa shifted slightly to look up at her. "Any regrets?"

Devin stroked her hair. "Are you kidding? I get to put everything I've ever learned into practice here. I'll help develop a place that will protect people who live here. I'll play in the dirt, and in caves, and with special clay made by Native Americans." After they'd dropped their gear, Van had taken them on a tour and shown Devin the special mixture they were using at Balcony House, which was apparently working. Still, they were hoping to improve on it, and Devin couldn't wait to get started. "And, to top it all off, I've got the woman I love in my arms. Life is awesome."

Karissa snuggled in against her. "I'm so glad you feel that way. I was worried you'd resent not going."

"Nah. Granted it would have been a hell of an adventure, but I can still have an incredible one here. And no adventure was worth losing you." Devin couldn't imagine a minute without Karissa by her side, and she meant every word.

Karissa kissed Devin's shoulder. "Did you see the way Van was looking at the doctor?"

Devin laughed. "No doubt those two are in deep. Crazy that Dr. Sandish is the one who should have been on our convoy pickup. They're lucky she made it to them. Imagine finding a cure for fever."

Karissa moved to straddle Devin and leaned down to kiss her. "I can't believe how lucky I feel. If I hadn't been chosen, if you hadn't...we'd never have found one another."

Her kisses grew more ardent, more searching. Her hair tickled Devin's exposed skin and made her tingle. She slid her hands up Karissa's back and unhooked her bra so she could slide her hands beneath the cups. She tugged at Karissa's nipples the way she knew made her back arch. Holding her tightly, she flipped her over so she was on top.

"I love you, Karissa. With everything I'll ever be."

Tears fell from Karissa's eyes as she cupped Devin's face in her hands. "And I love you, Devin. In this world and the next."

Their lovemaking was slow, filled with promise and a future. Devin took her time, wanting to feel every muscle clench, every moan, every cry of pleasure. After, she held her close, thankful for the moment not just that they were chosen, but for the moment they'd chosen each other.

About the Author

Brey Willows is a longtime editor and writer. When she's not running a social enterprise working with marginalized communities on writing projects, she's editing other people's writing or doing her own. She lives in the middle of England with her partner and fellow author and spends entirely too much time exploring castles and ancient ruins while bemoaning the rain.

Website: http://www.breywillows.com

Books Available from Bold Strokes Books

A Fighting Chance by T. L. Hayes. Will Lou be able to come to terms with her past to give love a fighting chance? (978-1-163555-257-7)

Chosen by Brey Willows. When the choice is adapt or die, can love save us all? (978-1-163555-110-5)

Death Checks In by David S. Pederson. Despite Heath's promises to Alan to not get involved, Heath can't resist investigating a shopkeeper's murder in Chicago, which dashes their plans for a romantic weekend getaway. (978-1-163555-329-1)

Gnarled Hollow by Charlotte Greene. After they are invited to study a secluded nineteenth-century estate, a former English professor and a group of historians discover that they will have to fight against the unknown if they have any hope of staying alive. (978-1-163555-235-5)

Jacob's Grace by C.P. Rowlands. Captain Tag Becket wants to keep her head down and her past behind her, but her feelings for AJ's second-in-command, Grace Fields, makes keeping secrets next to impossible. (978-1-163555-187-7)

On the Fly by PJ Trebelhorn. Hockey player Courtney Abbott is content with her solitary life until visiting concert violinist Lana Caruso makes her second-guess everything she always thought she wanted. (978-1-163555-255-3)

Passionate Rivals by Radclyffe. Professional rivalry and long-simmering passions create a combustible combination when Emmett McCabe and Sydney Stevens are forced to work together, especially when past attractions won't stay buried. (978-1-163555-231-7)

Proxima Five by Missouri Vaun. When geologist Leah Warren crash-lands on a preindustrial planet and is claimed by its tyrant, Tiago, will clan warrior Keegan's love for Leah give her the strength to defeat him? (978-1-163555-122-8)

Racing Hearts by Dena Blake. When you cross a hot-tempered race car mechanic with a reckless cop, the result can only be spontaneous combustion. (978-1-163555-251-5)

Shadowboxer by Jessica L. Webb. Jordan McAddie is prepared to keep her street kids safe from a dangerous underground protest group, but she isn't prepared for her first love to walk back into her life. (978-1-163555-267-6)

The Tattered Lands by Barbara Ann Wright. As Vandra and Lilani strive to make peace, they slowly fall in love. With mistrust and murder surrounding them, only their faith in each other can keep their plan to save the world from falling apart. (978-1-163555-108-2)

Captive by Donna K. Ford. To escape a human trafficking ring, Greyson Cooper and Olivia Danner become players in a game of deceit and violence. Will their love stand a chance? (978-1-63555-215-7)

Crossing the Line by CF Frizzell. The Mob discovers a nemesis within its ranks, and in the ultimate retaliation, draws Stick McLaughlin from anonymity by threatening everything she holds dear. (978-1-63555-161-7)

Love's Verdict by Carsen Taite. Attorneys Landon Holt and Carly Pachett want the exact same thing: the only open partnership spot at their prestigious criminal defense firm. But will they compromise their careers for love? (978-1-63555-042-9)

Precipice of Doubt by Mardi Alexander & Laurie Eichler. Can Cole Jameson resist her attraction to her boss, veterinarian Jodi Bowman, or will she risk a workplace romance and her heart? (978-1-63555-128-0)

Savage Horizons by CJ Birch. Captain Jordan Kellow's feelings for Lt. Ali Ash have her past and future colliding, setting in motion a series of events that strands her crew in an unknown galaxy thousands of light years from home. (978-1-63555-250-8)

Secrets of the Last Castle by A. Rose Mathieu. When Elizabeth Campbell represents a young man accused of murdering an elderly woman, her investigation leads to an abandoned plantation that reveals many dark Southern secrets. (978-1-63555-240-9)

Take Your Time by VK Powell. A neurotic parrot brings police officer Grace Booker and temporary veterinarian Dr. Dani Wingate together in the tiny town of Pine Cone, but their unexpected attraction keeps the sparks flying. (978-1-63555-130-3)

The Last Seduction by Ronica Black. When you allow true love to elude you once and you desperately regret it, are you brave enough to grab it when it comes around again? (978-1-63555-211-9)

The Shape of You by Georgia Beers. Rebecca McCall doesn't play it safe, but when sexy Spencer Thompson joins her workout class, their non-stop sparring forces her to face her ultimate challenge—a chance at love. (978-1-63555-217-1)

Exposed by MJ Williamz. The closet is no place to live if you want to find true love. (978-1-62639-989-1)

Force of Fire: Toujours a Vous by Ali Vali. Immortals Kendal and Piper welcome their new child and celebrate the defeat of an old enemy, but another ancient evil is about to awaken deep in the jungles of Costa Rica. (978-1-63555-047-4)

Holding Their Place by Kelly A. Wacker. Together Dr. Helen Connery and ambulance driver Julia March, discover that goodness, love, and passion can be found in the most unlikely and even dangerous places during WWI. (978-1-63555-338-3)

Landing Zone by Erin Dutton. Can a career veteran finally discover a love stronger than even her pride? (978-1-63555-199-0)

Love at Last Call by M. Ullrich. Is balancing business, friendship, and love more than any willing woman can handle? (978-1-63555-197-6)

Pleasure Cruise by Yolanda Wallace. Spencer Collins and Amy Donovan have few things in common, but a Caribbean cruise offers both women an unexpected chance to face one of their greatest fears: falling in love. (978-1-63555-219-5)

Running Off Radar by MB Austin. Maji's plans to win Rose back are interrupted when work intrudes and duty calls her to help a SEAL team stop a Russian mobster from harvesting gold from the bottom of Sitka Sound. (978-1-63555-152-5)

Shadow of the Phoenix by Rebecca Harwell. In the final battle for the fate of Storm's Quarry, even Nadya's and Shay's powers may not be enough. (978-1-63555-181-5)

Take a Chance by D. Jackson Leigh. There's hardly a woman within fifty miles of Pine Cone that veterinarian Trip Beaumont can't charm, except for the irritating new cop, Jamie Grant, who keeps leaving parking tickets on her truck. (978-1-63555-118-1)

The Outcasts by Alexa Black. Spacebus driver Sue Jones is running from her past. When she crash-lands on a faraway world, the Outcast Kara might be her chance for redemption. (978-1-63555-242-3)

Alias by Cari Hunter. A car crash leaves a woman with no memory and no identity. Together with Detective Bronwen Pryce, she fights to uncover a truth that might just kill them both. (978-1-63555-221-8)

Death in Time by Robyn Nyx. Working in the past is hell on your future. (978-1-63555-053-5)

Hers to Protect by Nicole Disney. High school sweethearts Kaia and Adrienne will have to see past their differences and survive the vengeance of a brutal gang if they want to be together. (978-1-63555-229-4)

Of Echoes Born by 'Nathan Burgoine. A collection of queer fantasy short stories set in Canada from Lambda Literary Award finalist 'Nathan Burgoine. (978-1-63555-096-2)

Perfect Little Worlds by Clifford Mae Henderson. Lucy can't hold the secret any longer. Twenty-six years ago, her sister did the unthinkable. (978-1-63555-164-8)

Room Service by Fiona Riley. Interior designer Olivia likes stability, but when work brings footloose Savannah into her world and into a new city every month, Olivia must decide if what makes her comfortable is what makes her happy. (978-1-63555-120-4)

Sparks Like Ours by Melissa Brayden. Professional surfers Gia Malone and Elle Britton can't deny their chemistry on and off the beach. But only one can win… (978-1-63555-016-0)

Take My Hand by Missouri Vaun. River Hemsworth arrives in Georgia intent on escaping quickly, but when she crashes her Mercedes into the Clip 'n Curl, sexy Clay Cahill ends up rescuing more than her car. (978-1-63555-104-4)

The Last Time I Saw Her by Kathleen Knowles. Lane Hudson only has twelve days to win back Alison's heart. That is if she can gather the courage to try. (978-1-63555-067-2)

Wayworn Lovers by Gun Brooke. Will agoraphobic composer Giselle Bonnaire and Tierney Edwards, a wandering soul who can't remain in one place for long, trust in the passionate love destiny hands them? (978-1-62639-995-2)

Breakthrough by Kris Bryant. Falling for a sexy ranger is one thing, but is the possibility of love worth giving up the career Kennedy Wells has always dreamed of? (978-1-63555-179-2)

Certain Requirements by Elinor Zimmerman. Phoenix has always kept her love of kinky submission strictly behind the bedroom door and inside the bounds of romantic relationships, until she meets Kris Andersen. (978-1-63555-195-2)

Dark Euphoria by Ronica Black. When a high-profile case drops in Detective Maria Diaz's lap, she forges ahead only to discover this case, and her main suspect, aren't like any other. (978-1-63555-141-9)

Fore Play by Julie Cannon. Executive Leigh Marshall falls hard for Peyton Broader, her golf pro…and an ex-con. Will she risk sabotaging her career for love? (978-1-63555-102-0)

Love Came Calling by CA Popovich. Can a romantic looking for a long-term, committed relationship and a jaded cynic too busy for love conquer life's struggles and find their way to what matters most? (978-1-63555-205-8)

Outside the Law by Carsen Taite. Former sweethearts Tanner Cohen and Sydney Braswell must work together on a federal task force to see justice served, but will they choose to embrace their second chance at love? (978-1-63555-039-9)

The Princess Deception by Nell Stark. When journalist Missy Duke realizes Prince Sebastian is really his twin sister Viola in disguise, she plays along, but when sparks flare between them, will the double deception doom their fairy-tale romance? (978-1-62639-979-2)

The Smell of Rain by Cameron MacElvee. Reyha Arslan, a wise and elegant woman with a tragic past, shows Chrys that there's still beauty to embrace and reason to hope despite the world's cruelty. (978-1-63555-166-2)

The Talebearer by Sheri Lewis Wohl. Liz's visions show her the faces of the lost and the killers who took their lives. As one by one, the murdered are found, a stranger works to stop Liz before the serial killer is brought to justice. (978-1-635550-126-6)

White Wings Weeping by Lesley Davis. The world is full of discord and hatred, but how much of it is just human nature when an evil with sinister intent is invading people's hearts? (978-1-63555-191-4)

CPSIA information can be obtained
at www.ICGtesting.com
Printed in the USA
LVHW022027311018
595438LV00001B/56/P